DIARY OF A
Broken Cinderella

BROKEN WHILE BROKEN

Engage Lyfe™

BALBOA.
PRESS
A DIVISION OF HAY HOUSE

Balboa Press books may be ordered through booksellers or by contacting:

Balboa Press
A Division of Hay House
1663 Liberty Drive
Bloomington, IN 47403
www.balboapress.com
1 (877) 407-4847

Print information available on the last page.

ISBN: 978-1-9822-1329-9 (sc)
ISBN: 978-1-9822-1331-2 (hc)
ISBN: 978-1-9822-1330-5 (e)

Library of Congress Control Number: 2018911635

Balboa Press rev. date: 10/18/2018

CONTENTS

ABOUT THIS BOOK

Diary of a Broken Cinderella is a 2017 romantic comedy-drama novel written by Engage Lyfe™. This ordinary girl named Cynthia (Cyn) goes through a life changing tragedy and misfortune of losing her mother. Her father remarries and she must live with evil stepsisters that always did everything in their power to make her life pure hell. On top of the wicked stepsisters, the nefarious stepmom doesn't give a hoot about her. Just like every other cliché story, she wonders if her own life story would have a joyful ending?

In this novel, when she gets older, Cyn struggles to find true love and true happiness. She doesn't have a seemingly perfect life with the American dream fulfilled with money, mansion and the perfect love story. She deals with countless torment from her stepfamily that only want to see her fail in her life. So many curveballs are thrown Cyn's way. Faced with the harsh reality of her struggle to remain good in a world of evildoers. This faith-based novel follows the journey of trials and tribulations that she will face and overcome. She must reassess her life, her purpose and her faith. Cyn is forced to not be easily broken, regain love, trust and forgiveness.

Everyone has a story...

PROLOGUE

"Preston! Preston!" Cynthia gripped his hand tightly while staring into his irresponsive face.

The color was completely drained from his pigment and his body lay limp as did his hand smothered by her loving hold. The machines attached to him began to beep loudly and erratically. This couldn't be happening. Tears blinded her eyes as she glanced over to the one device which flashed a consistent flat line as it squealed its truth relentlessly. She was no medical professional, but Cynthia had seen enough movies and hospital-based television shows to know that this was a fatal sign. She dropped his hand immediately and grabbed his face as if her touch would somehow return energy to his body.

"Preston!" she screamed, becoming irate and emotional. She was practically kneeling on her knees beside him on the hospital bed as she peered down into his face. Her hands moved down to his chest and she began to press sporadically against his flesh hoping that her actions would be fruitful. "Don't do this! You can't do this to me! I can't do this without you. Please … please … don't do this to me."

Pandemonium took place as the room began to fill up with nurses, doctors, and techs all trying to respond to the code they'd been alerted to. Cynthia's focus was centralized on Preston and her body strength became greater than she knew. Two of the male techs tried to remove her from the body but she refused to let go and step aside.

"Ma'am, please," a nurse begged of her. "We need you to get off of him."

"Get her out of here!" one of the doctors ordered.

"Come on, Ma'am," the tech to her left pleaded. "You have to let us do our job. You have to give us space to do our job."

Their words were falling upon deaf ears as she continued to pound on the chest that she'd spent years of her life falling asleep on, crying on, and inhaling the scent of. They wanted her to give it up; to move aside and just let him go, but she couldn't do it. She owed it to Preston to fight for him even when he couldn't fight for himself any longer. She owed it to him to hang on with love until the absolute very end when God stepped in to say that the fight was over. Right now, her spirit wouldn't allow her to throw in the towel. Her heart was shattering into a thousand pieces as the hospital staff around her barked orders, tinkered with equipment, and tried to force her out of the way.

"You can't do this!" she yelled at Preston. "You can't leave me. You can't leave me."

The techs managed to remove her from her semi-straddled position over Preston's body, but she didn't venture far despite their instructions. Time was of the essence and no one in the room knew what to expect from their attempts to save the man on the table. His chest was exposed and the defibrillator was readied. The leading physician stepped forward and shut his eyes for a brief second before grabbing the paddles from the nurse to his right.

"Charge to 200," the doctor ordered.

His request was fulfilled and immediately he pressed the paddles against Preston's chest and issued a volt to the man's body. All eyes flew over to the monitor which failed to report a change in his status.

"Charge to 250," the doctor ordered, determined to get a satisfactory outcome. He mimicked his earlier actions, feeling the surge of the shock as he tried to rejuvenate activity within Preston's body.

Still, there was no change. The room fell silent minus the consistent beep that magnified the intense depression surrounding the team's failure. Cynthia stood clutching her chest with large, blood shot eyes. She could feel it; the end. The end of an era, their marriage, their friendship, and his life. At that complete instance, it was over. The staff was conceding finding it pointless to advance their efforts and there was nothing that she or anyone else could do about it. In that instance, she felt her life shift to a cold emptiness that she knew she'd never be able to cope with, never be able to accept. A life without Preston wasn't a life at all, it was a tragedy.

"Time of death," the doctor stated morbidly as he handed the paddles back over to the nurse."2:59 P.M."

"No!" Cynthia screamed out, her strength finally weakening as she lurched forward and threw herself over Preston's lifeless body. "Nooo! I can't do it, Preston! I can't do it. I can't live without you. What am I supposed to do?" she cried out. Her tears began to create a puddle along the ridges of his abs. A flashback of a dream she had jumped to the forefront of her mind. She'd been huddled over on her knees in a distraught manner. She remembered waking him up to tell him about the dream but they'd both gone back to sleep, neither thinking much of it. Now, here she was feeling a sickening sense of dejavu as she felt the rip in her spirit due to reality tearing her apart. "What am I supposed to do without you?"

No one bothered to pull her away this time. She was grieving and they all understood that. As Cynthia cried and held on to the man she'd never again have the opportunity to hold a conversation with, the man who would never again embrace her, the hospital staff went about business as usual. The machines were turned off, the coroner was called, and the room was vacated. Cynthia was lost in despair and heartbreak. Preston was all she'd known for years. He'd been her sunrise and sunset, the lifeline that kept her going. Without him she knew she'd live a mediocre existence devoid of love aside from that of their three children. The thought of going through it alone now without him by her side and no real support system frightened her.

"What am I going to do, God?" she asked in a whispered cry. "What am I going to do?"

Chapter 1

How beautiful the beginning is when everything is pure
How the euphoria engulfs you, the anxiety grips
you, and the endless possibilities fill your mind while
the overwhelming joy of it all fills your heart
When a commencement occurs, bittersweet
emotions run rampant and practically
nothing compares to the bliss of it all
The saying goodbye to an era whose
ups and downs shaped you
While saying hello to the future that awaits
you with memories yet to be determined
How beautiful the beginning is when
you're so sure, so certain, so in love
How beautiful it is when two hearts mesh to
create one entity defying mathematical logic
The magic of it all supersedes any
expectations previously had
For this moment could have never been
preconceived in a manner which compares
to the grandeur of the overflow of glee, tears
of happiness, and eternal optimism
How beautiful it is
To start anew

- Kenni York © 2016

he wind whipped through the cracked patio door, causing the white sheer curtain to fan outward. In the mirror, Cynthia Grayson saw it swaying behind her. She smiled as the air danced into the room and kissed her skin. The glow that radiated through her reflection was undeniable; even she was in awe of the joy she exuded. This was it! Today was the day that all of her dreams would come true and she'd truly begin to live the life that she'd desired for so long. Her fingers grazed over the pearl embellishments that covered the bodice of her gown. The halter dress, with its floor-length straight skirt, was simple in its appearance yet fit Cynthia's personality perfectly. She, much like the dress, was a classic beauty with features that weren't too showy but were charismatically alluring in their own way. The material hugged her voluptuous breasts but was forgiving in her midsection, especially thanks to the full bodysuit and additional shapewear that she wore to give herself a more slender appearance. Never one to be looked upon as conventionally pretty, today the plain woman she was used to being looked ravishing following her prewedding spa day and makeover, compliments of her intended.

Cynthia smiled at the glimmer in her own eyes and then caught herself in a one-woman stare down. The hotel was beautiful, and she loved the fact that they'd been able to get a wedding package without having to break the bank. In the past, though whimsically wonderful and majestic in concept, weddings had seemed to be nothing more than a gross display of a couple's alleged affection for one another that almost always ended up being an overpriced show for hundreds of people who probably didn't even believe that the couple would make it to see their first anniversary. While weddings were beautiful, with all of the color coordination, fluffy white dresses, and over-the-top decorations, Cynthia had heard tell of enough of them where the guests were more cynical than supportive of the bride and groom. She hadn't been to many herself, but she'd listened to her stepsisters and stepmother following their many invites. She'd made a mental note that should her day ever come, she'd limit the wedding to only those closest to her in order to ensure that the day was truly about her and her new husband, a true celebration of their union.

Cynthia's smile faded at the thought of family. She'd gotten dressed alone, having no bridesmaids to attend to her. The silence in the room and the loudness of her thoughts forced her to remember the absence of her mother. This was the very moment that every young girl envisioned: having your mother by your side to help dress you before you took your glide down the aisle to your future. The hurt was still agonizing nearly a decade after the death of her mother, Miriam Grayson. At twenty-three, Cynthia could still recall her mother's scent, the gentle feel of her caress, and the softness of her tone. Miriam had died just before Cynthia's twelfth birthday. It was a day that would forever be etched in Cynthia's memory alongside the sorrow that never quite seemed to evaporate from her heart. A tear threatened to do damage to her perfectly applied eyeliner, and Cynthia placed a fingertip against the corner of her eye to stop it. Emotions of all kinds were flying high today, but it was to be expected.

"Gone 'head and fix ya face now." The voice boomed from the doorway with authority.

Cynthia quickly turned around and smiled at the sight of her aunt Thea standing to her left and beaming at her proudly. Thea was her father's sister, and from the moment Cynthia's mother had passed, Thea had been like a godmother to Cynthia. Whenever she needed advice, tough love, and a little feminine connection, it was to Thea that she turned. By the time Cynthia was thirteen, her father, Elton Grayson, had remarried. It had taken forever for Cynthia to get used to her stepmother, Ebony, who pronounced her name as "can-daw-say." They'd never developed a bond nearly as tight as that she had shared with Thea.

"How do I look?" Cynthia asked, holding out her arms so that Thea could survey her.

Thea walked deeper into the room, breathing heavily. Her large, round body was clad in a lilac-and-white floral dress with pearls dangling from her neck. Cynthia had never seen Thea without her infamous pearls. Per Thea, a true lady always donned pearls to distinguish herself from the other rotten oysters in the sea of women. A lady stood out without showing out; that was a lesson she'd once taught Cynthia. But for as long as Cynthia had known aunt Thea, if anyone could be counted upon to show out or turn it up, it was Thea.

"Beautiful," Thea answered her. "Just beautiful. Miriam would be proud to see her baby all grown up, happy, and 'bout to be a Mrs." She smiled so wide that it looked as if her face would pop. "She'll be even happier to know that you're wearing white. You're not perpetrating the white now, are you?"

Cynthia blushed and turned away from her aunt. "Thea! That's a personal question."

"What's a little girl talk between ladies?" Thea teased.

"Is my dad here?" Cynthia was excited about her father walking her down the aisle.

"Mmm hmm. He out there with Cruella and her minions."

Cynthia laughed. "Now, you know you're not right."

It was no secret that Thea and Ebony didn't get along, but Cynthia was hoping that everyone would be cordial on her special day. She'd be lying if she said she felt any connection to Ebony and her daughters, Ana and Ella. But at the end of the day they were family, and they were all she had to call her own.

"You oughta see her standing out there with her nose tooted up and that hat looking like an Easter egg–colored tire sitting on her head." Thea laughed at her own insult. "Sitting there with her nose tooted up like this." She mimicked her disdain for Ebony with her head thrown back and her nostrils aimed to the ceiling and flaring wide. "She likely to have a whole swarm of bees shoot straight on up there." Thea doubled over with laughter at the thought of Ebony's nostrils being riddled with bee stings.

"You're too much," Cynthia said, shaking her head and trying not to laugh. It was a hard task because as crass as Thea could be, she was equally as hilarious. There'd been times when Cynthia had wanted nothing more than to ball up and cry from all the misfortune and depression that had plagued her life, but it was always Thea who had pulled her out of the funk and made her laugh while seeing things from another perspective.

Thea began to prance around the room, still in character with no shame at all. "Helloer, I'm Cruella-er. I'm saddity." Her laughter resounded throughout the room.

It was then that the door opened and in walked her stepsisters, Ana and Ella, decked out in varying cuts of lavender bridesmaid dresses. Cynthia's eyes grew wide as she saw them, and immediately she tried to correct Thea's behavior.

"Thea," she called out. "We have guests."

Thea turned in midlaughter, and her hilarity transitioned into a forced cough in an attempt to play off her theatrics. "Helloer," she stated, composing herself but still using her comical tone.

"Guests?" Ana piped up, rolling her eyes at Cynthia. "Honey, we are the living centerpieces that are making your little wedding pop."

Ella looked Cynthia up and down but didn't speak.

"Could you have picked a more common place to have a wedding?" Ana complained. "I mean, this just screams lower class trying to be elegant."

"It's simple," Cynthia replied, defending her decision.

"It's low-grade. A hotel, and you didn't even bother to rent out the most extravagant ballroom or the entire lower level of the hotel to accommodate your guests."

"I was going for simple yet elegant," Cynthia pointed out. "And the terrace is beautiful this time of year. It'll be nice. You'll see."

"Nice," Ana replied. "When I get married, my wedding's going to be far better than nice. It's going to be grand. Watch. Mom and Elton are going to hold back nothing regarding expenses, and I'm sure every society column in Atlanta will be clamoring for an invite and trying to get an exclusive story."

"Hmm," Thea murmured. "And where's this fiancé of yours?" She laced her fingers together and sat her clasped hands on her rotund belly while looking at Ana over her oversized glasses.

Ana sneered at Thea, a woman she'd never quite taken to. "Excuse me?"

"I mean, you're talking about your wedding like there's a real possibility of it occurring."

Ana rolled her eyes. "I'm a catch. I'm just waiting on the right one to come along. You know, the one with the right size bank account." She turned to look at her sister, and together they shared a laugh sparked by their vanity and materialistic personalities.

Thea nodded. "Mmm hmm, honey, and I'm sure he'll come right along and catch what you got."

"Thea!" Cynthia quipped.

"I mean, he'll just snap you right on up," Thea commented, trying to clear up her rudeness.

"Anyway, dear," Ana went on, returning her attention to Cynthia. "It's just as well. Your little wedding's a reflection of you. You do what you want. Whatever makes you happy." She gave her a tight smile before continuing. "I'm just surprised that you were the first of us to get married."

"Excuse me," Ella cut in, looking disgusted as if she'd just been slighted. "She wasn't the first."

"Shhh," Ana stated. "That doesn't count."

Ella looked over at Cynthia with a glare that she quickly tried to get rid of before anyone else took notice of the emotions that were dangling from her sleeve.

"Imagine that," Ana went on. "You, a married woman. I suppose that Preston's not too bad of a guy either, for you. A little too common for me. What's he do again? Massages?"

"He's a physical therapist," Cynthia stated, standing up for her husband's occupation. "Preston's going to start his own practice one day."

"Is that right?" Ana smirked. "Good for him."

"We make an honest living. Nothing flashy but … we're good. He's a good man. He's good to me."

"You don't have to defend your relationship to nobody, honey," Thea spoke up. "You's happy and that's all that matters."

"Yes," Ana replied. "We're happy that you're happy."

"Your dress," Ella cut in. "It's nice. I'm glad you were able to find something to fit your body type."

Although she instantly turned her back to look herself over in the mirror, the look of hurt was still detected in her eyes by Thea. Thea opened her mouth to speak but was interrupted by a knock on the door.

"We're ready to start when you are," the hotel's event coordinator announced, poking her head in the door.

"Thank you," Cynthia called back.

"Alright now y'all just go on," Thea instructed the stepsisters. "I'll help Cynthia out to the terrace."

"We'll see you once you're married," Ella told Cynthia.

Both Ella and Ana took turns hugging Cynthia before stepping out of the door in their stilettos. Thea stood behind Cynthia and watched her saddened expression as she surveyed her curves and appearance one last time in the full length mirror. She wanted to see herself for the blushingly, beautiful bride that she was, but it was moments like these when she couldn't help but to recall the chubby, out casted young girl she'd been upon her father and Ebony's union.

TEN YEARS AGO

"Shame, shame, shame! I don't wanna go to Mexico no more, more, more." Ana and Ella sang in unison on the playground at Piedmont Park. Their perfectly pressed ponytails dangled against their shoulders freely as they sat crossed-legged at the top of the landing leading to the slide, prohibiting the younger kids from going down the slide as if they owned it. In their cute little pastel rompers, they were adamant about staying put and not getting dirty like the other kids playing. Their mom was taking them to lunch after at Mary Mac's Tea Room after getting a little sun at the park and they dared not get messy and embarrass her with unkempt appearances. Besides, they were ladies now and ladies didn't run around and play like little babies.

They continued to clap their hands together, recanting the timeless rhyme that had them in stitches giggling. "There's a big fat policeman at the door, door, door. He'll pull you by the collar and make you pay a dollar. I don't wanna go to Mexico no more, more, more."

Simultaneously, they clapped their hands and laughed, ready to play another round or a different game of the same manner. Behind them stood Cynthia, waiting patiently with her hands behind her back. Her cut-off jean shorts had ragged edges were a complete contrast to the neatness of Ana and Ella. Her stripped t-shirt was a half size too small and her portly belly peeked out underneath. Unlike her stepsisters, Cynthia's hair wasn't newly groomed. She was sporting corn-rowed braids that had been done nearly a month ago. Her hair had long since become worn-looking and fuzzy from weeks of laying on it.

"Is it my turn?" Cynthia asked innocently. Her eyes were hopeful as she awaited their answer.

Since her father had moved into their new lavish house with Ebony and her daughters, Cynthia had to adjust to not only a new family but also a new neighborhood. She had no friends and looked to Ella and Ana to welcome her in on their hijinks. Although they allowed her to follow them around, very seldom did they actually allow her to participate in their activities. Still, she yearned for their acceptance, tagging alone faithfully feeling as if she was the third Musketeer although she was merely their shadow.

Ana turned around and looked at Cynthia as if she'd just grown a second nose. "You want to play this game? You know only two people can play right?"

Cynthia nodded. "I just wanted a turn, please."

"You can't play this game," Ella stated bluntly. "Unless you're gonna be the fat policeman."

Ana burst out into laughter and readily agreed with Ella. "Yeah, Cyn. You can do that!"

Cynthia's eyes swelled with tears as other kids on the playground stopped to take notice of the scene. "But I don't wanna be the policeman," she protested.

"You have to be because you're fat," Ella advised.

"You either have to be the fat policeman or you can't play with us," Ana chimed in.

Cynthia's lower lip trembled as she tried her best to not break down in front of the crowd of her peers. "But whhhhhyyyy?"

"Because you're fat!" Ana answered.

"And because we told you so and we're older than you so you have to listen to us," Ella went on.

"Ha, ha!" Some random kid standing across from them took that moment to add his assessment of the situation. "Look at your belly! You got a big belly just like a policeman! Fat belly! Nobody wants a fat belly around!"

"Fat Belly, Fat Belly," the other kids began to chant, taunting Cynthia and falling over with laughter.

Cynthia's cheeks flared out as she huffed to keep from crying like a baby in front of the others. She became self-conscious as she tugged on her t-shirt and made a mental note to ask her father to take her shopping for decent clothes since she knew that Ebony wouldn't think to take her the way she did her birth children. Embarrassed and hurt, Cynthia turned away and walked through the crowd that was teasing her relentlessly. With her head down she climbed down from the playground and walked away from the group that was still laughing as if the joke was fresh out of her stepsisters' mouths. Cynthia found her stepmother situated upon a park bench with her cell phone to her ear and back to Cynthia's approaching figure.

"Yes, yes, I understand all of that," Ebony snapped into the phone. "But I am Mrs. Elton Grayson and I am authorizing the transfer of the funds. I can do that. We are both listed as co-account holders so what is the problem?" She paused to listen to the person on the other end and apparently was displeased with the response that she received. Ebony rose from her seat and her tone matched her action. "What kind of incompetent organization are you running over there? This is ludicrous! No matter the amount I shouldn't need a babysitter or approval to make a transfer. I'm entitled ..." She spun around in the midst of her rant and her words trailed off at the site of Cynthia staring at her. Quickly she covered the microphone of her cell and hissed at Cynthia. "Didn't anyone ever tell you that it's rude of you to listen in on grown people's conversations? Surely your mother at least taught you very basic manners!"

"I wasn't listening," Cynthia replied meekly, feeling further hurt by being chided for something she wasn't actually doing. "I was just waiting ... I was being patient ... waiting to tell you something."

"What is it?" Ebony asked, annoyance laced in her tone.

Cynthia looked over in her stepsisters' direction and tried to explain to her stepmother what was going on. "It's Ana and Ella. They're making fun of me because I'm bigger and making the other kids laugh at me and—"

"Ugh!" Ebony huffed. She looked away from Cynthia and hurriedly spoke into her phone. "I'm going to come in and you buffoons better handle my transfer or have someone else available that can rectify this situation otherwise I'll have my husband take our business elsewhere!" She disconnected the call, dropped her cell over into her Burken bag sitting on the bench, and then stroked her hair as if tidying up her appearance and calming down. Then, she refocused her attention upon Cynthia. "Poor little Cynthia," she said sarcastically. "You're not a very popular girl are you? And now you're tattle-telling like you're eight years old. Get over it! You're going to have people talking about you your whole life especially because of your weight and your lack of pedigree so you might as well get used to it. Coming to me about it isn't going to work because unlike your mother, I'm not a coddler … I'm not holding your hand your whole life or handling your affairs for you. Grow a backbone!" She grabbed up her purse and started to walk towards the playground. "And you can forget bothering your father with such trivial matters. If you're really that concerned about your weight try losing it." Ebony looked over towards the playground and motioned for her daughters. "Girls! Girls! Time for our lunch date!"

CURRENT DAY

"Don't you do it," Thea advised.

Cynthia looked up at her in the glass. "Do what?"

"Don't you let 'dem witches get you down on yo day. This yo day. And you're more beautiful than either of them could ever be inside and out. You got you a good man that loves you and you're happy. They don't know nothing 'bout that 'cause they too busy being hungry. They need a sandwich and some business of they own, up here worried 'bout you and yours. Now come on here, let's go get you married."

Cynthia smiled and turned to face Thea. "I love you. Promise me that you'll never leave."

The request was sincere; since losing her mother Cynthia had been so regaled with fear over those she loved leaving her. That was part of the reason why she continued to maintain a relationship with her stepsisters despite the horrible way in which they treated her. They were all she had and the thought of being completely alone in the world with no support system at all scared her. Cynthia had to take what she could get even though what she was getting often left her feeling empty, insecure, and sad.

Thea grabbed Cynthia's hand. "Child, you don't need me. You got you a man out there waiting on you and y'all gon' have a whole slew of babies. But I ain't going nowhere even when you try to drop dem babies off at my do'." Thea laughed and squeezed Cynthia's hand. "Come on."

Cynthia allowed her aunt to lead her out of the door and to the designated waiting spot where her stepsisters and the wedding coordinator were waiting. Her parents in front of the closed double door and turned to see Cynthia as she and Thea approached. Ebony pursed her lips and didn't say a word as her husband smiled grandly. He dropped his hold of Ebony's hand and walked over to Cynthia who looked up at him approvingly.

"I swear you look more and more like your mother every day," Elton told his daughter as he embraced her tightly.

"Let's hope that I instilled a little more classic good taste in her," Ebony whispered loudly enough for her daughters to hear her and snicker.

"Do you really like it, Daddy?" Cynthia asked, feeling like an adolescent all over again.

"You're gorgeous, baby. And I'm sure that Preston will love it."

Thea nodded her approval of the father-daughter moment before patting her brotther on the shoulder and walking away from the family in order to head out to the terrace and find a seat right near the front.

Ebony stepped forward and slid her arm through Elton's. "We need to take our seats now, dear. It's in bad taste to leave the guests waiting for so long." She smiled curtly at Cynthia. "Stand up straight, love, and remember to smile." Ebony ushered her husband back towards the closed patio doors and nodded at the event coordinator who quickly hopped into action.

The doors were opened and Ebony and Elton began to descend the aisle in pursuit of their seats. Ella took her position and followed behind them being sure to take her time walking down so that everyone could get a good look at her yoga toned body in the deep cut, V-neck knee-length gown she wore. Behind her was Ana whose longer dress with the split up the side drew in the attention of several eligible bachelors in the crowd. The sisters took their positions across from Preston whose eyes were glued to the doors anxiously. He, like all of the seated guests, were eagerly awaiting the main attraction.

Kenny G's "The Wedding Song" began to play as the flower girl, the granddaughter of one of Ebony's acquaintance's, took her walk down the aisle tossing silk flowers onto the path for Cynthia's entrance.

"Here's your moment," the event planner said enthusiastically.

Cynthia nodded and swallowed hard. At the end of that aisle her future was awaiting her. Her heart was pounding in her chest as if she was about to walk into a room of a stern hiring team in hopes of landing a job. The nervousness was equivalent to that since she knew that she'd be putting herself on display for a crowd of critics. But it didn't matter. Like the event planner had said, this was her moment. This was her opportunity to grab a slice of 'happily-ever-after' and she was ready. Remembering to stand tall, she placed a smile on her face and slowly began to step out onto the rose petal covered walkway. Everyone rose to their feet and watched as the youngest member of the Grayson family moved closer and closer to her destiny. Some oohed and ahhhed over how stunning she looked, some stifled petty remarks, and others wished that they were walking in their own essence of love and happiness.

As she moved along with a genuine smile kissing her lips, Cynthia's eyes never left Preston's. Even across the short distance that separated them she could see the look of love in his eyes and it caused her entire face to light up. Nothing else in the world mattered aside from the feeling that this man evoked within her. As she approached him and placed her hand in his she felt something that she hadn't felt in years: safe, loved, and secure. They were about to begin a new life where she'd never have to fear her heart being broken or being left alone. This was their beginning.

Chapter 2

What's for me is for me
You can't change it, can't take it, can't stop it
If I earned it, it's mine
God will see to it
If I need it, I'll get it
I trust in HIM enough to know it's true
If my heart desires it
No malice on your end can reshape my aspiration
Words hurt,
But I've been made strong
Betrayal is heartbreaking,
But my spirit is resilient
Family can scar you,
But I'm wise enough to know that it
isn't blood that bonds you
What's for me is for me
You can't steal it, can't claim it as
yours, can't wish it away
You only hamper you own blessings when you try …

-Kenni York © 2016

arried life was great. Cynthia couldn't believe just how much Preston actually loved her, but there wasn't a doubt in her mind that he was completely genuine in his adoration. The way he doted on her, reminded her daily of how beautiful she was and how lucky he was to have her, and the way he made her feel like the single most important person in the world was like heaven. She'd never known affection like this, never had such a kismet bond with another person until now. And the truth of the matter was that it scared her. All of her life, she'd been the ugly duckling, the unfortunate one to whom bad things happened and who people never really gravitated to. To know that there was now someone who thought the world of her and to be living her version of a fairy-tale existence felt unreal to her. At times she wondered if she would wake up and find herself alone in a studio apartment instead of their quaint three bedroom ranch-style home, realizing that neither Preston nor their beautiful marriage actually existed. It was a silly thought, but a real one none-the-less, so every night Cynthia got down on her knees and prayed to God to keep her husband by her side always and thanked the Lord for the blessing that he'd bestowed upon her.

Preston Durden was an honest, hardworking, stand-up guy. Standing at six feet, one inches, he donned an appearance reminiscent of Justin Timberlake with his penetrating eyes and short haircut. Although he wasn't much of a religious man, he was a spiritual being with great morale and a set of values that mirrored Cynthia's. Working as a physical therapist for a small clinic in Atlanta, Preston had dreams of opening up his own rehabilitation facility. His ambition and entrepreneurial spirit was one of the things that Cynthia found most attractive about him. They'd met by accident one day when she'd bumped into his buggy at the grocery store, but had been inseparable from that day forth.

They'd been married for nearly a year and everything about their union seemed blissful; from the way they supported one another to the way that they were friends above all. While Cynthia adored the time spent with Preston's parents, George and Pamela Durden, whenever they visited from Florida, the same was not true for time spent with her own family. In fact, Cynthia did all that she could to keep Preston out of the company of her immediate family with the exception of Aunt Thea. With her fears of anything tainting her relationship, there was no way that she would let Ana, Ella, and Ebony get in her husband's ear and turn him against her in their unique little way. While they were practically all of the family that she had, she still didn't trust them. Cynthia did her best to be kind to them while keeping her distance. They had a way of being condescending and nice-nasty to her face while all the while being completely treacherous behind her back. Devoted to keeping her marriage together if it was the last thing she did, Cynthia felt it was imperative to leave her family out of the equation. Unfortunately, her family had other plans.

"Your father's requesting that you and your husband join the rest of us on vacation next month," Ebony revealed.

Cynthia was at her parents five bedroom home in the heart of Covington, Georgia. Standing by the large stainless steel refrigerator drinking a glass of orange juice, Cynthia felt small in the oversized kitchen with all of the sparkling top of the line appliances and the black and tan granite décor that covered everything from the cabinets to the floor to the backsplash over the sink. It was a grand kitchen ironically owned by a woman who could barely boil an egg. Like everything else in Ebony's life, Cynthia knew that the kitchen—truly the entire estate in general—was merely for show. No one lived in the home except for Ebony and her father. Between them they had no grandchildren and rarely did Ebony allow guests to stay over. The home was more of her stamp in the community; it was Ebony's way of showing all of elite-Atlanta and surrounding areas that she had arrived. Elton's net worth of over $300,000,000.00 made it possible for Ebony to buy whatever she wanted whenever she wanted and she certainly did.

Cynthia wasn't intrigued by the vacation that Ebony was mentioning. Every year her father planned some extravagant summer getaway and every year it had turned out to be tumultuous for Cynthia. This year she had no intentions of going along because she had no desire to trap herself and Preston in close quarters with the vultures that she called her family. She simply sipped her juice as she waited for her father to come down and take her out to their monthly father-daughter lunch.

"We're going to the Poconos," Ebony went on. "Everyone has their own suite and we'll be there for four days and three nights. Of course, Elton's paid for everything already so you don't have to worry about a thing."

Cynthia's eyebrow went up at the remark. Sure, her father typically did cover all of the expenses for their family vacations, but she knew there was much more of a malicious meaning in her step-mother's words. Because she wasn't in her father's pocket and was living solely off of the modest income from Preston's job and her own employment as a dental assistant. Together they made a decent living but it was nothing compared to the extravagant lifestyle of her parents. At times it felt as if Ebony went out of her way to remind Cynthia that they lived a better life than she did, forgetting that her 'better life' was compliments of Cynthia's father's hard work, sacrifices, and determination. As the owner of one of the largest record companies in America, GMG, short for Grayson Music Group, Elton Grayson did remarkably well for himself and his wife did equally as well with flaunting around his money and his achievements.

"I don't think we're going to be able to make it," Cynthia said politely.

Ebony raised a brow. "And why not?"

"We can't just take off from work on a whim like that. More advance notice has to be given."

Ebony waved her off and pressed the button on her Keruic to pour herself a cup of green tea. "Nonsense. Just let them know that you have to go off with your father, they'll understand."

Cynthia chuckled. "The work force doesn't operate like that. They're not going to care that my dad wants to go on vacation."

"They will when they know that your father is Elton Grayson."

Cynthia remained silent. That was an area in which they differed. While Ebony didn't miss an opportunity to make it known that she was related to the Elton Grayson, Cynthia would just as soon keep it quiet. She didn't want to get by in the world on her father's name and money. She was her own person and wanted to be seen as such. Ebony on the other hand lived to be recognized as Mrs. Elton Grayson.

"Besides, your father will have a fit if you don't come and I really don't want to deal with that so you're coming," Ebony said with finality.

"Really, it isn't that simple," Cynthia protested. Perhaps it could be, but she was adamant about not wanting to spend any more time with her family than she necessarily had to.

Ebony turned around to face her step-daughter with a tight grin and her hands on her hips. "Listen to me closely dear, it wasn't a question or an invitation. It was a mandate. Elton doesn't ask for much, just this cumbersome family vacation and a dinner. For God's sake, you can manage to squeeze in some time for your father and come up for air from that little love nest you've been hiding in with Preston."

"Preston," Cynthia corrected him, noticeably agitated.

"Whatever. You'll give your father what he wants and you will not make life hard for me, is that understood? Really, you'd think that you'd be a little more grateful with all that we've done for you."

Cynthia was astonished by the statement. She stood stark still staring at her step-mother clad in a Donna Karen pant suit and draped in pearls with her face remarkably made up as if she was expecting photographers to swoop in at any minute. Unfortunately, Cynthia could still see the signs of aging in her cheeks and the cynical look in her eyes only made her unattractive. She tried to run down a mental list of the things that her parents had done for her which would constitute the guilt trip that Ebony was attempting to lay on her, but all she could remember from the time that her father had linked up with Ebony was being treated like an unwanted, forgettable, waste of space. For that, she felt she owed them nothing but familial respect because of the ties that bound them.

"Besides, this'll give us the chance to get to know this husband of yours better since you've done such a stellar job of keeping him to yourself all this time," Ebony continued. "Had we not met him once or twice before the wedding I would have bet money that you were making the whole engagement up." She laughed dryly and turned around to fix her tea to her liking.

Cynthia held her tongue, not wanting to snap back and be disrespectful to her stepmother in her father's home. Ever since Ebony came into her life Cynthia had been keeping silent whenever she felt slighted. Only once had she ever attempted to call her stepmother out on the way she treated her and that hadn't gone over too well. Since then, she'd made it a habit of simply keeping quiet and praying that one day her father would see Ebony for the monster she truly was on the inside. In the meantime, Cynthia did her best to remain respectful and loving because after all, she couldn't change the fact that Ebony didn't seem to be going anywhere any time soon.

"Seriously, dear, we're all so glad that you're married and happy," Ebony said with her back still turned to Cynthia.

No you're not, Cynthia thought.

"We're surprised that you managed to pull that off," Ebony stated, "because we would have never thought you a bride in a million years … but look at God! So, you should be proud to display your husband, dear. You should be proud to show that our lord is definitely in the blessing business and that miracles happen every day."

Cynthia turned away to rinse her glass out in the sink and place it in the dishwasher. Her cheeks burned and her eyes got misty. She hated that she was so sensitive to the way that her step-family spoke to and regarded her. Even as an adult she couldn't seem to shake the feeling of worthlessness that they seemed to constantly instill in her. Closing the dishwasher, Cynthia stared out of the kitchen window peering out into the back of the house where the water from the pool glistened in the sunlight. The water looked so clean and inviting, but even poolside memories evoked pain within her that she thought she'd long since overcome.

SEVEN YEARS AGO

It was summer and the sun was blazing hot. Never one to let an opportunity to show off her home, possessions, and body, Ebony had decided to host a pool party for the girls and their friends as well as her own circle of cronies, other socialites who spent more time gossiping and boasting than anything else. Both Ana and Ella had invited five friends a piece but Cynthia had invited no one. Most of the people that spoke to her in school only did so because of her connection to her popular step-sisters. Still, she wanted to enjoy the luxury of the pool and the barbeque lunch that her father had catered especially for them.

While Ana and Ella sported patterned bikinis and took selfies all day with their friends to post on Facebook, Cynthia wore a more modest one-piece solid black bathing suit. Because she hadn't filled out as well as her step-sisters yet and because of her self-consciousness, she didn't feel comfortable wearing anything more revealing. Ebony hadn't made it any better on the day when they'd all gone shopping.

"You have to be sure to shop for your body type," Ebony told her. "No one wants to see your jiggly belly or those thick thighs. Really, dear, you're going to have to start coming to the gym with me if you ever intend to do something with that round body of yours."

Despite the difference in her attire verses her step-sisters' and her lack of companionship, Cynthia tried her best to enjoy the festivities. While the other girls sat around the pool looking cute, she actually dove into the pool and swam. She enjoyed the feel of the cool water engulfing her body and caressing her skin. She wasn't the least bit concerned with her hair getting wet. She'd pulled it into a ponytail at the top of her head and went on to have a good time. However, Ana and Ella refused to get their hairdos messed up sense they'd just got their hair done the day before in preparation for today's party. Just like their mother, they never missed an opportunity to put themselves on display.

Growing tired of the water aerobics, Cynthia pulled herself out of the pool and walked past Ebony and her friends in route to the towel caddy positioned behind them. She pulled a towel from the waterproof caddy dried off quickly. Leaving her towel on a chair situated at the patio table nearby, she brooklynyed through the opened back door of the kitchen to get herself a glass of lemonade. The caterers were bustling around, moving in and out of the kitchen, setting up the barbeque buffet near the patio table. After getting her beverage, Cynthia sauntered back outside in the direction of the chair she'd claim, but the mention of her name coming from the huddle of women laid out on the lounging chairs nearby stopped her.

"Cynthia's her own train wreck," Ebony stated.

"What are you going to do with that child?" Rochelle Jones, the wife of a former basketball player, asked shaking her head. She was seated two chairs down to Ebony's right with her oversized sunglasses covering her eyes.

"What can I do other than pray for her? We can't all be born with good genes."

"But with the money Elton has," Tenniel Elder, a twice married boutique owner, chimed in, "you should be able to at least make her look acceptable on the surface."

"Darling, no amount of money can replace classic good taste, etiquette, and grace," Ebony replied. "I can dazzle her in gems and it still wouldn't increase her value because she'll still be that same lump of clay underneath."

"Clay is meant to be molded," pointed out Darla White, a well-known gossip columnist that Ebony kept around just to make sure that her name stayed in print. "Work with the girl. At least put her in somebody's gym or get that cute trainer of yours to give her a one-on-one."

Ebony readjusted the large beach hat covering her newly hairdo and leaned her head back. "Ana and Ella have never been this much work. Really, I can't put more effort into someone else's bastard child than my own children."

"Wasn't Elton married to Cynthia's mother?" Darla asked, checking the facts. "That makes her more of an orphan than a bastard."

"All the same, I can't tire myself out trying to give her class when I don't have to go to such extreme measures with my own children. If I could get away with sending her off to boarding school I would but I know that Elton would have a fit if I so much as mention it." She shook her head. "I can't phantom what it's like to go through life being the ugly duckling especially when she's surrounded by beautiful girls like Ana and Ella. Did I tell you that the girls were invited to prom by some senior classmen?"

A series of oohs and ahhhs occurred in response to Ebony's news.

"Even Cynthia?" Tenniel asked in astonishment. "Where there's your opportunity to get her made over."

Ebony looked over at her friend as if she'd grown a third head. "Of course not Cynthia. I've never seen one boy give her a second glance, much less invite her to prom.

She relaxed in her seat once more and hesitated. "Hmmm … I worry about her future."

"What do you mean?" Rochelle asked.

"I mean, suppose no man ever marries her. Then she'll forever be Elton's responsibility and be in his pockets all of the time. That is simply not acceptable."

"Cynthia's a smart girl," Darla commented. "I think she'll do well to be self-sufficient … man or no man, I don't see her as the type to live off of Daddy forever."

"I certainly hope not. I didn't sign up to be permanently responsible for some other woman's spinster daughter. She better have a plan because there's no way that I'm going to let Elton carry that child through life."

"You don't think you're being just a little hard on the girl?" Darla asked. "Sometimes it's the ugly ducklings who actually grow up to be the beautiful swans."

Ebony laughed. "Right. That would be the day. Honestly, I'll be the first to admit that I was wrong if some man ever comes along and asks for Cynthia's hand in marriage."

Rochelle chimed in on the laughter. "The girls are getting older. If she's going to transform at all, now would be the time."

"Don't hold your breath," Ebony stated. "Elton should have reserved his sperm or at least met me first before peddling away his formative years with that sickly woman. We could have bred the perfect child."

"Do you at least get along with her?" Tenniel asked. "I know how that step-child thing can get ugly at times. Thank God my step-children are either grown or live with their mothers."

"She's mindful," Ebony answered. "Severely needy and childish for her age, but she minds. And lucky for her that she does. Otherwise, there'd be no peace in the valley. Elton knows, a happy wife makes for a happy life. So long as the girl gives me no trouble, everyone's happy. And I don't care if she finds a man, a career, or what … once high school's over she better have a plan because I'm cutting off loose the apron strings. I want my husband and our money to myself."

"I'll drink to that," Rochelle stated, holding up her half empty margarita glass.

The women clinked glasses and shared in a laugh, completely oblivious to the sulking teenager positioned within earshot behind them. Cynthia felt humiliated listening to her stepmother's declaration of how no man would ever want her and how she planned to cut her off financially in the future. Never had Cynthia felt so worthless in her entire life. Before anyone could notice her, she wrapped her chubby frame as tightly as she could in her beach towel, and slid into the house through the open patio door. For the remainder of the pool party Cynthia stayed in her room out of sight of all the others. There was no use in being surrounded by people who thought so little of her and felt that she was nothing more than an ugly burden.

Sitting on the floor in her room with her door locked and her back against the side of her bed, Cynthia held in her hands a framed photo of her mother. Since moving into the house with her new family there'd been no memories posted of her mother. She understood that Ebony didn't want to be constantly reminded of her husband's first wife, but Cynthia desperately needed something to feel close to her mother. So, she kept that one framed picture by her bedside making it the first thing she saw in the mornings and the last thing she laid eyes on at night.

"It's not true, is it, Mom?" she asked the photograph of her mother's dazzling smile staring back at her. "I'm not an ugly duckling, am I?"

Her tears dripped down onto the glass protecting the photo. Overwhelmed with emotion, she hugged the frame tightly against her chest as if willing her mother's image to come out of the glass and hug her back. She couldn't remember the last time she'd had a sincere hug or the last time she'd actually felt like she was important. She spent many days locked away in her room so that she wouldn't have to face the scrutiny of her stepsisters or her stepmother. Her father was so busy with work and pleasing Ebony that he didn't even seem to notice anything else going on within his family, Cynthia's unhappiness included.

After a few moments, she looked back down at the frame and stared into her mother's eyes. "I promise to never be anything like them. I'll never go around hurting other people and making them feel bad no matter what. I don't ever want anyone to feel like this. I need you, Mama. I miss you so much." She sniffed and climbed up on her bed to curl up, still holding on to the photo. "I don't care what she says, I don't need their money and someone will love me one day for me. Right, Mama?" she whispered unsurely as if her mother would truly confirm her statement.

CURRENT DAY

"There's my girl," Elton's voice boomed out as he entered the rather quiet kitchen.

Cynthia turned away from the window to see her father approaching her with open arms. He was an amazing handsome and fit older man of fifty and his graying beard and close-cut hair cut looked great on him. Cynthia smiled warmly. It was always a pleasure seeing her father, her true family, and even more of a pleasure whenever they were able to spend some time alone. Cynthia rose and spread her thick arms to greet him. "Hi, Dad!"

Ebony watched them embrace with a sour expression on her face. With her tea cup in hand, she stood by the island and shook her head. "Really, Elton? Must you yell throughout the house? We're the only ones here. We can hear you just fine, dear."

Elton paid no mind to his wife's nagging; it was just her way of trying to get him to have some couth. Instead, he squeezed his daughter lovingly and took a step back to take in her appearance. "Preston treating you right?"

Cynthia blushed, feeling great to know that her father was concerned about her wellbeing. "Of course he is."

"Good deal because if he isn't I have a lawyer that can make him a thing of the past like that." He snapped his thick fingers and laughed. "Tell 'em he doesn't want to play with me."

"I'm sure that Preston and Cynthia are perfect for each other dear," Ebony cut in. "No need in expending your resources to settle any of their minuet differences."

"Nonsense," Elton replied, pulling his iPhone out and glancing at the screen. "I wouldn't let a day go by with anyone mistreating my only daughter. Money's no object."

"Don't be absurd," Ebony mumbled, her words lost in her tea cup as she took a sip of the warm liquid. She gave her husband a tight-lipped smile. "Besides, you have *three* daughters. Let's not be petty."

Although Cynthia knew that Ebony cared very little about the success of her marriage and only wanted to ascertain Cynthia wasn't cashing any checks courtesy of her father, she still had to agree with her stepmother. "Ebony is right, Dad. Put the checkbook away. Preston and I are fine." She smiled brightly. "Can we go to lunch now, please?"

"Long as you're happy," Elton stated, sticking the phone back into his pocket. "Come on! Your chariot awaits." He crooked his arm and held it out to his daughter.

Cynthia gladly hooked her arm through his and together they exited the kitchen.

Ebony watched them walk out and fought back the sickening feeling bubbling in her stomach. She hated the little lunch dates that Elton took Cynthia on regularly. Not because she felt left out of the experience, but because she wanted to hear every syllable being uttered to make sure that the girl wasn't saying anything disparaging about her or talking Elton out of any money. As it stood, she managed most of his affairs and she had no intentions of letting little Miss-Orphan-Annie step on her toes where Elton's finances were concerned. The way Ebony saw it, if Cynthia wanted to secure any kind of fortune she had best do it on her own or through her little physical therapist, lowly paid husband. Everything about Elton belonged to her and sooner or later she'd be the sole beneficiary of his estate.

For each daddy-daughter date, Elton allowed Cynthia to choose where they would dine. Today she chose Longhorns, a simple steak house. As they seasoned their entrees and concluded small talk, Cynthia felt a tiny sense of nostalgia. Time with her father was great, but if her mother were there things would have been perfect.

"You know we could have gone anywhere," Elton told her. "Ruthie's has the best steaks I've tasted in a long time."

Cynthia cut up her sirloin steak and smiled at her plate. Traces of Ebony's influence seemed to linger within her father's conversation from time to time. Only his wife would have a low opinion of their current eatery. "This is fine, Dad. I know it's nothing like the fine dining experiences you've become accustomed to but I like it."

Elton buttered a piece of bread and laughed. "You make me sound privileged and pompous."

"Maybe a little elitist," Cynthia replied jokingly. "Seriously, when's the last time you've been to just a regular restaurant with no VIP sections, no meal over $25.00, and no coat check?"

"I can't say. You know, Ebony likes a certain caliber of places … but that's not to say that anything's wrong with here. I like Longhorn's just fine."

"Mmmhmmm." Cynthia didn't comment on the matter further. She chewed her steak and enjoyed the flavor of the red meat that she probably should have passed on.

"So, I'm sure that you've heard about the family trip."

Cynthia nodded.

"I'm expecting you and Preston there."

"I don't know, Dad. Like I was telling Ebony, I'm just now sure that we can both take off from work to—"

"This is important to me, Cyn. Make it happen." The authority in his tone was a tad bit alarming. "No excuses. Besides, I'd like to get to know Preston better. I need to be better acquainted with the young man who's responsible for my daughter. How's he coming along with the therapy thing? Wasn't he setting his sights on starting his own practice?"

Cynthia sighed. "Yeah well, these things take money so—"

"A man should never let money stand in the way of his dreams. You have to succeed by any means necessary."

"Understandable, but all things happen in time. We just have to do a little more aggressive saving, put in for a loan, and be prayerful."

"You need capital, not prayers."

"You saying you don't believe in the power of God's will for us?"

"Not at all. I'm just wise enough to know that faith without works is dead and—"

"We're working, Dad," she interjected defensively.

"Yes, I'm sure that you are, but sometimes you have to give a little more effort, Cyn. Sometimes you have to put your pride to the side. Have your husband call me."

Cynthia cocked her head to the side. "For what?" she asked slowly and skeptically.

"You're my daughter. There's no reason you should have to struggle. Have him call me and we'll work out the details."

Cynthia put her fork down and looked at her father with a serious expression. "The details?" She shook her head. "No, Dad. I didn't say any of this in request for a handout."

Elton chewed his steak and shook his head. "There's that pride," he said, pointing his knife at her. "And anyway, this is man business. Just ask Preston to call me."

"Daddy, I'm serious! We don't need you to break the bank to fund our dreams. We're responsible adults and can handle our affairs ourselves."

"Everyone needs a little help here and there, Cyn. Everyone. I didn't start GMG on my own. I had help."

"I get that, I do ... but ... please. Just let us do things our way." Her brain was rapidly turning over thoughts. Cynthia knew that Preston was the kind of man that didn't want to feel burdened to any other man. It was a sentiment that they shared and she appreciated him for the being the self-made man that he was. Aside from that, she knew that Ebony would never allow her to live it down if her father went out of his way to give them a contribution or even a loan unless there was some exuberant amount of interest tacked on to it. She'd gone all of her adult life without asking for a cent from her parents, there was no way that she was about to start now. Ebony seemed to believe that she was an opportunist, simply standing by and waiting for the chance to milk her father. Her stepmother's snide remarks about how her dad was covering all of the expenses for their family trip had driven home her assumption that Cynthia and her husband were broke vultures looking for any handout that they could get. The opinion couldn't have been any further from the truth; Cynthia wanted nothing but love from her family. She could care less about the digits in their bank accounts and no amount of money would make her ever want to bow down to her stepmother.

"You know, you have a lot in common with your mother," Elton stated, forking his sweet potato.

At the mention of her mother, Cynthia stood stark still. "I do?" she asked. They never talked about her mom, especially after Elton married Ebony. Before Cynthia knew it, it was as if her mother's existence had become but a mere memory that was a taboo subject in the Grayson household.

Elton nodded. "You're both stubborn as hell. But I always admired that about Miriam. She was relentless and stood firm in what she believed in." He stared off into the distance past Cynthia's shoulder as if lost in the past. "She was a great woman."

Cynthia noted the shimmer in his eyes and looked away. She'd never seen her father tear up before and certainly had never witnessed him having a tender moment with regards to her mother. There'd been times that she'd wondered if he'd forgotten her; if he still loved her even though he'd moved on. In this moment she knew that there was still some feeling there and that he hadn't completely put her mother out of his heart and mind despite Ebony's attempts to do just that.

Elton shook his head and pulled himself out of the trance he'd been caught up in. His eyes fell upon his daughter and the radiant glow of her skin. He'd never seen her look so beautiful. "There's something different about you," he stated.

Cynthia looked up and donned a perplexed expression. "What do you mean?" she asked, sitting up straighter in her seat and adjusting her white blouse.

"You're glowing," he said. "You're stunning, Cynthia."

She knew that it wasn't altogether true, but she was grateful that her father saw her as more than the pudgy daughter that often remained in the shadows. "Thank you."

"You look ... happy."

She smiled brightly and reached across the table to grab her father's hand. "Yes, Dad. I'm so happy and for the longest I didn't think that I ever would be."

"Ridiculous. You've always deserved nothing less than a great life, love, and happiness."

"And I have that."

They sat still for a moment, holding hands and communicating with their eyes. He was truly happy for her and Cynthia was glad to know that her father sincerely cared about her wellbeing.

"How was lunch with Elton?" Preston asked as he came out of the bathroom wrapped in his favorite tan and brown terrycloth towel. He had a ritual of coming straight home from work every day and getting right into the tub to wash off the work day he'd experienced.

Cynthia put away freshly folded laundry and took a good look at the man whose last name she bared. "It was great," she answered with a smile. "I really appreciate the time that I get to spend with him alone."

"I think it's nice how you carve that time out for one another. If I ever have a daughter I hope I'm as close to her as you are to Elton."

Cynthia frowned slightly.

"What's the matter?" Preston asked, catching her expression, as he searched through his drawer for underclothes.

"Nothing … I mean, it's just that Dad and I aren't as close as I'd like for us to be. I know he loves me, I just feel like there's this long-standing gap between us that limits us to these little lunches."

"And your family vacations."

Cynthia stood still eyeing her husband's back. "What did you say?"

He closed the drawer and faced her. "The vacations. It's a tradition right? I got an email this afternoon from Ebony about it."

Cynthia bit her lower lip. It infuriated her that Ebony would go behind her back and extend an invitation to Preston when she'd already kindly declined on her family's behalf. "It's no big deal," she replied nervously. "It's something Dad likes to do but I already let them know that we couldn't make it so …" Her words trailed off as she turned to leave the room, hoping to dead the conversation right where it was.

"Well, I shot her a message back accepting the offer," Preston stated nonchalantly. "I think it'd be good to get away for a while. I mean, I know you're not that tight with your sisters but it's not like we have to be up under them the whole time do we?"

Cynthia's stomach turned somersaults as she reached out to grab the frame of the door. She had no desire to go away a secluded resort with the people who loved to pick her apart the most. So far her relationship had remained untainted by her stepsisters' and stepmother's scrutiny. What would happen now if she allowed them to judge her husband and tear her down at the same time? The thought of the possible humiliation made her want to vomit right there on their cream-colored carpet. She turned to look at her adorable husband who simply smiled at her in return. He had no idea the hell he'd just signed them up for and Cynthia was almost certain that she wouldn't be able to get him to renege.

"It'll be good for us," he said, walking over to her. "A little relaxation. A little get away. I can't wait to see you strut your stuff in your swimsuit."

Cynthia blushed. No one had ever been interested in seeing her round figure in a swimsuit. "Stop it," she said, unable to hide the smile that crept upon her lips.

Preston stroked her face gently. "You're the most beautiful woman I've ever met."

"You're just saying that so that I'll agree to go on this trip."

He shook his head and pressed a kiss against her forehead. "No, I'm saying it because it's the truth and I love you." He kissed the bridge of her nose, followed by the tip, and then graced her lips with a tender peck. "I put in for the time off and already got the green light. I'm sure your job won't mind letting you off for a few days, so go ahead and take care of that. It'll be good, I promise. Any time that we're together is guaranteed to be a good time."

She looked up into his bright eyes and couldn't help but concede to his wishes. Maybe she was overreacting. Maybe Anna and Ella wouldn't be as difficult to tolerate as she anticipated. Maybe it was a good thing for her family to see that things between her and Preston were going really well. With any luck, perhaps they'd develop a new perception of her instead of seeing her as the ugly-duckling of the family. Cynthia threw her arms around Preston's waist and brought her face upward so that their lips could meet yet again, this time in a sweeter, more passionate, lingering kiss. Seconds later, she pulled away and smiled at her husband. "Fine," she said softly. "I guess we're going on vacation."

"We sure are." Preston's right hand found its way to give her a firm squeeze. "Sexy," he leered with that knowing look in his eyes.

Cynthia never tired of him showing her how much he was attracted to her. She eyed him lustfully and focused on the towel knotted around his waist. "So um … how about you show me what you have in store for me doing this little get away." Her hand glided down to the towel.

Preston licked his lips as he reached down to pull the bottom of her shirt upward. Cynthia accommodated him by raising her hands over her head. With ease, he removed her top and wasted no time in lowering his face into the welcoming of her bosom. He kissed and nibbled the tops of her voluptuous mounds, squeezing them as he did so. Cynthia moaned softly, enjoying the feel of his cool kisses caressing her bare skin. With no hesitation, she pulled at the towel until it finally gave way and fell to the floor exposing his most private extremity. With her left hand, she reached down to bear witness to the physical evidence of Preston's excitement. His enthusiasm escalated the moment she took him into her hand. He quickly reached around her and fumbled with the clasp of her bra until her breasts were finally freed. Tossing the garment to the ground beside her shirt and his bath towel, he took both of her breasts into his respective hands holding as much of her D-cups as he could.

Right there in the doorway of the bedroom, they engaged in foreplay that had them both burning with sensual heat. Preston lowered his head once again and took her left nipple into his mouth. He'd done this many times during the course of their sexual relationship and each time it had sent shivers up Cynthia's spine. But this time, she practically climbed up the frame of the door in response to the intense stimulation his actions were causing. Her nipples were increasingly sensitive and each flick of his tongue or suckle of his lips drew her towards the brink of climax and he hadn't even touched her love mound yet. She relished in the moment feeling beautiful, loved, and wanted. After years of feeling as if she could never measure up to others she finally was realized her worth and felt desired. As her husband preceded to lead her to their bed where he would then undoubtedly make passionate love to her, Cynthia knew that this was her heaven on earth: Preston was her everything. No matter what, she knew there could never be a life worth living without this man and the way that he made her feel physically and emotionally.

When Elton set out to do something, he always did it big. With the help of Ebony making decisions, plans, and reservations, the Graysons' family vacations were always a big to do. Elton spared no expenses and Ebony made sure of it. This time no one could deny the grandeur of their lavish accommodations at the Sky Top lodge in the heart of the Poconos. The lodge itself sat within the mountains and looked like a large manor fit for a king and his queen. Everyone had a private, deluxe suite on the fourth floor of the main edifice, much to Cynthia's pleasure. It was a far better setup than forcing them all to share living space in one of the resorts cozy cottages. The décor of the room was simply breathtaking from the exhilarating garden view, the combination of vaulted and sloped ceilings, the fancy king sized antique oak bed decked out in satin linens, the uniquely patterned wallpaper that adorned the walls, and the antique vases that housed fresh flowers; and that was just the bedroom. The adjourning parlor area equipped with a fully stocked bar, sofa and love seat, and custom designed dinette tucked off in the far right corner of the room had an equal air of charm and grace. The couple was touched by the welcome basket situated in the middle of the dinette table whose contents included two bottles of Dom Perignon, a box of white and milk chocolate covered strawberries, customized champagne glasses with their initials, and gift certificates for a pre-arranged spa-date.

"Your father seems to think of everything," Preston said, looking over the gift basket.

"Hmmm. I'm sure he has more than a little help," Cynthia replied, sinking down onto the plush fabric of the loveseat.

Preston picked up a card resting on the table beside their goodies. "Looks like we have correspondence from your folks."

Cynthia's interest was piqued as she looked over in Preston's direction. "What is it?"

His eyes poured over the words and he read the message aloud to his wife. "Dinner's at six sharp, do try not to be late. We're meeting in the Windsor Dining Room, attire is business casual." He chuckled. "Signed C.G."

Cynthia's eyebrow raised a bit as she threw her head back onto the back of the sofa. "Ebony," she stated. She knew what this dinner was; it was one of the organized events of the weekend where they were all expected to come together like one happy family. It was an opportunity for Ebony to get in everyone's business and try her hand at playing mother while showing off for the other vacationers just in case someone of importance was nearby.

Preston looked at his watch. "Well, we have a couple of hours before our dinner reservation. Shall we explore the grounds?"

Cynthia shook her head. "Can we just enjoy each other in the privacy of our room before we have to go out and share ourselves with the others?"

Preston eased next to her on the sofa and pulled Cynthia into his embrace. "We could do that but I'm worried."

"About what?" she asked skeptically.

"I'm worried that I'll lose myself in you while isolated up here in this magnificent display of ambiance and then we'll miss dinner and upset your folks." He smiled as he watched the corners of her lips spread and the look in her eyes soften.

She readjusted herself so that her head was laying in his lap and reached her arms up to pull him downward. "Well, that's a risk I'm willing to take."

They laughed and kissed, relishing in the moment of quietness and serenity while enjoying their bond which had only grown tighter over the course of their first year of marriage. *This isn't so bad*, Cynthia thought, as her husband's tongue did the tango with hers. *Maybe this vacation was a good idea after all.*

"Why isn't that a quaint little get up," Ebony commented as Preston and Cynthia approached her and Elton waiting to at the hostess stand to be seated.

Cynthia ignored her stepmother's wayward compliment and focused on greeting her father with a hug. Dressed in a strapless black cocktail dress which hugged her snuggly at the bust and flared out from the waistline to the bottom of her ample thighs, Cynthia felt beautiful. Preston had marveled over her attire the whole way from their room to the elevator, making her secure in her decision to wear the dress she'd never before had the confidence to do.

Preston was quite dapper himself in his black suit and white collared shirt. He stood proudly next to his wife with one arm around her waist and one arm outreached to shake his father-in-law's hand. "I've got to thank you Elton for the immaculate accommodations," he said graciously.

Elton gave him a firm shake and a head nod. "Anything for my daughter and her betrothed. How about that view?"

"It's awesome, sir. Everything is great. Couldn't have asked for a better setup."

Elton winked. "Stick with me kid and this'll be nothing compared to what you can experience over your lifetime.

Ebony smiled proudly as she looped her arm through Elton's being sure to flash her diamond cocktail ring and shiny bracelet in the process. "If anyone knows class it's the Graysons."

"No argument there," Preston replied politely.

Elton and Ebony looked as if they were ready for a full spread magazine layout photo shoot for Essence. Ebony's makeup was flawless and she the cream colored A-line dress that she wore accentuated her perfectly round breasts and gave everyone a great view of her long, firmly toned legs. Diamonds sparkled everywhere around her from her earlobes to her hands. Elton's attire complemented hers as he pulled off his own GQ look in a finely tailored cream-colored suit, chocolate collared shirt, and chocolate Stacy Adams shoes. The only diamonds he possessed were in the platinum wedding band that Ebony made sure he never left home without.

Ebony looked past Cynthia and Preston and smiled. "Ah, there's Ella."

Everyone turned to watch as Ella swayed through the walkway to approach the group. Her gold sequined, backless, bodycon mini-dress was a sight to behold. It was a direct reflection of Ella's flashiness. With her hair swept up into a bun on top of her head and long tear drop gold earrings dangling from her ears, Ella knew that she was the center of attention. Many men turned to get a second look as she strutted by in her five inch gold pumps. She lavished in the attention and smiled to herself thinking about how many were lusting after her body.

"Hi, everyone," she greeted the family as she looked over at a gentlemen at a nearby table who was peering at her over the top of his cognac glass while his unsuspecting date yammered on.

"You look stunning, darling," Cynthia complimented her oldest daughter with no sarcasm in her tone. It pleased her to see her daughters taking pride in their appearance and being sure to be head-turners whenever they stepped out in public.

Ella stroke a pose and smiled. "I try," she replied vainly.

"Where's your sister? We had a reservation for six."

Ella frowned as she opened her clutch bag to retrieve her compact. "I don't know, mother. We're not joined at the hip you know." She checked her makeup to ensure that she was still dazzling and dropped the compact back into her bag upon satisfaction.

Ebony's lips tightened. She had a thing for organization and obedience. Seeing that Ana had no regards for her instructions irritated her.

"Grayson?" a male voice called out.

The family turn to see the maitre'd standing behind them.

"Yes," Ebony spoke up. "We're the Graysons."

"Party of seven?" the maitre'd questioned.

"We uh ... we seem to be missing two of our guests," Ebony explained.

"Not a problem. I can go ahead and seat you now if you'd like and then we'll escort your other guests back once they arrive."

"Very well," Ebony agreed, holding tight to Elton's arm with her head held high as the group began to follow the gentleman to their table.

Once everyone was seated, he passed out menus and left two laying in front of the two empty chairs. "Your waiter will be with you shortly," he advised before walking off.

As everyone opened their menus and began perusing the listings, Cynthia's curiosity got the best of her. "Who else are we expecting?"

"Hmmm?" Ebony murmured, trying to decide which cocktail would be appropriate before dinner.

"The seventh chair," Cynthia stated, pointing at an empty seat across from her. "Who is it for?"

Cynthia smiled and clutched her menu to her chest. "I wasn't going to say anything because I wanted it to be a surprise. But Ana's got a suitor."

"You make it sound like they're going to get married tomorrow, Mom," Ella replied sounding unimpressed.

"Well you never know, dear. She did ask if it was okay for him to come on vacation which says a lot. No respectable woman goes away with a man on vacation if she doesn't have serious intentions upon making their relationship permanent."

"Some people are just looking to have a good time."

"Nonsense," Ebony snapped. "At a certain age you stop prancing around having a good time and start taking serious stock of your future. Getting married and having a family is the natural order of things and the young women I raised are worth more than just being some man's good time." She shot a stern look at her eldest child and quickly composed herself.

Knowing how her mother felt about appearances and marrying well, Ella tried to smooth things over and then drop the subject. "You're right, mother. I was just saying that we shouldn't get too excited not knowing for sure what the status of their relationship is. But I'm sure that Ana's very astute when it comes to picking a quality mate."

"Of course she is," Ebony agreed, returning her glance to her menu. "As you both should be. You've learned from the best."

Preston and Cynthia shared a look and both worked hard to stifle their laughs. Cynthia nervously broke their glance and looked down at her menu before darting her eyes over in Ella's direction. Ella didn't notice her stepsister watching her. She was too busy looking to her right and making eye contact with the man near the front who'd been eyeing her from the moment she entered the dining room. Cynthia followed Ella's gaze and slightly shook her head as she realized what was going on. Leave it to Ella to be openly flirting with a man who was with another woman. At times, the girl simply had no shame.

"Good evening, family," a tall, slender man of Hispanic descent approached their table gaily. "I'm Hector and I'll be your server for this evening. May I start you off with cocktails and appetizers or shall I give you more time to peruse the selections?"

"We'll have the kale salad all around," Ebony spoke up. "And the pan-seared crab cakes for starters."

"And for your missing guests?" Hector inquired. "Shall I set out salads for them as well?"

"Please do," Ebony answered. "I'll have Ana's hide if she lets this salad welt," she turned and mumbled to Elton.

"And to drink?" Hector asked, scribbling on his note pad.

"A Cosmopolitan for me," Ebony replied. She looked over at Elton. "And uh ... a simple gin and tonic for the gentleman."

Hector looked over at Ella.

"Oh, um ... a sex on the beach is fine," she ordered.

Hector nodded and looked to the Durdens.

"What would you like dear?" Preston asked Cynthia.

"Just water," Cynthia replied. "Thank you."

Preston looked at Hector. "Water with lemon for my wife and a Heineken for me, please."

"Beer?" Ebony asked with disdain. "At dinner, Preston. Surely you can think of a more appropriate beverage."

Preston laughed. "I'll take the beer," he instructed Hector.

Hector nodded. "I'll put this in and be right back."

Preston looked at Ebony whose nose was still turned up as she continued to review her menu. "You know, I'm just a simple man with simple tastes."

"We can see that," Ebony remarked without looking up.

"No cocktail for you, Cyn?" Ella questioned. "Are you cutting back on the empty calories?"

Ebony gave her stepsister a tight-lipped smile. "No, my stomach has just been kind of unsettled lately. I figured it's safer just to go with water."

"Hello, hello, hello everyone," Ana's voice called out jovially as she approached the table dragging a man along behind her by his hand. She stood before the family and smiled widely with her left hand on her hip. Her coral-colored embroidered lace sheath dress was a colorful contrast to the plain dark suit that her date wore. "I'd like for you all to meet Trey."

Ebony looked and took in Trey' appearance. He was 5"8 with broad shoulders and well groomed edge up, an earring that shined a little too much like pure crystal for Ebony's taste, and an overall rugged demeanor that made her wonder where Ana had found him.

"Sorry we're late," Ana said, taking her seat beside her sister.

Trey took the other vacant seat between Ana and Preston. "Right, we kinda lost track of time."

"Well, you know what they say," Ebony said, still eyeing her daughter's friend. "First impressions are everything and tardiness is uncouth."

"Who says that?" Preston whispered to Cynthia who elbowed him and giggled.

"Mother, we apologized," Ana said with a smile. Her eyes glared at her mother, begging the woman not to embarrass her.

"Your salads," Hector injected, returning to the table with the family's first course. He busied himself with setting everyone's salad plates before them only stopping to retrieve the drink orders of the late arrivals. Then, he departed yet quickly returned with the crab cakes which he placed in the center of the table.

Everyone then placed their entrée orders, Ebony ordering for Elton, Preston ordering for Cynthia, and Ana and Trey going last since they needed the extra time to go over the menu. Once that was done, everyone began to dig into the salads. Preston hesitated before picking up the fork closest to his plate and began to try the dish his mother-in-law had forced upon them all. Trey toyed with his salad, pushing the kale leaves from one side of the plate to the other. Ana noticed her beau's skeptical behavior and tried to nudge him before her mother could say anything.

"Do you dislike the salad, Trey?" Ebony asked as she slowly and meticulously buttered half of a roll.

Trey looked up at the older beauty. "Uh … no, it isn't that … I've just never had this kind before. I'm not really the type that tries knew things, you know?"

Ebony nodded. "I see. So we know that you aren't well versed in culinary delights and that your table etiquette leaves a lot to be desired, much as Preston's, seeing as though you're both using your dinner forks to eat your salad."

Trey looked at Ana who quickly snatched his fork and replaced it with the appropriate salad fork. Preston looked at Cynthia who was holding her stomach and taking small bites of her own salad. She shrugged and continued eating. Preston followed suite.

"Why don't you give these young people a break?" Elton finally spoke up, reminding everyone of his presence. "We're all here to have a good time, not to harm on anyone's shortcomings."

Cynthia was stunned that her father had mildly put his wife in her place, but not as stunned as Ebony.

"Dear, I know you're not suggesting that good manners is of little importance," Ebony quipped.

"Of course not," Elton said, chuckling and looking over at Trey reassuringly. "But even I sometimes forget which fork is which."

Seeing that Elton was a lot more down to earth than Ebony, Trey noticeably relaxed and began to give his salad a fair chance with the correct fork.

"So Ana, love," Ebony said, redirecting her attention to her daughter. "You've yet to properly introduce your friend to your family."

"Of course," Ana replied, setting down her fork and covering her partially full mouth. "Where are my manners?" She went around the table letting Trey know who everyone is. "Trey, this is my mother Ebony and my stepfather Elton, my sister Ella, Elton's daughter Cynthia and her husband Preston."

"It's really nice to meet all of you," Trey said with a toothy grin. "Especially you, sir," he said to Elton. "I've followed your career for quite some time."

"Is that right?" Elton asked. "What do you do?"

"Um, Trey is in marketing," Ana quickly answered. "He's very creative, Elton. He's done work for a lot of local businesses around Atlanta. Top notch companies."

Elton nodded. "Sounds impressive."

Trey looked at Ana unsurely before responding. "It pays the bills."

"And that's very important," Ebony cut in.

Ana smiled at Trey. "He's thinking about branching out. Expanding his portfolio and such."

"It's always a good thing to propel yourself further in your career and not remain complacent in your current position," Elton stated.

"Exactly. I was hoping to speak with you in the future about my endeavors, if you're open to it," Trey said.

"Well, I don't know how much help I can be in marketing since my realm is music, but sure, I don't mind at all. We'll set something up."

The excitement radiated all over Trey' face. "Sure thing."

"I'm sure you'll find that you two have more in common than you think," Ana replied. "I'm very proud of Trey' initiative and drive. I just know that he's going to be big in his own rite."

"Thanks for the support, baby," Trey said, leaning over to kiss Ana on her cheek.

For the first time Ebony smiled at the sight of the couple. She was all for any man who was making something of himself and could afford to adequately take care of a woman. "You know we'll do anything that we can to make sure that you girls and your beloveds have everything you need to succeed. We're all about ambition and making a name for yourself in this family. And my Elton is as benevolent as they come. Just look at how he's helping Preston."

Cynthia choked on her salad and dropped her fork. Preston's eyes darted nervously from his coughing wife to his obviously caught off guard father-in-law. As Preston patted Cynthia on her back, Elton shot his wife a look of annoyance.

Cynthia reached for her water glass and took a tiny sip to get herself together. "What do you mean, how he's helped Preston?"

"What?" Ebony asked innocently. "You didn't know?"

"This is supposed to be a vacation," Elton cut in. "I'd rather not discuss business especially at the dinner table."

Cynthia looked at Preston, ignoring her father's request. "What's going on?"

"It's nothing, babe," he answered. "Your dad just reached out to me a few weeks ago regarding the clinic."

"What clinic?"

"My clinic. My private practice. He's helping me with the start up."

Ebony smiled. "Oh the benefits of coming from money," she remarked before taking a sip of her cocktail.

Cynthia looked at her father pointedly. "You deliberately went behind my back and offered him the money after I told you that we didn't need a handout."

"I'm going to thank you to watch your tone at the table, young lady," Ebony snapped.

"Don't think of it as a handout," Elton told his daughter. "It's more of a hand up." He smiled.

Cynthia shook her head. "No matter how you describe it, it's still the same thing. This is something we wanted to do on our own."

"My god!" Ella exclaimed. "What's the big deal? Let your rich father help your husband get his little slice of the American pie. What? Do you want to be poor forever, Cyn? Lord. Try saying thank you."

Cynthia was flustered. "It's not that I'm not grateful for his help it's just—"

"Then leave it alone already," Ella said, growing bored with the entire discussion.

Cynthia looked over at her husband as meaningless chatter began to ensue amongst the rest of the family. Preston's eyes were sorrowful. "Why are you so upset?"

"You don't know what you've done," Cynthia whispered.

"He offered, Cyn. I didn't ask."

Feeling the bile rising up her throat, Cynthia threw her cloth napkin over her unfinished salad plate and rose from the table. "If you'll excuse me," she said in a trembling voice before leaving the table.

Preston turned in his seat watching his wife's retreating figure and instantly stands to follow her.

"Let her go," Ebony advised. "She can be overly emotional sometimes."

"She's not really like the rest of us," Ella stated, waving her hand. "Cynthia doesn't really understand how business and networking works. I mean, she's a smart girl and all but she's meek and passive at best. Ignorant if you will where these types of enterprising situations are involved. You on the other hand seem like a real go-getter, Preston. Handle your business, don't let Cynthia's pride stand in the way of your come up."

Preston looked to Elton, unsure of what he should do.

Elton nodded and took a bite of his appetizer. "I wouldn't have exactly worded it that way, but trust me, son, she'll come around. She was just a little caught off guard." He shot a look at his wife as she nursed her drink giving him back her most innocent expression. "Sit, sit," Elton urged Preston. "Give her a minute to collect herself and she'll be back. Everything'll be fine."

Reluctantly, Preston slid back into his chair and toyed with his fork. He knew his wife and felt that she was a lot more understanding and perceptive than her family was leading him to believe that she was. Sitting there verses running after her didn't exactly feel like the right thing to do, but if her father was right then the last thing she needed was for him to crowd her space when she was clearly upset with him at the moment. He took a deep breath and made up in his mind that if Cynthia didn't return to the table with ten minutes, he'd disregard the popular opinion of the group and chase her down. It was their vacation; he didn't want it to be ruined over his pending business plans or a difference of opinion.

Cynthia hurried through the crowded dining room in search of the ladies room. The moment she was inside of one of the sparkling stalls, her chest heaved and her body involuntarily expelled the contents of her stomach. She dropped her purse on the decorated tile of the bathroom floor and had just enough time to lean over the commode before vomit spurted everywhere. She gripped the porcelain for dear life, afraid that she'd soon pass out given the violent way that her body lurched and her head become light.

There was a knock on the door of her stall as she tried hard to compose herself only to fall prisoner to yet another horrid bout of regurgitating.

"Miss? Miss are you okay?" called out the voice of a kind, older woman.

Cynthia placed her hand over her chest as she finally lifted her head and pushed the lever to flush the toilet. "Yes!" she cried out weakly. "I'll … I'll b-be fine. Thank you."

Although she said the words she wasn't at all certain that it was the truth. Never had she been so sick in her life. For a few weeks she'd been experiencing a queasy stomach, dismissing it as stress. Now, after hearing that her father had gone against her wishes and her husband was in cahoots with him, Cynthia was sold on the fact that she was suffering from severe stress. She'd never been in her parents' pockets before and purposefully so. It was one thing for Ebony to lord the money and riches of her father over her head making her to feel as if she was merely the peasant of the family. It would now be a totally different hell with her believing that she and her husband were now indebted to them because of her father's generosity.

Cynthia pulled some tissue from the roll beside her and shook her head. She knew that she needed to talk Preston out of including her father in his business plans, but something told her that he wouldn't be so willing to listen to her. Starting his own clinic was Preston's dream. She didn't want to do anything that would hinder him from being able to realize it. Cynthia loved Preston so much that she'd give anything to make sure that he was at least half as happy as he made her, even if it meant selling her soul to the devil. As she wiped her mouth the irony of the situation brought tears to her eyes. If in fact she did allow Preston to take the money they may as well see it as selling themselves out to Satan's little helper because everyone knew that Ebony was the overseer of the Grayson estate and finances. Hell had just opened its door a little wider and made a special spot for Cynthia and Preston. The thought sent shivers up her spine.

"Are we going to talk about what happened at dinner?" Preston asked.

Cynthia had returned to the table nearly fifteen minutes after departing, just as Preston was about to search for her. Though her demeanor had been a little frosty and she remained silent through the course of the meal, he'd just been glad to have his wife back by his side. Now, in the privacy of their hotel suite he was eager to resolve their differences so that they could get on with enjoying their vacation. Sitting on the plush king sized bed with his back against the pillows, Preston watched Cynthia as she walked over to her side of the bed and sat with her back to him.

"I haven't been feeling well," she stated. "That's why I excused myself. I was sick."

"And it had nothing to do with me partnering with your father?"

Cynthia sighed, unable to lie to her husband. "It had everything to do with it." She turned around slightly to face him. "This was something I thought that we'd agreed to do on our own. My father has money, yes, and he's contribution can be very helpful. But, as with anything, there's consequences to that, Preston … consequences that I'd just as soon avoid for everyone's sake."

Preston reached over and grabbed her hand. "Honey, your father's a very fair businessman from what I can tell. I listened to his pitch thoroughly and he's having some papers drawn up for me to go over with an attorney. Don't tell me that you don't trust your own father."

Cynthia looked down at the sparkle of Preston's wedding band. "It isn't that," she mumbled, feeling her stomach begin to churn again.

"He's done very well for himself so it's clear that the man knows what he's doing."

"Yes, yes of course. I've never once doubted my father's business sense."

"Then what is it, Cyn?"

She looked up into his eyes and gave him a pleading expression. "I just wanted this to be something that we accomplished without my parents having to pave the way for us."

"It's the same as me finding any other investor or getting a loan from the bank. At least in this instance we know the morale and ethics of the person we're dealing with." Preston pulled her closer to him and placed his arms around her protectively. "Trust me on this."

One of us knows who we're dealing with more so than the other, Cynthia thought. She looked up at her husband and could feel the excitement radiating through his body. He was on the brink of realizing his dream. Who was she to take that away from him? "I wish you'd told me yourself," she said softly.

Preston kissed her forehead. "I wanted to wait until the papers were signed and everything was worked out. We're going to be up and running within a year with the business plan that I have laid out, Cyn. We're on our way, baby. We're on our way. Between you, me, and God there's nothing we can't do, baby."

He leaned down to press a kiss upon her lips that was so tender and sweet that Cynthia nearly forgot what it was that they'd been discussing. In his embrace she felt loved, secure, and safe. Maybe she was worrying too much about the evil potential of her stepmother. Maybe she was overly cynical in general giving her upbringing. But, sitting there in the arms of the man that made her feel like silk, she realized that she didn't have to worry about such things because she had a life partner who held both of other best interests in mind. In that moment, Cynthia relaxed and gave herself over to Preston mind, body, spirit, and soul. Theirs was a bond like no other and not even money or the evil that lurked behind it could alter what they had.

Cynthia heard the ding of the elevator as she strolled down the hall. She hurried hoping to catch it but just as she approached it she was stalled in her movements. Her eyes bulged as looked into the cavity of the elevator to see Ella wrapped around a familiar looking mocha complexioned, bald man who at least a decade older than her. Giggling as his face was nestled in her cleavage, Ella looked up to see Cynthia standing there in shook as the doors of the elevator closed on the scene, hiding the creeping couple from the rest of the world. Instantly the truth dawned on her. Ella's companion was the leering man at the front table from the night before; the one who had been dining with some other woman. Shaking her head, Cynthia pressed the down button for the elevator. She knew that her stepsister could have little shame at times, but felt that creeping with someone else's man was low even for Ella. Still, it was none of her business and in honesty she wished that she hadn't witnessed the incident at all.

Cynthia went on to join Ana at the resort's spa where Ebony had arranged for the girls to have a little quality sister time. Cynthia was surprised that she'd been invited along with the others. The outing seemed like something her stepmother would have much preferred her biological children enjoy alone, thinking that Cynthia would have no appreciation for the experience. Quite the contrary, Cynthia looked forward to the opportunity to relax and try to ward off some of the stress that had her relentlessly sick to her stomach.

As Ana and Cynthia settled into their chairs to prepare for their mani-pedis, Cynthia vowed to herself that no matter what she would enjoy this time. Later she had plans to explore the grounds with Preston following his golf game with her father. Preston knew nothing about golf and secretly Cynthia hoped that the invite wasn't a ploy for her father to get Preston alone to discuss business. Either way, she was here now and it was time to unwind and make the most of the next couple of hours with her stepsisters.

"Where's Ella?" Ana asked, looking down at her iPhone tucked away in a pretty pearl case. "It's not like her to be late."

It was the truth; that was a trait more fitting of Ana herself.

Cynthia remained silent though she wondered if Ella had any intentions upon joining them at all considering she appeared so caught up in her secret love interest earlier.

Ana put her phone down on her lap and frowned. "She sent me to voicemail." She rolled her eyes. "I know she's not trying to bail on this little bonding session. Had I known then I would have stayed in bed with Trey." She giggled and looked over at Cynthia devilishly. "He is simply the most amazing lover."

Cynthia shifted uncomfortably. She was no prude, but she had little interest in hearing about Ana's latest conquest.

"Tell me, does Preston even come close to giving you multiple orgasms during sex?" Ana asked as the nail technician placed her feet into the bubbling water of the foot bowl.

"That's kind of a private question don't you think?" Cynthia asked in response.

"What? It's just us sisters here. This is girl talk, honey." She sneered. "Unless of course little Ms. Married isn't having great sex."

"What would Cynthia know about great sex?" Ella said, entering the room and taking her seat on the other side of Cynthia placing her in the middle of the trio. She kicked off her flip flops and smiled over at the others. "I'm sure that you were a virgin until you married Preston. What a shame. Marrying the first dick that comes along. You wouldn't know if you were having great sex or not since you have nothing to compare it to."

Cynthia was offended but she held her tongue, refusing to allow

Ella to push her out of character. "I'm more than satisfied with my husband in every aspect of our relationship."

Ana laughed. "Really, Cyn? Is that code for the sex is mediocre? Poor girl."

The nail tech ushered Cynthia's feet into her bowl and then started up the water for Ella, trying hard to ignore the banter between the women. Soon they were all soaking their feet and waiting for their avocado face masks to be applied.

"So really, Cynthia, how is married life?" Ella asked.

"We're doing well," Cynthia answered. "I couldn't be happier."

"I still can't believe that you're actually married," Ana sneered.

"Believe it," Cynthia said smugly, looking down at her modest wedding rings. "Honestly, sometimes I can't believe it either. Preston's the best husband a girl could ask for."

"Really? He seems pretty dull to me," Ana commented. She quickly looked over at Cynthia and faked earnestness. "No shade, girl. But until last night I didn't really see anything so appealing about your husband. I mean, as long as you're happy."

"I am very happy," Cynthia said defensively as she wiggled her toes in the warm, bubbling water. "And Preston's very appealing. He's a kind, loving, hardworking and—"

"Well go ahead and add entrepreneur to that list," Ana cut in. "I'm telling you, honey, money makes a man thousand times more appealing especially after he hasn't had any to start with."

"Money isn't everything," Cynthia replied meekly, wishing that she'd bailed on the sister spa session.

"Ha! It's a whole lot of something especially in compensation for mediocre sex," Ella chimed in, stretching in her seat.

Ana laughed, but Cynthia simply shook her head.

"Preston's great in bed thank you very much!" Cynthia snapped. "There's nothing wrong with our sex life so can we please put that to rest?"

"Touchy, touchy," Ana joked.

"What you need is a man with an impressive investment portfolio that matches his vigor and then you can say you have a great sex life, honey," Ella stated.

"What does a man's financial worth have to do with his … his sex drive or his skills?"

"When he's worth something, he acts like it and you definitely reap the benefits."

"Say that," Ana cosigned.

"Oh, so your little thug-marketing exec really has some impressive dividends?" Ella shot back at her sister. "And here I thought he was sniffing around trying to jump on Elton's coattails."

Ana tooted her nose up at the comment, somewhat put off by the fact that her sister would take a shot at her. "Well, however he gets it honey, so long as he gets it. Trey has potential. Mom always said that sometimes you have to show a man the way."

"Hmmm. I don't have time to bring some schlep up. If he can't come correct already then these cookies will remain in the jar. I can't get wet if his pockets aren't set." Ella laughed at her own joke.

"Why does everything have to always come back to sex?" Cynthia asked.

"Because that's the way of the world, honey," Ella answered.

"I disagree. Maybe it's just what you're focused on. Maybe if you focus on traits other than that you'd find a better quality of man."

Ella raised a brow at Cynthia. "Oh, so now that you've been married for a year you're the expert on relationships now? Thank you, but I think I'm doing just fine working with what I've got."

Suddenly, Cynthia was reminded of Ella's moment of indecency in the elevator earlier. She opened her mouth to speak on Ella's concept of what she had—more like what she was borrowing from another woman—but Ella's hardened expression practically dared her to utter a word about what she'd seen.

Cynthia took a deep breath, deciding to hold on to Ella's secret. It wasn't like her to sling mud just because the others were coming for her. "Whatever happened to love, intimacy, companionship, and just simply enjoying a person for who they are and not what they have?"

"I'll leave all of that to ole traditional thinking women like you, dear," Ella said. "I'm a little more evolved and my needs are simple: money and orgasms. Love fades."

"It doesn't have to," Cynthia said softly.

"But it does. People fall in and out of love all the time. It's the women who think that their men are so in love with them who are oblivious to the truth and end up heartbroken once they find out that their man is cheating on them. I refused to be disillusioned … I'm fully aware that a relationship based solely on the weak emotions of love is doomed for failure." Ella looked over at Cynthia sympathetically. "You think you're so happy now but it's only a matter of time before reality eventually kicks you in the ass. But, what do I know. My one little marriage doesn't count, right?" She leaned her head back and closed her eyes signifying the end of the conversation.

Cynthia disagreed with her stepsisters' outlook and tried to put the disheartening viewpoint out of her mind. It was just like Ella and Ana to try to make her feel small about her marriage. Being genuinely happy for her was just out of the question. Sure, they tried to make it seem as though they were educating her and had her best interest at heart, but it only came out sounding and feeling as though they were putting her down and trying to instill doubt and insecurity within her. *Don't listen to her,* she thought. *Preston loves you. No matter what happens or what anyone says, Preston loves you. We got good love.*

Chapter 3

You are embedded within my spirit
I feel when something's wrong,
I sense when there's excitement brewing within you
I hurt when you're troubled
No other connection could be so undeniably kismet,
So clearly etched in the stars of the universe
Than the one between you and I
I carry you with me,
In a special place in my heart
That has grown over time and will never lessen
Even in death.

-Kenni York © 2016

ith the financial backing of the Grayson empire, within months Preston was able to put his business plan into effect. He worked days at his current therapist position, taking his lunch breaks to run out and handle business matters for his own venture. After work, he focused on the building developments for the location he'd settled upon. Weekends were dedicated to interviewing potential employees, purchasing furniture and equipment for the practice, as well as going over the books to make sure that things stayed within budget. True to Preston's word, Cynthia noticed that Elton made little or no noise regarding what was going on with Right Touch Whole Body Therapy, as Preston so named his company. Not that Cynthia ever thought that her father would stake claim upon Preston's accomplishment; her worries initially lied within Ebony and her money-hungry, scheming nature. Still, all was quiet from the Graysons.

Cynthia did what she could to assist her husband, but for the most part she sat back and allowed him to handle his business without interfering. This was his thing and she could see how completely invested he was in making sure that the clinic was a success. Besides, between working and making it through her unplanned pregnancy, she already had her hands full. Shortly after returning from their family vacation, she'd learned that what she thought were nerves and stress getting the best of her was really morning sickness that was making a habit of sticking around all day. She'd been elated, to say the very least upon confirming that she was with child, but as the months flew by and her belly grew bigger, Cynthia began to wonder how she'd really make it through. All though Preston was excited about becoming a first time father, his time, energy, and focus was split between work and getting things in order with the clinic. With him being her greatest support system, Cynthia wondered just how much he'd be able to give her the help and encouragement that she felt she would need growing closer to childbirth and even more so once the baby was born. She didn't really have any close friends to call upon for parenting advice and help and the only family she really had to call her own was her dad, step-sisters, and step-mother. Ebony didn't really appear to be the grandmother type in Cynthia's eyes so she didn't want to rely on her weak relationships with her family to sustain her through this new era in her life.

At a time like this, a girl wanted her mother more than anyone else. Preparing for motherhood was beginning to weigh heavily on Cynthia's spirit as she was constantly reminded of the fact that her mother was not there. It was a bittersweet time period and as the third trimester carried on, Cynthia felt the burden of loneliness and wasn't sure of how to cope. As with any other time that she needed a strong maternal figure, Cynthia called on the only person that she knew would never steer her wrong: Thea. Feeling the need to be close to her mother but also have the opportunity to reach out to her aunt, Cynthia invited Thea to meet her at her mother's gravesite.

The cemetery was quiet during Cynthia's mid-afternoon visit. The wind blew restlessly, swaying the tree branches and fallen leaves all around her. Cynthia stood for a moment staring at the tombstone she visited often as soon as she'd stepped into adulthood. No matter how many times she came out to reconnect with her mother, she could never quite accept the fact that she'd watched her mother lowered into the ground at that very spot, changing her life forever. Cynthia struggled to lower herself to the ground despite the weight of her belly so that she could wipe away the debris from her mother's tomb and lay down the bouquet of fresh red roses that she'd brought her. Touching the coolness of the stone marker, Cynthia stared at her mother's name etched eloquently across the front.

"I'm having a baby," she said softly. "I can't believe that I'm having a baby, a little girl, and that you're not here to see her when she comes out." Tears began to form at the corners of her eyes as she went out. "I never thought I'd get through school, Daddy's marriage, or getting married myself without you. I still don't know how I'm still surviving -it still comes as a surprise to see that I'm still living ... but I know that you're with me, Mom. I know you're here in spirit ..." She sniffed and lowered her head, picking at the leaves of the flowers. "But is it selfish of me to wish that you were here in person instead?"

A chill ran through Cynthia's body that made her stand up straight and look around. Certainly someone had to be there, but as she looked down the aisles of the cemetery there was no sign of life at all. She wrapped her arms around herself, giving her body a hug as she shook off the feeling that another presence was near her. Looking back at the tomb, she cocked her head to the side and simply stared. *Are you trying to tell me something,* she wondered of her mother. Over time, Cynthia had become a strong believer in the supernatural and the universe finding various ways to connect with, warn, or redirect humans. If anything, she hoped that her mother's spirit was lingering over her watchfully and protectively.

A rustling sound occurred behind her and Cynthia quickly turned around again. There was no way that this was all in her imagination. If she was experiencing some kind of supernatural occurrence, she was ready to take in all aspects of it so that she'd be able to give Preston a full count when she returned home.

"Whew! Chile, you know how to pick a meeting place." Thea paused just by a tree to catch her breath, finally coming into Cynthia's line of vision.

Cynthia clutched at her chest and exhaled. "Aunt Thea, you scared me."

Thea picked back up the trek towards Miriam's grave. "That's you being out here with all the graves and spirits that's got you spooked. Don't pin that on an old woman." Thea approached Cynthia and smiled wide. She reached out to pat Cynthia's protruding belly. "Lord, you's mighty pregnant."

Cynthia laughed. "Don't remind me." She placed a hand on against her lower back as she spoke. "This weight is beginning to wear my back out. If this girl doesn't hurry up and get out of here I might have to evict her."

"You know what they say 'bout that don't cha?"

Cynthia raised a brow, not sure that she was ready for whatever old wives tale her aunt was about to share. "What's that?"

"It's 'bout three sure fire ways to make a baby get on up outta there. First one is to drink you some red tea."

Cynthia shrugged. "Sounds simple enough but what does the tea do?"

"It's a natural stimulant that makes yo' muscles down there contract." Thea made a pushing motion with her hands facing downward. "And it just makes ya' walls push that youngeon on outta there."

Cynthia laughed, not at all sold on her aunt's theory. "What's the other ways, Aunt Thea?"

"You can just walk."

"Just walk?"

"Just walk, chile. Walk, walk, walk. Make the baby get all dizzy and tired of ya' moving around so they just wanna break free." Thea chuckled at her own comical advice. "Last way been working for centuries. You know that saying, start how you wanna finish?"

Cynthia nodded.

"How you get that baby in ya belly?"

Cynthia squinted. "What in the world?"

Thea shook her head and smiled. "Come on now, this ain't rocket science. How you get that baby in yo belly? It was Immaculate Conception. You was doing the wild monkey dance right? Like married folk 'pose to, you had sex."

Cynthia doubled over with laughter.

"That's what you do. You have sex and startle that child 'til she slide right on outta there. Start how you finish." Thea joined in on Cynthia's laughter.

Once the comedy of the moment died down, Thea looked down at Miriam's grave. She stepped forward, pulled a handkerchief out of her purse, and wiped down the marker. "Shame that your mama's not here to see how beautiful you are while you with child."

The somberness returned to Cynthia's demeanor as she too fixed her attention on her mother's grave once more. "I was just thinking that myself."

"She'd be a proud granny, I'm sure of that." Thea smiled. "Nice flowers."

"Thanks. Wanted to bring her something with some color."

"Thanks." Cynthia said with a growing smile as she reminisced in the all the times that her father brought home a bouquet of red roses. They were always her mother's favorite as well as Cynthia's too.

Thea turned to face Cynthia and gave her a serious once over. "What we doing out here, chile? What's troubling you?"

Cynthia couldn't hide her emotions from her aunt. "Oh Aunt Thea, I don't know what I'm doing. I don't know anything about being somebody's mother. I'm still trying to get it right with being someone's wife."

"You getting yourself all worked up over nothing."

Cynthia shook her head. "I don't know … I mean who am I supposed to call when something's wrong with the baby?"

"The pediatrician."

"Who do I call when I'm exhausted and can't get the baby to stop crying? Or I'm trying to do some house work and she needs attention?"

"The Fahter," Thea answered, purposely mispronouncing the word.

"Well, who do I call when Preston's busy with his clinic but I'm tired or overwhelmed?"

"The lordt."

Cynthia gave her aunt a stern expression. "Aunt Thea, I'm serious. I have no support circle. Not a real one. Who's going to show me the parenting ropes?"

"Chile, what you going through every woman to ever give birth done gone through. Parenting don't come with no instruction guide. You wanna know who gon' show you the ropes? That baby gon' show you the ropes. Hell, you ain't never been a mama and she ain't never been a baby. Y'all gon' learn together."

Cynthia couldn't contain her laughter. "You always have an answer for everything don't you?"

"Naw, I just look at a situation and take it for what it is." Thea opened up her arms to invite Cynthia in for a hug. "Stop worrying about who gon' have your back. You got all the love and support you need. You got a good man, me, your savior, your dad, and push comes to shove that woman and her shadows will be there."

"Hmmm. I'm not so sure of that. You know they'd just as soon watch me fail and have my child taken by social services than to ever reach out and help me."

Thea pulled back. "You never know. Folks get a baby in their lives and their perspectives change. Only a heartless person can turn their back on a baby. I'm not saying put all ya' eggs in one basket with them, but at least give 'em the benefit of the doubt."

Cynthia smiled. "I'll try."

"Now, when is the baby shower?"

Cynthia frowned. "I'm not having one. Between work and trying to rest as much as I can now, I haven't had the time to plan one."

"Well, we can't welcome a baby into the world without a shower. We gotta do things properly. Leave everything to me. Your Aunt Thea's gon' take care of this."

Cynthia smiled. "Thanks. You're the best."

Ebony took a sip of her mimosa and smiled at the handsome gentleman sitting in front of her. Perched on top of her husband's grand oak desk with her legs crossed at the knees, she took in the expression on his face. Kori Remington was the advisor and attorney for the Grayson estate. She'd met him many years ago when he was just starting out in the legal field, striving to garner the accounts of Atlanta's most prominent and elite figureheads. Upon the origin of their acquaintance, he hadn't had as much potential and income as Ebony would have liked causing her to pass over him and take to Elton whose career in the music industry was much more promising and lucrative. Still, once she had Elton where he needed to be per her satisfaction, something had nagged at her regarding Kori and his status. She felt compelled to push him along and get him on a winning team. It had taken very little convincing to get Elton to agree to let Kori represent him and his brand. It was a win-win situation for all as far as Ebony could tell. Elton had his affairs properly managed, Kori had a handsome retainer and build an impressive resume based off of the connections developed as a result of being on Elton Grayson's payroll, and Ebony was in the know about everything pertaining to Elton's money, ventures, and plans. She was pulling the puppet strings and calling the shots as the go-between, making sure that everything lined up to her specifications. She couldn't have been happier, at least until now.

"Why are you giving me this static all of a sudden?" Ebony asked Kori, pouting her pink-painted lips as she dangled her champagne glass through her fingers. "Haven't I been good to you?"

The fine waves of Kori's neatly cut, graying hair disappeared from her view as he raised his chocolate face to look at her. "I could say the same to you."

Ebony threw her free hand in the air. "Then why rock the boat? If everyone's content then what's the problem?"

"The problem is that what you're now asking me to do isn't legal."

She cocked her head to the side and looked at him knowingly. "As if this is the first time that we've bent some of the rules."

"That may be so, Ebony, but you're asking me to commit insurance fraud and that's something that I'm going to have to draw the line at. Why can't you just get him to knowingly sign off on the increase? Why do you have to apply for the increase in the first place?"

Ebony sat her glass down and leaned forward giving Kori a close-up view of her ample bosom popping over the open top of her low cut blouse. She stroked the side of his strong jawline and smiled at him seductively. "Now, when have you ever been in position to question my requests? To question me? If I didn't know better, it sounds as if you're having some a lapse in memory of who the conductor is of this money train." She lowered her hand to rest in his lap, dangerously close to his impressively sized member threatening to bulge within his pants. "Do I need to issue you a little reminder?"

Kori cleared his throat, noticeably bothered by the way she was beginning to stroke him. "I'm just saying ... Elton's worth a couple of cool millions, Ebony. I don't understand the need to increase the policy. When he dies you'll have plenty to keep you comfortable within the lifestyle you're accustomed to. I mean, with what he's leaving you and what you've already managed to—"

"Ah ah ah," Ebony chastised, daring him to give voice to her history of foul financial dealings.

"What you've managed to save up," Kori finished up with emphasis in his tone, "you should be more than well off."

"I'm the judge of that."

"But what you're doing to Cynthia isn't right."

Ebony frowned. "I'm not doing anything to her. Spoiled brat. We all get one life to live and it's up to us to make the most of it. She's living her life ... it's up to her to figure out how to capitalize on her opportunities. Surely you can't blame me for trying to make sure that my future is secure."

"Yes, but at whose expense?"

"Funny, but I didn't realize that I was paying you to have a conscience."

"Funny, but I was pretty certain that it's your husband who's paying me."

Ebony smiled. "And you and I both know that I'm the reason he's paying you ... and I can be the reason he stops paying you." She leaned even closer and kissed him gently on the nose. "Now, be a good little estate manager and do what I've asked you to do."

"You might be able to fool Elton because let's face it, the man obviously gives you free reign over his entire life," Kori said sarcastically.

Ebony chuckled as he reached back for her glass.

"But in the event that he does pass away, how are you ever going to explain things to Cynthia when she finds out what you've done?"

"I don't explain myself to anyone, dear. Besides, if she has any hard feelings it'll be towards her beloved father, not me. I'm not responsible for how anyone feels." She opened her legs slowly and re-crossed them in the opposite direction.

Kori licked his lips, unable to resist the plushness of her thighs which were calling to him. He reached out and caressed her smooth, exposed skin. "You're hell on wheels, Ebony."

"You better believe it. I've come too far to end up with less than everything I want ... everything I deserve."

"And what about Cynthia? Doesn't she deserve something?"

"Ha! You know what she deserves? Cynthia deserves—"

Without warning, the office door popped open and in walked Thea with her large purse dangling from her arm, eyes wide through her thick glasses, and expression all-knowing as she watched her brother's wife jump to her feet and the young man she was consorting with snatch back his hand and snap his neck around to lay eyes on her.

"Hello-er," Thea called out. "Sounds like I'm right on time. You were in the middle of talking about what Cynthia deserves."

Ebony held her glass with both hands as she glowered at her sister-in-law. "Didn't your mother ever teach you to knock? I was in the middle of a private meeting."

"I can see that you and this fella were being very private," Thea shot back, looking from Kori to Ebony and raising her brow. "All tucked away in my brother's office with the door closed."

"Who let you in?" Ebony inquired, fuming on the inside but trying with all of her might to remain composed.

"Your underpaid, overworked maid," Thea answered. "Po woman look like she gon' just tilt over the way she's all exhausted like some slave."

"Maria's fine."

"I hope you giving her some decent benefits. She looks like she needs to go on that CMLA leave."

"What?"

"CMLA ... cleaning my life away ... that's what she's doing. Gon' kill herself taking care of this big ole' house. She needs some leave fo' she fall out in here."

"I think you're referring to FMLA," Kori corrected her, laughing. "It's in reference to the Family Medical Leave Act."

"Yes," Thea replied, looking him up and down. "Aren't you smart?"

Ebony massaged her temples with the tips of her fingers. "What can I do for you, Thea?" she asked, getting increasingly irritated.

"I came to talk to you about Cynthia's baby shower but it sounds like you're already in here making some plans of your own."

"Uh." Ebony looked over at Kori. "Well, I … I was making some plans, yes." She smiled.

"And is this gentleman the event coordinator?"

Kori rose to his feet. "I'm the Grayson family attorney, Ma'am. Kori Remington." He held his hand out to shake Thea's.

Thea slowly extended her left hand to engage in the shake. "Family attorney? You planning on doing something illegal at this here shower?" she asked Ebony.

Ebony laughed off the question and placed her hand under Kori's arm. "Of course not. We were handling some monetary matters to see if I could afford a particular … uhhh … (could take out the uh just to show how easily she lies without even having to think about it gift for Cynthia. Kori works closely with our banker making sure our transactions go through and that our accounts are good and balanced. But, we're about done here so …". She looked to Kori to cosign her lie.

"Yes, yes," Kori piped up, catching on. "We're all good to go." He looked at Thea and smiled. "It was nice meeting you." He turned to look at Ebony before stepping away from the two women. "I'll look into that matter and get back to you."

"Sooner rather than later," Ebony called after him as Kori made a hasty exit from the office. She took a sip of her mimosa and rounded the desk to take a seat in Elton's plush office chair. "Now what about this baby shower?"

Thea smiled. "Well, if you're already in the planning stages you can just clue me in so that can execute."

"No, no. By all means, I'd love to hear your ideas."

"No need," Thea insisted. "Your money, your party, your way. I'm sure that with all the consulting you were doing with Mr. Remington that you've got it all under control and that Cynthia will have a very nice shindig. We all know how you like to go above and beyond. I can't wait to see all the media coming to get exclusive pictures of Elton Grayson's first grandchild's welcoming celebration." She crossed her arms over her large chest and smiled. "Yes … I know you've got it all under control. When's the big day?"

Ebony's nostrils flared. There was no way that she could back out of the lie now. "Next Saturday," she said through clenched teeth.

"Fine, fine. You're not half bad, Ebony," Thea said, purposely pronouncing the woman's name in the common style of its spelling verses the lavish pronunciation that Ebony preferred. "With you being a new grandma and all I wasn't sure that you'd do right by my little Cynthia and her new baby. But, I see that you're gonna be just fine."

Ebony grimaced. "Grandma? Ugh! Please, do not call me that." She patted her hairsong. "And Cynthia isn't all that little. She doesn't need anyone to do anything for her or lord over her the way you do. She's a big girl. She better start tending to her own affairs and stop walking around like some pitiful orphan."

Thea shook her head. "My hearing's not all the way right 'cause for a minute there it sounded like you wanted me to call my brother and tell him 'bout how close you and his little attor-ty are. But I know I couldn't have heard that right. But just to be clear …" Thea squinted her eyes and looked over the top of her glasses so that Ebony knew she meant business. "You will do right by this, Chile. I don't wanna hear no tale of otherwise 'cause when you mess with mine, you mess with me."

Ebony laughed, seemingly unfazed. "Is that a threat?"

"It's whatever you want it to be." Thea pushed her glasses up on her face and took a breath. "Good meeting," she said, turning to walk out. "I'll be here bright and early next Saturday for the festivities. Have a blessed one."

Ebony watched Elton's sister waddle out of the office without closing the door back. She sucked her teeth and downed the remainder of her drink. She could care less about the woman's idle threats. Ebony had been doing what she wanted for years now and there was no one that could stop her. Still, she'd put it out there that she was coordinating some lavish baby shower for her husband's daughter and now she'd be obligated to make good on it. It was just as well. She could afford to throw the shower of the year even though it unfortunately wouldn't be for one of her own daughters. She'd give Cynthia the bash of all times to pacify Thea, make Cynthia feel loved, and show her husband how benevolent she was. They'd all be content for now and later she'd be the one enthralled and laughing all the way to the bank.

"That was really nice of her, don't you think?" Preston asked, leaning back against his pillows and scrolling through his social media messages.

Cynthia pulled back the covers on her side of the bed and climbed in beside him. "She's only doing it because Thea lit a fire under her. Honestly, I thought that Thea was going to assume responsibility for the shower since it was her idea. But leave it to her to con Ebony out of some money I'm sure she didn't willingly want to spend on me."

"Well, it's done," Preston stated, reaching over and rubbing her belly. "And from what I hear it's going to be really nice. You deserve it, baby. You're going to be the best mother ever."

"How do you know that?"

Preston looked into her eyes. "Because you're the kindest, sweetest most loving person that I've ever met. You're patient and understanding, nurturing and caring. You're going to be a natural at this."

She covered his hand with her own. "Sometimes I wonder about that. I don't know what I'm doing ... I don't want to fail this child."

"You could never fail our child, Cyn. As long as just love her like I know you will, everything'll be fine." His eyes rose and lingered at a spot near their dresser.

Cynthia followed his glare over. Seeing nothing, she looked at her husband and gripped his hand. "What's the matter?"

"Huh?" Preston shook it off and looked back at his wife. "Nothing ... just uh ... something caught my attention. It's nothing." He smiled. "I love you Mrs. Durden. Thank you for having my child."

She touched his face lightly. "Besides your love, bearing your offspring is the greatest gift in the world." She kissed his lips and felt a spark shoot through her body. A dark vision flickered through her mind and quickly disappeared. The intensity of the moment caused her heart rate to quicken and she pulled back and looked at her husband intently. She had no clue what was going on but certainly felt that something was looming around them. "You sure you're okay?"

He smiled reassuringly. "Never better."

Elton took a sip of his cognac and grimaced at the burn. His body lurched forward and his left hand cradled his midsection. It had been a long, exhausting day at the office and now he was doing his best to relax for the evening, but his body hadn't gotten the memo. He sat his glass down on the table beside him and threw his head back. He was growing tired of the ups and downs his body experienced and longed for mere peace.

"Here," Ebony said, handing over two oxycodone pills from his medicine bottle resting in her right hand. "No need in sitting there in pain."

Elton shook his head. "No need in taking those when they're not going to do help. It won't change anything."

"It manages your pain."

He shot her a look of indifference. "We both know better. That stuff will constipate me and make me a zombie." He shook his head. "I don't have time for that ... got stuff to do. I'll be fine."

Ebony sighed dramatically and threw the pills back into the bottle. She wasn't going to force him to take them if he wanted to sit there in pain. Besides, she was only trying to be a good wife. There were really other more pressing concerns on her mind to be honest. She sat the bottle down and perched herself on the arm of Elton's chair. "So, like I was saying, I think that it will do a world of good if we go ahead and be proactive about your affairs."

"I have a business to run. I don't have time to think about insurance and wills and such."

"Exactly, baby. You're a businessman with so many other daunting tasks to tend to. As your wife it only makes sense that I should take care of the finite things, the little odds and ends of your life so you don't have to worry about them."

"Then why are we discussing it?"

He was being short with her but he knew that it was only his pain talking. For the greater good of her bottom line, she was willing to take the verbal lashing. "Because this is a matter that you have to attend to in order to hand all other responsibilities to me. I need you to make me your power of attorney, dear. Then you won't have to be concerned about these kinds of details and can just tend to your business."

"Doesn't that make it seem like I'm senile or something? Can't manage my own affairs."

"You're looking at it all wrong, Elton. Who cares how anyone else would perceive it. We know that we're doing it so that you can focus on your legacy and I can make sure you're good and that your family's good." She reached down and grabbed his hand lovingly hand portraying flawed love. "And when the time comes to make hard decisions for the business and your estate in general, I have the ability to do that with no qualms."

Elton thought about it. "You are my wife, that should go without saying." He pondered further. "But Cynthia—"

"Is starting her own life, her own family dear," Ebony replied, cutting him off. "You don't want to burden her with the responsibility of handling your affairs or tending to GMG. Isn't that why you're keeping things a secret in the first place? Not wanting to add any stress to her life? We owe it to her to let her walk her own path in life and not put any of our stuff on her. You know how independent she is. Remember how pissed she was about you fronting Preston that money?"

Elton remained silent though he was taking in his wife's argument.

"I love you, Elton. I just want to make sure that you're taken care of and that everything you've worked so hard for is protected. I'm all about preserving your legacy and taking some of the stress off of you." She smiled and kissed his forehead. "It's your decision." She stood up as if she was done with the situation.

"Do it," Elton mumbled.

She smiled to herself as she picked up the paperwork from the table and handed it to him along with a pen. "Just sign all the places that are highlighted. You'll see, baby. I've got your back."

As Elton mindlessly placed his John Hancock on the documents, Ebony picked up his glass and replenished it with the toxic liquor. She stood beside his chair and waited for him to hand over the signed forms. She smiled lovingly as she traded him the glass for the papers. "You can relax, Elton. I've got your best interest at heart. Drink up and relax. I'll go check on your dinner." She hesitated for a moment, watching him guzzle his alcohol. Then, walking out of the room she did a little shimmy knowing that she'd conquered the world by just a stroke of Elton's pen. She had real power now: the power to take everything she ever wanted while making others wish they were dead. The irony of the situation made her drop her smile for a moment. Her come-up came with a price but she wasn't responsible for that. Obviously, it was God's will, right? Who was she not to capitalize upon it?

"I can't believe that you did all of this," Ella exclaimed, biting into a strawberry and looking out over the white and gold glamor of the baby shower décor that decked the back yard of the Grayson estate. "I didn't know that you were that gung-ho about this baby." She looked at her mother, partially being sarcastic and partially wondering if her mother really was smitten by the idea of becoming a grandmother if it was to Cynthia's baby.

"Anything for my husband," Ebony said through tight tips, smiling for the camera that was trying to get a candid snap of her. "Besides, who doesn't like an opportunity to dress up and be seen?"

Ella looked across the yard at Cynthia situated in an oversized chair dressed in a thin white dress that looked like a sheet merely wrapped around her belly. Without meaning to, Ella's face scrunched up in a frown that was caught by the cunning photographer in the distance. She watched as people who were all associates of her mother greeted Cynthia and rubbed her belly as if they really cared about the child she was carrying. Cynthia was glowing as she held her spot as the queen of this outdoor ball and all Ella really wanted to do was take the elaborate cake designed as a tiara and smash it in Cynthia's face. As Preston stood walked by and placed a kiss on his wife's forehead, Ella became even more disgusted. They had this way of always appearing so happy when in fact she knew that they couldn't possibly be that in love all the time. She rolled her eyes and reached for a glass of sparkling wine. "Bitch," she muttered.

Ebony shot her daughter a look as she gave a member of the catering staff an approving nod to head out with tray of appetizers. "Excuse me?"

"I'm just saying, all of this fuss over Cynthia and her little peasant baby. You and I both know that she would have been more than happy to have a little family gathering at some greasy buffet instead of spending all of this money for something she has no class enough to appreciate."

"However either of us feels, let her have her little moment," Ebony advised. "It isn't as if she'll have many of them so what's a couple of hours in the spotlight?"

"I don't understand at all how this became her life. She isn't cute, she isn't all that special, and I've never known any guy other than Preston to have the slightest interest in her." Ella took a sip of her wine and glared at her stepsister. "And she does this thing ... like, looks down on us because we have money. Like she's better than us because she chooses to be poor."

"Honey, don't worry yourself with such trivial matters. Instead of complaining about Cynthia you should be more like your sister and find a man to marry of your own." Ebony looked over to her right at Ana and Trey as Ana fed him a stuffed mushroom. She wasn't all that thrilled to see her daughter fawning all over some man, but at least the girl had a man who seemed stable enough to provide Ana with a decent lifestyle if she could manage to rope him in.

Ella looked her mother up and down but bit her tongue. Something about Ana's beau didn't sit well with Ella, but who was she to judge? However, she had no desire to attach herself to the likes of someone like Trey nor to be a love-sick puppy like Cynthia. In her eyes, she was the strongest, most independent of the three sisters. If she was attached to a man it would be because of how he elevated her worth, not because she needed him to make her feel giddy. Her eyes found Preston in the crowd once more. Toying with the rim of her glass she again wondered to herself just how it was that he'd gotten involved with Cynthia. He had to be like Trey and just be gunning for an opportunity to advance in life courtesy of Elton Grayson. It was the only logical explanation. Although he was hardly her type, Preston still seemed as if he could have pulled a different caliber of woman; someone a notch or two above Cynthia's status. *He must be gay*, she thought.

Ana sauntered over to her mother and sister and smiled as she retrieved two glasses of wine from the bar. "Your horns are showing," she teased Ella.

"Screw you," Ella retorted.

"Your mouth," Ebony chastised her daughter.

"What you really wanna say is screw this shower," Ana replied knowingly.

"More than you know." Ella looked to her mother once more. "Really mother, I really can't stomach this charade as if I really care about that kid she's toting around. I mean, watching Cynthia act as if she's the queen of all Atlanta isn't really my idea of a good time. That bitch can choke on a cucumber sandwich for all I care." In her mind, she could clearly recall the look of judgment on Cynthia's face when she'd caught her in the elevator during their family vacation. "Sick of subjecting myself to her shenanigans. I mean, that pauper of a wedding last year, the way she looks down her nose at us, and now this baby shower where we're supposed to act like one big happy family. Please." She looked over at Cynthia. "You can't tell if she's really pregnant or if it's just her normal round body." She laughed at her own joke.

"White is definitely not her color," Ana agreed. "Why'd you pick white, Mom?"

Ebony smiled, feigning innocence. "It's a baby shower and babies are pure. I thought it was cute."

"Ha! I bet you did," Ella remarked. "She'll look like a whale in every picture taken today." She downed her wine and reached for another. "Fat Bitch."

Behind them, Aunt Thea picked up a cup of lemonade and shook her head. It was just like the three wicked witches to be standing around taking shots at Cynthia when she wasn't there to defend herself. Thea considered addressing them, but when she looked over and saw the radiance that exuded from Cynthia's smile she decided that now wasn't the time. She'd promised her niece a baby shower and she was having the grandest one of all time, despite Ebony's reluctance to shell out the cash. It was done and Cynthia was happy, that was all that mattered. As long as Ebony and her minions didn't do or say anything to disrupt the joy that Cynthia was experiencing, Thea felt comfortable allowing her .9mm to remain in her purse.

Walking away, Thea spotted Elton having a conversation with Trey. She wouldn't run up on Ebony, but she would certainly drop a bug in her brother's ear. Approaching the men, each dressed in their own and variation of a white ensemble, Thea couldn't help but notice that there was something shifty about Trey. Something in his eyes didn't set well with her.

"Hey there, Elton," Thea called out, taking a seat beside her brother. "Hey there, fella," she acknowledged Trey.

"Hello," Trey said, shifting in his stance. Feeling uncomfortable with their company staring at him, Trey looked over at Elton. "So, I'll uh … call and set up that session."

Elton nodded and let out a small sigh. "Yeah. Call Ronnie on Monday. He'll book studio time. I'll come down and see what you're working with."

Trey looked as if Elton had just awarded him a million dollars. In all honesty, he might as well had because every artist with even the slightest bit of knowledge about the game knew that an Elton Grayson project was guaranteed platinum.

"Yes, sir," Trey said. "Aight then." He walked away with an enthused pep in his step.

"Yes suh, massah," Thea mocked the young man. "You's gon' make me a star for ya, massah and hold all rights and masters for the duration of my career, massah."

Elton frowned. "You don't know what you're talking about."

Thea laughed. "Honey, I know mo' than you think I do. I probably know mo' than you."

"Did you walk all the way over here to antagonize me, Thea?"

"Nah, I walked all the way over her to tell you to open yo' eyes."

"What?"

Thea leaned forward and stared hard at her brother. "Open yo' eyes, Elton."

He looked at her long and hard. "And what is it that I should be looking at?"

"Why you yeller?"

"What?"

"You yeller. Yo' eyes look, yeller. What's wrong with you?"

Elton leaned back and looked at the partygoers around him. "Nothing's wrong with me. You came over here to give me a once over? Is that it?"

Thea wasn't convinced. "I came over here to tell you to watch your little gold digger and now I'm sitting here asking you why the hell you's yeller?"

"My little gold digger?" he questioned.

"Ebony," she replied, once again, purposely mispronouncing the exaggerated, preferred enunciation of his wife's name.

Elton cocked his head to the side. "Why do you do that?"

"Do what?" Thea asked innocently.

"You know what. You do that to get under her skin. I wish you'd stop. And stop calling her names. We've been married over a decade now, Thea. You'd think that you would have learned to get along with my wife by now."

"You'on know your wife."

"What don't I know?"

"If you knew like I did you'd be calling her a couple of names too."

Elton was tired of the bantering. He held his hand up to silence his sister. "Enough of this. Get off it, okay, Thea. Ebony is my wife.

We're all family. You're going to have to start showing her some more respect."

"Hmmph. Soon as she show you some."

"And what's that supposed to mean?"

To their left, the crowd was migrating over towards the gift table to watch as Cynthia opened her presents.

Thea rose from her seat. "Lemme go help this chile'." She looked back at her brother. "Open yo' eyes, Elton. I done told you … don't let all that yeller stop you from seeing what's going on in yo' own family." She walked away without saying another word. Sooner or later, Ebony's mess would surface, of that Thea was certain. She didn't like the way Ebony regarded Cynthia and that would be addressed in time, but her spirit told her that the woman was up to something far more devious than just disliking her husband's daughter. Yes, in time Thea would uncover the truth one way or the other and Ebony had better hope that she was bullet-less once her transgressions came to light.

"This was really nice, Thea," Cynthia gushed as she stood by her Acura MDX while Trey and Preston finished loading up the back with the baby shower gifts they'd received. She smiled at her aunt appreciatively. "Thank you. Even though I didn't really know half of the folks that showed up …" She laughed. "It was still very nice."

"Yeah, it's something what a lil' money can do for you." Thea's eyes glanced over at Elton and Ebony sitting on the bench that over looked the coy-pond in their garden on the left side of the front lawn. "Mmmhhmm, money can do all kinds of things."

Not really understanding her aunt's tone or her statement, Cynthia remained silent for a moment, studying the woman's expression. Suddenly, a chill ran through her body and she couldn't help but to shake off the feeling.

Thea looked at her quizzically. "What's the matter with you, chile'?"

Cynthia shrugged and shook her head. "I can't explain it … I just keep having these weird feelings … these ripples running through me and chills … like at Mom's grave. I felt like she was with me maybe. But I'm not sure … I just have this feeling … maybe it's something about the baby. I don't know."

"What feeling?" Thea asked concernedly.

"Like maybe something's wrong," Cynthia admitted.

Thea's eyes darted back over to her brother who looked frailer than she'd ever seen him before. Next to him Ebony sat straight up looking like she was still posing for the snooty press photographers that she'd invited to their family's private event. In her bones she felt that something was amiss and she was determined to get to the bottom of things. Refocusing her attention on her niece, she wondered if the younger woman was experiencing some of the same misgivings. "Hmmm," she let out, pursing her lips. "That baby's fine, honey. Spirit's just trying to tell you to look around you. Something's happening around you."

Cynthia looked at her aunt and instantly became filled with trepidation. "What is it? What's going on? Is something wrong with someone?" She hugged her belly. "Are you okay?"

Thea waved her off. "I'm fine, chile'. I don't know what it is and don't you fret none over it. Whatever it is will come to light sooner or later."

The thought of someone close to her going through something or some dark secret looming within her family concerned Cynthia. She prayed that all would be revealed sooner rather than later in light of Thea's comment. Whatever it was, she didn't want to go crazy with the signs that the universe was throwing her way. She needed some answers and had no clue where to start searching for them. With her own fears, worries, and responsibilities consuming her she wasn't sure if she could handle anything traumatic.

Thea could see her wheels turning. "Nuh-uh, don't you sit there and let this run you looney. You got that baby to worry 'bout. Whatever it is, it'll be okay."

Preston walked up and placed his palm against Cynthia's lower back. "You ready, babe?"

Thea smiled at the young couple. "Y'all so in love. Go on, take yo' wife home. Y'all go on. Enjoy each other before that baby comes."

Preston smiled back at her. "Thanks, Thea."

Thea nodded.

Cynthia hugged her aunt and waddled over to the open passenger side door. She looked over in her parents' direction and waved wildly but Elton and Ebony were too engrossed in their current conversation to notice. Not thinking too much of it, Cynthia slid into the car and within moments they were off with Thea standing in the middle of the circular driveway watching them depart.

The birth of Amelia, Cynthia and Preston's first born child was a miraculous, impactful event of Cynthia's life. From the moment the tiny baby girl being slipped from her body wailing and Cynthia got an opportunity to look into her perfectly rounded face, she fell in love. It was a love like no other; a love that was different and more intense than the deeply rooted love she had for her husband. She was a mother now and the feeling was unparalleled to any other emotion she'd ever experienced. From the day of Amelia's birth Cynthia couldn't be away from the child longer than a couple of hours without feeling separation anxiety. Amelia became her life. No one had warned her that she'd be stricken in this manner upon giving birth, but she was ever so grateful for the opportunity to be Amelia's mother. So thankful for the gift bestowed upon her, the moment she was able to get out of the house with Amelia, she made certain to attend church. It was only fitting that she take her baby to the house of the lord to give thanks to him for the miracle she would have a lifetime loving.

Parishioners from the church wasted no time in flocking to Cynthia to oooh and ahhhh over the precious addition to her family. She was proud to hold her daughter in her arms as she swayed to the melodic sound of the youth choir belting out their rendition of Kirk

Franklin's "Imagine Me". Her eyes misted over as the choir sung her testimony about gaining strength and not allowing others to break her down. Suddenly, she wondered if all of the majestic feelings she'd been consumed with was really the spirit shielding and embracing her as she moved forward into this new era of her life. Maybe Thea had misinterpreted things; maybe the feelings were positive and not so much cautionary. She felt her spirit lift as the words gave life to her feelings of the Lord coming in and removing all of the hurt and pain from her life the moment he brought her Preston and now Amelia. Without thought, she cradled Amelia in the crook of her left arm and raised her right hand to the heavens. "It's gone," she sang out in harmony with the choir. "It's gone." It was a true statement. All of the misgivings she'd had over the years following her mother's death—the feelings of being unloved, the mistreatment from her extended family, the insecurity—it was all gone. That life was behind her and now she knew what it was like to be whole and to have purpose, to be loved and accepted, to feel worthy. The lord had restored her faith in love and family. For that she'd be eternally grateful.

Ana checked the time on her phone and rolled her eyes. Trey had promised to take her to brunch since he'd had the audacity to stand her up for dinner the night before. She was trying to be understanding, knowing that he'd been waiting for this opportunity for a minute. True to his word, Elton had gotten Trey cleared for studio time down at his private studio. Although his first session had been scheduled over a month ago following Cynthia's baby shower, it seemed that he was so engrossed in studio-life that he simply couldn't come up for air. He was at the Grayson Sound Center every waking moment, every chance that he got, laying down tracks that he spent the remainder of his free time writing on. Whenever she saw him, all he talked about was music, Elton's keen sense of talent, and the people that he was meeting while working with her stepfather.

She was glad that he was making moves, but felt that a little more gratitude should have been thrown her way. After all, if it hadn't been for her he wouldn't be in the throes of living his dream. Ana took a deep breath and dialed Trey' number one more time. Crossing her legs while sitting on the plush pastel couch in her living room, she counted the number of times the phone rang, ready to blast him on his voicemail.

"Hello?" Trey' voice boomed in her ear.

In the background she could hear the thud of a fast-paced beat and the jumbled up sound of multiple voices trying to speak over the music.

"Did you forget about me?" she asked, pouting as she spoke.

"What?" he hollered back.

Becoming increasingly annoyed, Ana sat up straight and gripped the phone tightly. "I said, did you forget about me? About brunch?"

"Naw … naw … it's just that I'm down here with DJ Flex and this shit is epic."

Ana turned up her nose. "Is it me or are you sounding way more hood than usual?"

"What?" he yelled.

She shook it off. "Nothing. Look, are you on your way or what?"

"Uh … I'm gonna have to get back with you later."

"So you're just going to stand me up again?"

"It's business, alright? I'm down here networking and making connections that's gon' take my career to the next level. I thought you understood how this music business works being that Elton's your pops and all."

Ana didn't like his tone nor did she appreciate his snide remarks. She was sure that he was putting on for whoever was around him and it didn't make her feel good at all to know that he would clown her with such ease after everything she'd done for him. "He's not my father, he's my stepfather," she corrected him.

"Dance with me, baby." The female's request was loud and clear in Ana's ear from Trey' end of the call.

Ana's eyes widened as she began to clue in to what the scene was really like in Trey' current environment. "Who was that?" she demanded.

There was a series of muted words exchanged and Ana assumed that Trey was covering up the extension so that she couldn't hear anything else that the hoochie on his arm was saying.

"Trey!" she called out.

There was rustling sound that almost blocked out the noise of the music, but Trey still failed to respond. Ana could just imagine what had him unable to speak.

"Trey, you better answer me!" she screamed.

"I'll come over later tonight," he finally told her.

"Later tonight when?" she asked, dissatisfied with his resolution. "How do I know that you're not just telling me whatever to get off of the phone so you can go play with the groupies hanging around in the studio?"

"Come on, don't do that! I'm working."

"Uh-huh."

"Look, I'll see you later, alright?"

Before she could respond, Trey disconnected the line. Ana stared at her cell phone angrily. She had half the mind to go down to Elton's studio and catch Trey in the act, but her ego wouldn't let her do it. No way was she about to go out and humiliate herself in public. Besides, she'd put too much into trying to mold Trey to let things just fall apart now. If his music was any good and Elton actually decided to sign him then she wanted to be sure to be right there to reap the benefits of his new found wealth. She just had to remind him who had brought him to this lifestyle he was becoming accustomed to in order to avoid repeats of the crap that was occurring now.

Have your fun now, Trey, she thought. *But I'm going to have you by the balls before it's all over and done with.*

She was on a self-destructive path and didn't really care at this point. The man she'd been seeing for the past few months had cut her off completely after his wife found out about their liaison. That meant no sex, no money, and no more expensive gifts. Ella was livid.

She hadn't paid a bill at her Atlantic Station condo since the moment she started giving him the goods. She could care less about the man himself, it was the perks of being his mistress that had appealed to her. With him now out of the picture, she was back to spending her own money, tending to her own financial obligations, and making use of her exquisite yet mildly unfulfilling vibrating bullet. In time, she'd find a new benefactor she was sure but in the meantime, she was salty about being dumped. Though she had no real attachment to her lover, as a woman it made her feel some kind of way about being kicked to the curb. As a result of her bitterness, Ella was like a tornado, blowing around wreaking havoc upon the happiness of everyone else in her path just because.

While scrolling through Facebook she encountered a few pictures from the over the top baby shower that her mom had thrown for Cynthia. She was still mystified by how Cynthia had become the one married with children while she and Ana were still single. Sure, Ana had her thug-wannabe-rapper boyfriend but she knew that that liaison would only last for so long. Staring at the pictures from Cynthia's page, which was tagged in, Ella resisted the urge to hurl her stiletto at the screen.

"Ugh!" she let out in disgust, seeing a picture of Cynthia and Preston.

Preston was standing behind her with his arms wrapped around her waist and his hands planted firmly on Cynthia's belly. Cynthia was looking up into his eyes and they smiled at one another as if they were in the middle of some Disney fairytale. Again, Ella wondered what it was about Cynthia that made Preston the slightest bit interested in her, yet alone serious about marrying the girl. Sizing him up via the photo, she began to run through the list of possible reasons why he'd attached himself to Cynthia. The very first assumption and quite possibly the most logical one was that he was in it for the money. Everyone knew that Elton Grayson was worth millions and if Preston was as smart as Cynthia claimed he was then he probably assumed that he could slid his hand into Elton's wallet at any time, not to mention the fortune he'd come into as Cynthia's spouse once Elton died. The only problem with that was the way that Cynthia was dead set against using Elton's name or money. Ella recalled her stepsister's displeasure with learning about Elton and Preston's business arrangement. Still, maybe Preston was holding out for the big pay day in hopes that Cynthia stood to inherit quite a bit upon Elton's demise.

"He doesn't really want you," Ella said to Cynthia's image on her computer screen. A wicked smile spread across her lips. "And I'm going to prove it."

She checked the time and realized that she had to move quickly. She knew that Cynthia would be at church right about now. She also knew that Preston was taking it easy since his work schedule was so tight and that he'd be at home chilling on a late Sunday morning. Ella rose from her seat at her dinette table, grabbed her purse, and headed out of the door. There was no need to change; she was already flawless in her white lace skater dress and silver stilettos. She'd planned to do brunch with her mother since she now had no man to spoil her, but this new agenda was far more entertaining.

In record time, Ella hit up Babies R Us and made the trek out to Cynthia's quaint little home. Preston's truck was in the driveway but Cynthia's SUV was absent. Ella smiled knowingly as she pulled the shopping bags from the backseat of her Lexus and then brooklynyed up the walkway to the front door. After waiting a few minutes after ringing the doorbell, Preston opened up with a perplexed expression.

"Ummm, hey," he said confusedly. "Cynthia's not here."

"Yeah, I see that," Ella responded innocently. "I was hoping to see little Amelia. I thought it would be a good a time to drop by and surprise you guys." She held up the shopping bags. "I came bearing gifts."

Preston grimaced a little and looked down at his lounging pants and bare chest. "Um … I guess Cyn will be back soon."

"Let a girl in then. Don't you know that sugar melts?" Ella giggled.

Preston took breath and hesitated before stepping back and allowing her to cross the threshold. Ella held his stare as she walked by and moved through the house to get to the living room. She placed the bags on the sofa and sat her purse beside them. Placing her hands on her hips to accentuate her figure, Ella looked at Preston as he entered the room.

"So you're just sitting around enjoying the peace and quiet?" she asked him.

"Well, I was trying to get some work done before heading out back to put some salmon on the grill for Cyn."

"Hmmm. Salmon. That's a healthy choice. That's good for her."

Preston gritted at the shot taken at his wife and turned away. "I'll be right back. Let me grab a shirt."

"You don't have to run away because of me. You're at home. You have the right to be comfortable."

Preston didn't respond. He hurried upstairs and grabbed a shirt out of his drawer. On his way back down, he pulled the shirt over his head. By the time he hit the living room again, Ella was able to see his smooth abs disappear behind the fabric of his collegiate t-shirt.

"You didn't have to get out of your comfort zone for me," Ella told him, sitting on the edge of the sofa with her legs crossed, exposing her silky-smooth thighs.

"Right," Preston replied. "Just being respectful." He pointed at the bags beside her. "What you got there?"

"Just a few things," Ella answered, rising and bending over to give him a good view as she rummaged through the bags. After she felt he'd gotten a long enough glimpse of her firm behind, she turned around and held up a few outfits for Amelia. "I think she'll be adorable in these."

Preston nodded. "You'd know better than me. I'm not really up on the latest baby fashions."

Ella giggled and put the stuff back in the bag. "Well, take it from me she'll be the envy of all the little tykes at the playground."

"She's like two months, El," Preston said, chuckling. "She's not hanging out at anyone's playground right now. Shoot, right now her playground is that lil' play pen over there where she slobs over everything. You got an outfit in there suited for that?"

Ella laughed again. "You're a mess. So, how's everything going for you? Fatherhood, the new business. You've certainly got your hands full."

Preston moved forward to peek over in the bags to see what else Ella had brought over. "It's definitely an adjustment. Working all day nearly every day and then taking the night shift with Amelia."

"What?" Ella asked, faking her concern. "You mean, Cynthia doesn't take care of her when she needs to be fed and changed?"

"Like, she's here with her all day so I just try to give her a break when I'm home, you know? Give her an opportunity to relax and rejuvenate so she'll be good to go for the next day. Don't want her to get all burnt out."

"From taking care of her own child? Women have been child-rearing for years without burning out. It's not like she's back at work. She's a house mom right now. Basically, isn't this her job?"

Preston picked up a stuffed bear and gave it a playful squeeze. "Taking care of an infant's no joke. I'm worn out just from the few hours that it's my turn so I can just imagine how she feels by the end of the day."

Ella smiled lovingly. "That's so noble of you." She moved a tad closer to his body, completely invading his personal space. "But Preston," she said, her tone lighter and laced with concern. She touched the sleeve of his t-shirt and stared at him. "Who takes care of you so that you can be rejuvenated?"

Preston opened his mouth to respond, but was silenced the moment he turned his head and caught her glance. He swallowed hard and dropped the toy he'd been playing with. He could smell the sweetness of her perfume and hear her even breathing; because of this he knew that she was way too close to him. His eyes couldn't help but to venture downward to the swell of her breasts, but he immediately forced his attention back to her penetrating stare. "Um … I'm good. It's my job to m-m-make sure that my girls are taken care of. That's what I'm here for."

Ella licked her lips slowly and then smiled. She could see the sweat beads forming at his tapeline and the way that he continued to swallow back the lust that was creeping into his body and beginning to settle within his groin. His nervousness was cute and for a second she could see the slightest bit of attractiveness in him. If she said the right thing and made just the right movement, Ella had no doubt that she could have him on his knees in an instant sipping from the nectar of her womanly fountain. The thought tickled her and she strongly considered following it through.

"You're a good guy," she stated, knowing that flattery worked like a charm on men especially when they were already weakened with desire. She pouted a little for effect. "There should be more like you." She looked away and even took a step back to put some distance between them. She counted to ten in her head, waiting for him to make the next move.

Preston exhaled quickly and pulled at his t-shirt, glad that the awkward moment of closeness was over. He needed to excuse himself and leave her alone in the living room if she was adamant about staying to wait for Cynthia. If not, it was probably best to go ahead and walk her to the door. Knowing what the best option was, Preston looked at Ella and was halted in his speech. She was fingering the arm of the sofa and looking downward with a sullen expression on her face. Her entire demeanor had changed and he wasn't sure if she was about to burst into tears or what. The good guy in him couldn't just evade her at a time when it seemed like she was going through something. Whatever current dilemma she was facing must have been the true reason why she'd popped up to visit Cynthia, needing someone to love and dote on her in her time of need.

Preston stepped forward and placed a hand on her shoulder gingerly. "You alright?"

Ella nodded and smiled weakly. "I'm fine. It's nothing. Really."

"You uh ... you needa talk?"

She looked up at him with glossy eyes. "I didn't come over here to dump my problems on you guys, especially you."

Preston's eyes widened as he realized that she was indeed on the brink of tears.

"It's just that listening to you talk about how you're taking care of Cyn and the baby and seeing you be this ... this great guy just makes me so ... I don't know, disappointed that I keep picking such assholes," Ella let out. She dabbed at the corner of her left eye with her finger. "Damn it! I promised myself that I wouldn't keep crying over this jerk." She lowered her head and covered her face as if in shame.

Preston didn't know what to do as he watched her fall apart before his eyes. "Come on now, don't do that," he encouraged. With no other recourse, he placed an arm around her and squeezed her shoulders. "Whoever he is, if he's not treating you right then he's definitely not worth these tears. When someone loves you they don't wanna make you cry, El. They wanna make you smile forever."

She laughed through her faux tears. "See, that's what I'm talking about. You're so awesome ... you get women. I need someone who's interested in making me smile."

"Maybe you just gotta be mindful of who you're taking up with," he advised. "Sometimes we don't realize it, but the vibes we put out determine the type of people we attract."

Ella stood quietly in his arm, fuming over his statement. Had Cynthia told him about her little fling with the man at the resort during their family vacation? It would be just like Cynthia to paint her out to be some hussy, making herself seem like a saint in her husband's eyes. Infuriated by her stepsister's gall of tarnishing her character, Ella decided then and there to put an end to the other woman's happily-ever-after. Cynthia may have been the ideal good, God-fearing, mild-mannered wife that Preston thought he needed, but Ella knew how to be the one thing that every man definitely wanted: seductive.

She pressed her body up against his and positioned her hand flat against his chest with her forehead resting right next to it. She sniffled a little before speaking. "I need someone to show me ... I can do it on my own, Preston. How do I attract something different? Something good ..." She looked up into his eyes and batted her lashes. She removed her hand from his chest and caressed the side of his face, cupping his chin and focusing his face dead on hers. "Someone like you." Her words came out breathy and sexy her firm breasts meshed against his solid chest.

Ella held his glance and took a moment to draw him in. Although he dropped his arm, he wasn't pulling away and placing distance between them. That told her that she had his full attention. The next move could either be a winner or stall her efforts to bring the truth out of him. Either way, it was now or never and if anyone could sink their hoofs into a man and pull him deep into the darkness of fleshly excitement it was Ella. Slowly, she moved her face closer to his, her eyes fixated on his trembling lips. He was torn between whether or not he wanted to give in and do the right thing. As far as Ella was concerned, the right thing was overrated. She continued to stroke the stubble of his chin, as she the outer layer of skin covering her taunt lips barely made contact with his. She could feel his breath against her skin as well as the thudding beat of his heart through his chest. Excitement was rippling through him and Ella wondered how long it would take him to cum the moment she let him get a whiff of her goodies. She was ready to take it all of the way as she closed her eyes and parted her lips in order to initiate the tongue kiss that would spark her future claim of Preston's true lack of commitment to the woman who carried his last name.

The sound of the front door banging against the wall out in the foyer behind them brought Preston to his senses. If anything he'd been in shock and wasn't completely sure what was going on or where Ella's mind once. One minute she was crying and he was comforting her and the next minute she was crying out for the type of attention that he couldn't bring himself to give her. He took a step back, having been standing there motionless with his sister-in-law awkwardly pressed against him. He knew how the scene would look should his wife cross the threshold and catch them, but in his defense he hadn't done or said anything to encourage Ella's behavior.

"Pres!" Cynthia called out. "I see Ella's car out front."

Both Ella and Preston could hear the struggle in her voice as Cynthia worked to get herself, her belongings, and baby Amelia's things inside of the house. Ella looked at Preston, wondering what he was thinking and what he was planning to do or say. She fidgeted with her clothes, wiped her eyes, and tried to quickly compose herself just as her stepsister entered the living room.

"Hey," Cynthia said with a tone that was a little less than cordial. "What are you doing here?" She looked from Ella, who was giving her an awkward smile, and over to Preston who was avoiding eye contact. Suddenly, she felt uneasy.

"I … uhhh … I brought gifts," Ella said, turning slightly to point at the packages on the sofa. "For Amelia. Just felt like coming over and doing something nice for you."

Cynthia gave her a shocked expression. In all of the time they'd been affiliated, Cynthia had never known Ella to go out of her way to do anything nice for anyone. Surely there was some kind of ulterior motive at work here. Cynthia sat the baby carrier down on the couch beside the bags which she eyed suspiciously. She began to undo the straps that secured Amelia inside of the seat. "That was really … unexpected of you," she told Ella, unable to find any other way to describe the other woman's abrupt generosity.

Ella smiled. "Well, if you wanna be sure to keep your own blessings flowing you gotta make sure to bless others from time to time, Amen?" Ella threw out there, trying her best to be convincing.

Cynthia chuckled. "I'm pretty sure that's not exactly the way that works. You're supposed to be a blessing to others out of the kindness of your own heart and to please the lord. Not because you're looking to reap some kind of worldly thank you for it." Cynthia shook her head but wasn't the least bit surprised. It was just like Ella to misinterpret God's will for his children for some self-serving purpose.

Although her motives were fishy, Cynthia still appreciated the fact that Ella had gone out and spent the time and money to do something special for Amelia. Putting their differences aside for the sake of her daughter was something that Cynthia was more than willing to do. In fact, she was glad that they had a reason to impart some sort of shift in their otherwise toxic relationship. Cynthia pulled Amelia out of the carrier carefully and then turned and offered her over to her aunt. "You wanna hold her? Maybe spend a little time with her while you're here?"

The thought of a baby drooling, vomiting, or quite possibly throwing up on her outfit was none too appealing to Ella. "Oh no," she said, shaking her head and taking a step back. "I mean, I really have to go. I just wanted to stop by, say hi, and drop these things off."

"Oh," Cynthia remarked, a little disappointed that Ella was taking her skewed benevolence just a step further. "We understand." She looked down into her daughter's face and held her closely. "Don't we, Da-Da? Tell auntie we understand."

The baby voice that Cynthia cooed to her daughter in made Ella's flesh crawl. She was such a housewife / mother that it made Ella sick. She cursed the fact that Cynthia had returned when she had. If only she'd waited just a few more minutes, enough time to get Preston in a very compromising, completely undeniably shady position. Ella forced a smile and looked over into the chubby face of her only niece. The baby was kind of cute, but she didn't do children. "Maybe next time," she lied, knowing full well that if she ever came back it wouldn't be to coddle the infant; it would be to get the child's father caught up.

Cynthia looked at Ella and tried to read her expression and true intentions. "Thanks again. That was really nice of you."

"No problem," Ella replied. She turned to look at Preston who was still standing off to the side with his hands stuck into the pockets of his lounging pants and his eyes aimed downward as if he was lost in thought. "Thanks for the pep talk, Preston," Ella said sweetly. "I really hope I didn't talk your ear off or make you feel some kinda way with all of my drama."

Cynthia's interest was piqued. "What drama?"

Ella laughed it off. "You know how we girls get all emotional and caught up over guys. Preston here was kind enough to give me some brotherly love and some solid advice about a relationship."

Cynthia looked at her husband, surprised that he'd been privy to information that she knew nothing about. When last she'd checked, Ella had been just as single as a dollar. Now here she was ranting on about how Preston had helped her through some situation pertaining to this infamous relationship.

"Don't worry about it," Preston said, clearing his throat. "I was uh ... just trying to help."

Ella smiled at him and winked. "You were quite helpful. I had no idea how great of a guy your husband is, Cynthia," she said, turning back to give her stepsister another one of her phony looks of acceptance. "He's quite a brother figure."

"A brother figure," Cynthia repeated, rocking Amelia.

"Mmhmmm. Well, let me get out of here and let you get on with your Sunday. Thanks again for the pep talk and I'll see you guys soon." Ella grabbed her purse from the sofa and moved towards the front door. "Don't worry about seeing me out. I'm good. Y'all have a blessed day!" She threw up her hand without turning back and showed herself out of the home.

Cynthia took a seat on the sofa with the baby fussing slightly in her arms. She looked up at her husband who was still rooted to the spot and silent. He looked at her as though he wanted to say something, but no words escaped his lips.

"What was that all about?" Cynthia finally asked.

"Your sister is a piece of work," Preston finally stated. "I mean, first she pops up out of nowhere, not that her gifts aren't appreciated ... and then she stands here and starts having a meltdown about some dude."

"Hmm," Cynthia interjected. "It's really not like her to care that much about some guy, especially some guy that I haven't heard tale of before now."

"Yeah, so. I was just trying to keep her from having a full out tantrum. I must have struck a nerve with what I said because she then started nuzzling up to me like some love-starved child looking for attention."

"Nuzzling up to you?" Cynthia's blood pressure began to rise. "Preston, did Ella come on to you?" It was a shady thing to do, but Cynthia didn't put it past her stepsister.

Preston shook his head. "Honestly, babe, I don't know what the hell was happening. But I'm glad you came in when you did."

Cynthia nodded and mindlessly reached into the diaper bag near her foot to pull out a bottle for Amelia. "Yeah," she said slowly. "Me too."

Preston took a breath and finally shook it off. He walked over, bent down to kiss Amelia gently on her cheek as she sucked from her bottle, and then kissed his wife on her forehead. "Stop overanalyzing it," he told her. "Nothing happened and nothing would have happened. I'm a better man than that. I love you. I put my life on that." He caressed her head and then hurried off to get dinner started.

It's not you I'm worried about, Cynthia thought, fuming over Ella's gall. She'd stood right there in her home practically ready to strip naked for her husband with little regards for how she would feel. No, Preston hadn't said that it'd gone that far but she knew Ella. She could be downright devious, smiling in her face all the time stabbing her in the back. She had no scruples when it came to her sexuality and who she messed around with. Clearly, her lack of self-awareness and respect had escalated to an all-time high. Cynthia was furious. Who did Ella think that she was, coming into her space and attempting to threaten her marriage that way? It wasn't right and it wasn't fair. It seemed that her extended family would go to great lengths to make her miserable. As she turned Amelia over her shoulder in order to burp her, an image of Ella exiting and spewing out that line about having a blessed day infuriated Cynthia further. How could someone wrong you and then turn around and try to through some spirituality at you? It was the most sacrilegious thing she'd ever encountered.

She could hear Preston puttering away in the kitchen, getting his utensils and supplies to go out back and grill. She knew he was a good man and was thankful that the lord had a protective shield around him that kept him from succumbing to Ella's prowess. Cynthia trusted Preston completely, but she knew that in the end he was just a man. His love for her coupled by their ever-growing faith in the almighty were the only things that solidified his power over temptations of the flesh. Preston was a committed man, of this Cynthia was sure. But, with her failed attempt would Ella come for her husband again? Would she go stronger and be bolder next time? If she did decide to cross the line and commit to disrespecting Cynthia, would Preston continue to be the pillar of strength that she was sure he'd been on this day? There was no way to really tell given how weak she knew the flesh could be. Right there in that moment, as she repositioned Amelia to take her bottle once more, Cynthia lowered her head and prayed over her husband and their marriage. It was such a shame that the devil had come to her disguised as family.

Elton wasn't really up for it, but he knew that forever wasn't promised to him and he wanted to have as many familial moments as he could before it was too late. Besides, it was time to come clean and let the entire family in on the secret he'd been holding on to. For Elton's sixty-fifth birthday he was adamant about having the bash to end all bashes, which was right up Ebony's alley. But, much to her chagrin, he didn't want any one in attendance but family. The music industry was already buzzing with talk about hosting a roast in his honor, but the moment BET had called his office with the proposal he'd shot it down. He didn't want his birthday televised, didn't want to sit through his life being recapped or forced to laugh at himself, and he didn't want to sit in a room full of moguls, artists, wannabes, executives, and screaming fans. Elton had made an impressive living off of this lifestyle and via this industry, but his body and soul were tired and begging for peace.

So, Ebony rented a small ballroom at the Marriott Hotel in downtown Atlanta and advised their family to regard the birthday party as if they were attending the prom. This called for gowns, tuxes, limos, corsages, a catered buffet of tapas that was mouthwatering, and of course photographers on deck who would relay the evening's festivities to the general public via still shots released to the media. Although Elton wanted it to be a family only affair, Ebony still managed to find a way to link the event back to her husband's entertainment roots. She solicited the help of several artists whom Elton had either produced, signed to his label, or had some kind of alliance with. These few individuals headlined the private concert that Ebony put together as the entertainment portion of Elton's birthday party. Although it was more than he'd asked for, Elton couldn't help but feel honored that these artists had taken time away from touring, recording, or relaxing with their own families to come out and show love for him on his special day.

The family enjoyed themselves in the merriment of the moment. No one dared fail to put in an appearance unless they were ready to hear Ebony's mouth. If there was one thing she didn't stand for, it was not following her directions followed by making her look bad. In Ebony's eyes, when the paparazzi was about snapping candids, it made it look questionable if all members of their blended family weren't present and accounted for despite how any of them felt about one another. She was all about appearances and would be damned if any one of them caused her any static.

It took everything within Cynthia to make it out to the birthday-prom celebration. Dressed in her sequined gold, off the shoulder, floor length gown she felt amazing being swept across the dance floor by her well-dressed husband. He made sure to make her feel gorgeous every opportunity he got and for the most part his eyes never left her nor did he ever step far away from her side. Still, being in the same room as Ella who exuded sexiness in her short white and pink gradient, halter top evening dress that was ruffled out and layered just below her thighs, made Cynthia feel a tad bit self-conscious. She knew that Preston loved her and had no desire to bed her stepsister, but the thought of Ella getting out of line with him wouldn't escape Cynthia's mind every time her eyes fell upon her.

Ella was there with some gentleman of Italian descent with the darkest, waviest hair Cynthia had ever seen. The man's features were so sharp and defined and his accent was alluring. Ella never divulged where she'd met the man or how long she'd been involved with him, but no one seemed to mind because she never kept a guy around long. Ramaro, as she introduced him earlier in the evening, could have very well been a hired escort for the night as far as they all knew, but nonetheless as he danced in a borderline vulgar way with Ella, he made sure to look at her as if he was ready to devour her right there in front of the crowd.

Ana, dressed in a white, wrap around dress that hugged her figure, seemed more quiet than usual. She was there with her boyfriend Trey who had recently moved in with her and was set to release an album under Elton's label within the next couple of months. Together they danced beside the Durdens, but it seemed as if Trey was more interested in how he looked for the cameras that stalked them, than he was in having a good time with Ana who was trying her best to hang on to his arm. A small smile was plastered over her face, but her eyes told a much different story about her emotions.

Thea was there watching the group as they enjoyed the hits of the performers who belted out their lyrics as if they were performing for a full audience. She was content with sitting at one of the round tables with a royal blue candle burning in the middle of it, tapping her feet to the music. Her purse sat on her lap, her glasses were perched along the ridge of her nose, and her lips were turned up in a tight smile as she nodded to the beat and simply observed. Clad in royal blue and silver dress and silver flats, she too had spruced up for the occasion. However, something in her spirit told her that there was something far from happy about this birthday celebration despite the good food and music, expensive décor and attire, and the fixed grins that sparkled in the light of the glitzing ballroom lightening. She knew enough to hold her tongue for now and just watch, but the heaviness of the unspoken words and emotions lingering in that space was practically comical. It amazed Thea how some rich people could walk around and keep up the façade of having it all together, all the while they were miserable and dying on the inside. Surely the secrets that existed between members of the Grayson family were plentiful and hurtful enough to keep them all locked up in their own internal hell. Somehow at some point someone was going to have to be strong enough to start breaking down the walls that had long ago been built between them all, but Thea knew that much like everything else there was always a time and a place for such things to occur.

Ebony had done her best to get Elton to move a little bit with her around the ballroom, but soon he tired of the activity. All he wanted to do was sit down and take a good look at the people he called his family. He was enjoying the night and wished that they could have many more like it. He'd always done all that he could to bring everyone together although he knew that often times his efforts weren't always successful. Still, he prayed that now everyone was at some kind of peace with the next so that they could all enjoy one another and focus on that which was most important: family. Elton was no fool; he knew that Ebony worshipped the mighty dollar a little more than one could consider healthy, but deep down he felt the woman had a good heart. He owed her so much where his legacy and success was concerned. If it hadn't been for her pushing him to excel in music and leading him to his first real contact, there was no telling where he would have been. Surely, his health would have faded a long time ago from drowning his sorrow in drugs and alcohol after the death of the love of his life, Miriam. But, at a time when he wasn't sure that he had anything to live for, it had been Ebony who had reminded him of his gift and his music, eventually propelling him towards his destiny: music. For that, he hardly ever told her no, questioned her actions, spoke ill of her, or allowed anyone else to do so. His loyalty and honor for her ran deep and theirs was a relationship that most envied while others didn't understand.

"It's time," he said, trying to speak over the music.

Ebony, dressed in a custom designed red gown that was see-through at her midsection and her back, handed her husband his second glass of Remy. "Time for what?"

"Get everyone over here," he instructed, holding the glass and staring at the inviting liquid. He'd had quite enough liquid courage and was having difficulty passing up the opportunity to indulge.

Ebony gave him a questioning look. "It's not time to cut your cake yet, dear. We have a schedule for the evening, let's keep to it."

"Some things you can't schedule, Ebony. Get the kids." His tone was firm, a stance he rarely took with her, especially these days.

Standing up in front of her chair she looked at her husband with soft eyes, trying a different approach. "If you say so, but what is it that's so pressing that it can't wait until after the performance?" she asked, looking over at the sultry songstress who was now giving them a soulful performance of her latest hit.

"It's time," he said again, now rising to his feet as well and waving to the singer to wrap it up.

"Time for what?" Ebony hissed through a smile, embarrassed that he was cutting the young woman's solo short before she could get to the notable moment in her song.

"Time to tell them the truth."

"The truth?" For a moment Ebony was confused, but she quickly clued in on his meaning. "Now?" Her eyes bulged with disbelief. "Why on earth would you choose now? This is a happy occasion."

Elton ignored her as he signaled for the others to join them at the dining tables. He stood before his table as everyone took their seats. Some were smiling, some were chatting among themselves, and others were munching on the small plates that were so plentiful at the buffet. Over the ages he'd gone from being a struggling, depressed, single father to a married, successful mogul. He had a lot to be thankful for and in some way everyone at the tables around him impacted his life as well as he had theirs. It was only right that he provide them with full disclosure.

"It's my prayer that each of you are enjoying yourself tonight," Elton stated, looking from one to the next. "Even though it's my birthday, I feel that it's a celebration of all that we have together."

Trey raised his hand and stood from his chair with Ana looking at him in in shock, wondering what he was about to do or say. "If I can say a word."

Elton hadn't expected to be interrupted but was interested in hearing the young man out. He nodded and gave Trey his full attention as did everyone else around them.

"I just wanted to express my sincerest gratitude to you, Elton, for everything that you've done for me," Trey stated. "On everything I love, without you my dreams would be nothing but just that. You took an underpaid jiggle marketer with raw talent and molded him into an artist. Man, you're like the dad I never had, Elton. You're like my God ... my God of music and I just wanna wish you the happiest birthday ever. You deserve all the props and celebration a man can get."

From the table to Trey's left a light snicker was heard. Ella took a sip of her champagne and shook her head. "This isn't the Grammy's. Only released a couple of singles and already got your thank you Lord speech down."

Ana shot her sister a displeased expression and Ella simply shrugged her shoulders and returned an "what did I do" type of look.

Trey raised his glass and kept his eyes fixated on Elton. "To you E.G. Salute."

The rest of the family raised their glasses and followed suit. "Salute," they all called out in unison.

Elton was touched as he raised his glass in return, taking a moment to savor the liquor his wife had provided him with. "Thank you, thank you." He cleared his throat. "Family's so important. I've realized that more and more. I'm hoping that we can have more moments, more nights, like this where we're all able to come together as a family and celebrate each other."

From her seat, Ebony's eyes failed to blink as she stared at her husband, attempting to will him out of using this platform to start a riot. She'd planned this occasion for him from beginning to end and nowhere on her schedule had she allotted for a heart to heart.

"There's something that I wanted to share with all of you while we're here together," Elton stated.

Thea sat up straight in her seat beside Cynthia. She'd been paying attention all along but now her senses were heightened and she could feel the air of truth beginning to seep into the room. Elton's look was somber and she knew that whatever he was about to say would be something that would change the course of everyone's life in that room. Thea was ready for it, whatever it was. She was even more so ready to have a personal one-on-one with her brother following the party to inquire as to why he hadn't pulled her aside previously to share his little news. There was a time when they'd been close; she'd even had a special bond with his late ex-wife. But, over the years through his marriage to the wicked witch of the south, their relationship had become strained. Nonetheless, she had a sixth sense when it came to Elton and her spirit was telling her that what was coming would be quite interesting.

"Uh, if you don't mind, E. G., I want to piggyback off what you just said about family," Trey interjected yet again.

Majority of the glares in the room were focused upon Trey as he continued to stand across from Elton. However, Ebony's eyes locked with Ana's in a silent mandate for her daughter to get her man in check.

"Whose birthday is it?" Ella asked without trying to keep her voice down.

Ramaro, her companion placed his arm around the beautiful woman and simply watched to see what would happen next. He had no idea who any of these people were but he knew they came from money. If he had to sit through their strained family function in order to get with the sexually liberated vixen he was with and ultimately score his slice of the family fortune and a green card, then he was down for it.

"Family's very important," Trey said. "And I wanna thank y'all for bring me into your family and treating me like one of your own."

Ana tried to hide her embarrassment as she reached for her boyfriend's hand. Maybe he'd had a few too many drinks, but whatever the reason he was causing a scene and she was beginning to regret having invited him to come. "Okay, baby," she said softy. "Sit down now."

Trey shook her off. "Wait a minute, boo. I gotta say that I've never felt like I belonged in any arena or group until I met y'all. I feel like this whole thing, this whole union was meant to be. Like I was meant to be a Grayson, so to speak."

Even Cynthia had to knit her brows at that last statement. Who in the world had informed Trey that just because he was cutting an album he was now a member of their family? His outburst was a little weird and a series of hushed remarks spread around the tables, but it didn't seem to bother the man one bit.

Elton was a little stunned himself by Trey' proclamation of being his son, but he knew that alcohol tended to make emotions run high. "Thank you, son," he said, figuratively and hoping that Trey didn't take it literally. "We're glad to have you with us. Now I wanted to—"

Trey held his hand up to Elton which caused many to gasp. "Just a minute, just a minute."

"Ana!" Ebony hissed, becoming enraged by the nerve of her daughter's boyfriend. She raised her brow and nodded her head at the young man, warning Ana that she had better do something and quickly.

Ana was speechless. It was just like Trey to not listen to her and to capitalize on an opportunity to humiliate her. Never mind the fact that their relationship hadn't been going very well, but here he was in front of her family making an ass out of himself and asserting his self-importance all over the place as if anyone truly cared about him or what he was saying.

Trey turned to face Ana, whose mouth was moving yet he wasn't paying any attention to her silent pleas for him to stop. "I can't think of anywhere else I'd rather be or any move that's better or more meaningful than the one I'm about to make." He lowered himself to one knee and grabbed Ana's hand as he rummaged through his pocket.

Ana fell silent. This isn't happening, she thought to herself as she watched him through wide eyes. She'd been waiting forever for this moment and now it was happening in a ballroom where everyone was finely dressed and the décor was exquisite. It was like a fairy tale, being swept off of her feet at a ball. With all the strife that Trey had caused her over the last few months, she hadn't seen this coming at all.

Everyone was pretty clear on what was about to happen as marked by the dead silence that loomed over the room. Elton, once annoyed that Trey was interrupting him, was now touched and grateful that he was able to witness this moment in his stepdaughter's life.

Trey pulled out a small black ring box and opened it up. He smiled brightly at Ana as if he was presenting her with a three karat diamond ring instead of a karat and a half. "I wasn't joking when I said I was meant to be a part of this family, that I'm at home with this family. Ana, I wanna ask you here with your parents' blessing and in front of all your family ... will you marry me?"

"Oh my God," Ebony gasped, unsure of how she felt about the union. Sure, she knew that with Elton's name on the boy's album he was sure to be a success and make the money that would support a decent lifestyle for her daughter. Still, he was a rapper and Ebony knew what that life was like. She wanted Ana to marry well and have wealth, but she didn't want her daughter or their family to be subjected to any unfavorable antics that would shed negative light on the Grayson image.

Ana was overjoyed. Finally, she was about to join the club of other wealthy, married wives. Finally she was about to start her own family of which she could create a name for. Finally she would have a man to dote on her endlessly and take care of her forever. It was fated. She'd put in the grunt work of getting Trey to where he needed to be to gain confidence, notoriety, and status and now he was making an honest woman out of her and working to heighten her worth. "Yes," she answered him breathlessly. "Yes."

Trey slid the ring onto her finger and made a show out of tongue kissing her to commemorate the moment. Slowly, the others began to clap in congratulations of the couple's engagement. The men gathered around the shake Trey' hand and the women gathered around to hug Ana though giving her skeptical looks.

"Congratulations," Cynthia told her wholeheartedly. "I'm happy for you."

Ana smiled. "This is a night no one will ever forget." She laughed. "The date is more than just Elton's birthday now … it's epic."

Turned off by the statement, Cynthia simply fell silent.

"Leave it to your man to steal the show," Ella remarked.

"Go hard or go home," Ana shot back. She smiled at her sister. "I'm getting married."

Ella's brows rose and she nodded her head. "And so you are. To Elton's fair-headed boy. His protégé."

"Really, Ella?" Ana was noticeably hurt by her sister's comments.

Ella softened a little. "Hey, if you're happy so am I." She hugged her sister. "Just make sure you keep your pockets lined."

Cynthia making a smacking sound and shook her head. "Love isn't about filling your bank account."

"Not this again," Ella said. "You just keep being disillusioned."

Cynthia looked past Ella and stared at Ana. "I hope you have a long marriage that isn't tainted by greed or lonely women throwing themselves at your husband." She shot a look at Ella.

Thea heard the comment and a smile spread across her lips. She was proud to see Cynthia coming for Ella for once although her niece's statement troubled her.

"Why are you giving me that look?" Ella asked, raising her voice. "You got something you want to say to me?"

"Only if you have something you want to admit."

"I know you're not implying what I think you're implying."

"If the shoe fits then hey!"

Ella laughed. "Honey please, there isn't enough alcohol in all of Napa Valley to make me drunk or desperate enough to come after your leftovers. You think you're so high and mighty and so much better than the rest of us, but trust me sweetie ... if I wanted to I could pull your husband and any other man who'd trouble themselves to look twice at you."

The argument was getting loud and heated. The men were now surrounding them and Ebony was flustered that her lavish party had turned into an engagement party turned fighting match. She looked at Elton who looked as if he would pass out at any moment. It was all too much for him and she had to do something before he chose that moment to declare the end.

"What's going on?" Preston asked Cynthia.

"Nothing," she answered.

"That's right, nothing," Ella stated. "Really, Cynthia, you should be brooklynmed of yourself going around hurling insults and accusations like that, ruining Ana's moment and your own father's birthday party. I'm really surprised at you."

Ebony looked at her stepdaughter with disdain. "I'm appalled. Is this how we behave?"

Thea took a step forward and shook her head. "Nuh-uh, what we're not going to do is gang up on this chile'. Now, everybody needs to take responsibility for their own actions, including you," she said, looking at Ella.

"Excuse you?"

"Don't correct my daughter," Ebony snapped. "She's not a child and you're no authority on couth behavior and accountability." She snickered. "How many charges do you have on your rap sheet?"

"You want to help me add another one?" Thea asked, threateningly.

The smile quickly vanished from Ebony's face. "You're deplorable."

"And you're whore-able. You wanna talk about that?"

"How dare you!" Ebony exclaimed.

"Don't you talk to my mother like that," Ana piped up.

Thea wasn't one to back down once she got riled up. "She used to it. It don't bother her none. She know her name."

"Thea," Cynthia called to her aunt, pulling on her arm.

"Uh-uh, lemme show you," Thea said, brushing Cynthia off and looking back at Ebony. "Hey ho."

"Excuse you!" Ebony squealed.

Thea laughed. "See. She perk right up."

Trey and Preston couldn't help but laugh as Ramaro took a bottle of wine from the table and chugged it back, amused by the antics of such a prominent family.

"Elton!" Ebony called out. "Elton, are you just going to let your sister speak to me that way? Elton?" She turned around to look for her husband, shocked to see that he wasn't already standing by her side.

Not hearing him respond to her, everyone else turned and looked for the head of the family as well. With their commotion silenced, they could hear his little sputters as he struggled to cough from his kneeled over position at one of the tables.

"Oh my God!" Cynthia cried out, running over to her father's aid. She placed a hand on his back and peered over his arm as he held his hand to his mouth. "Dad? Dad? Are you choking? What is it?"

The others circled around and Ebony took up the other side of his body. "Elton?" she called his name weakly, wondering if this was just a momentary bout of discomfort he was experiencing or something more serious.

Elton tried to ward off his coughing but was weakened by the relentless pain that zipped through his body. He removed his hand from his mouth and looked over at his daughter. He tried to speak, but the pain claimed his words and he fell speechless as he lost his strength. Trey and Preston hurriedly caught him and eased the older man into nearby chair. From his mouth blood dripped and his hand was covered with it as well.

Cynthia was stunned to see her father in this condition. Sure, she'd noticed that he was a little frailer than usual and increasingly losing weight but at first she'd attributed that to him working out. As time went on she just figured that the aging process was claiming his body, but looking at him now she was sure that something much more serious was at play here. "Call an ambulance," Cynthia called out to no one in particular as she lowered herself to her knees before her father and took both of his hands in hers. "What is it, Daddy? What's hurting you? Tell me what it is."

Elton couldn't speak as he sat there staring blankly at his daughter and trying to continue breathing. Preston whipped out his cell phone and called 911 immediately. Ebony stood next to her husband, not knowing what to do or say as she watched the scene play out. Thea stood behind Cynthia resisting the urge to take her purse and knock it upside Ebony's head. Something was obviously very wrong with Elton and Thea was willing to bet that Ebony knew exactly what it was. He'd looked sickly to her for some time now and more likely than not, he was probably about to come clean before Ana's boyfriend decided to make the night about him.

Standing off to the side, Ana stood with her hand over her mouth watching as Trey stood behind Elton's chair, ready should the man fall over or something. Beside Ana was Ella who was just as shocked as everyone else to see the hit maker himself off of his game. Concern, fear, confusion, and shock filled the room as the family waited for help to arrive. Ana had been right about one thing: this would be a date that none of them would ever forget.

Chapter 4

Remind me what it is to keep the faith.
When my back is to the wall and I feel that
I can't take another step without succumbing ...
Remind me.
When my heart has shattered into a
million pieces and it seems
There is no glue plentiful or strong enough to repair it ...
Remind me.
When all the odds are against me
And I just can't see a way to make things right
Nor find a reason to keep trying ...
Remind me.
The moment I feel that I've lost everything,
The second I feel that I have nothing to gain,
The instant I feel that this set back, this
tragedy, this unbearable pain
Is all I'll ever know ...
Remind me.
Remind me what it is to keep the faith.

-Kenni York © 2016

ELEVEN YEARS AGO

t was Ella's birthday and she was having a slumber party in a hotel suite paid for courtesy of Cynthia's dad in light of the new venture he'd embarked upon. He'd just gotten into laying the foundation for GMG with two artists already on his roster which he'd handpicked, produced, and practically created himself. With things looking up for Elton financially and career wise, he was all too pleased to give his wife whatever she asked for, after all she was a major part of his success. In this instance, what Ebony wanted was to give her daughters a lavish girl's night in to impress the other mothers in the high society circles that she longed to dominate. Unfortunately for Cynthia, it was Elton's counter request that she be allowed to tag along with Ella and Ana during this celebration.

Sitting in the living room area of the Marriott executive suite surrounded by Ana, Ella, and Ella's five friends, Cynthia felt completely out of place. Not only did she have no clue who the classmates were that they were gossiping about or any desire to try out the makeup that they were all plastering over each other's faces, but she also didn't feel comfortable with the way the other girls looked at her. It was as if they all knew some secret about her and was looking down their noses at her. She considered turning in early and making her pallet in the left corner of the suite's bedroom, then thought against it. She didn't want them to pull some kind of prank on her, like covering her face in toothpaste, all because she'd been the first to go to sleep. So, she sat on the sofa with her legs crossed nibbling at a cup full of pretzels as the others giggled, talked, danced, and enjoyed themselves. There was no point in chiming in ever seeing as though her opinion or input was neither requested nor respected. Cynthia really didn't understand the point of her attendance and wished that she could just call her father up and have him take her home.

The music was blasting as Michael Jackson belted out the lyrics to "Pretty Young Thing". Some of the girls were going wild with hysteria, especially Bianca who was donning a PYT nightshirt. Cynthia couldn't help but bob her head to the music. It was definitely a classic and the rhythm was actually placing her in a more relaxed mood. Michael's work was timeless and Cynthia found herself escaping into the lyrical bliss shared by the other girls in the room. A smile was actually gracing her lips as she sung out.

"I would marry M.J," Bianca said, crashing to the floor and staring down at the front of her shirt as the song went off and the volume was turned down.

"What makes you think you'd be his type?" Ana asked.

Bianca smiled. "I'm everyone's type."

"I bet."

"I'd take Prince over Michael any day," Theresa, another partygoer chimed in. "Man, he be killing those instruments."

"Wait, wait, wait," Ella cut in from her position on the floor. "Are we talking talent or looks?"

Theresa shrugged. "Both, I guess."

"'Cause Prince might have the talent part over Michael but honeyyyyy … MJ is the truth!"

"What? Get outta here," Angel, Ella's ultimate best friend, stated. "Do you see the way Prince be looking into the camera all sexy like? Girl, he's so hot that he doesn't even use a name to identify him … just a symbol."

The group of girls burst out laughing in response to Angel's supporting evidence for her claim.

"Okay, okay, but anybody that can move like MJ can get my number," Ella said, getting over her fit of hysteria. "Can't nobody move like him at all point blank period."

"Who do you think is best, Cookie?" Angel asked another girl sitting next to Cynthia on the sofa.

Cookie smiled knowingly. "I gotta say Prince because I think he's got some real game … you see all the singers he's pulled in his time? Man … he can serenade me any day."

The others giggled.

"What about you, Gloria?" Cookie asked the fifth partygoer who was pouring herself up a glass of coke.

"Well, I think I'd go with Michael," Gloria said enthusiastically. "All that hair … I just wanna run my fingers through it. He's like, a musical genius."

"A musical God," Bianca said, as if correcting her. "There will never be another MJ, hands down. He's in a league of his own."

"Could you be crushing on him anymore?" Ella joked.

"What about you, Cynthia?" Cookie asked, cutting her eyes over at Cynthia and snickering as she took a bit of a candy bar.

"Huh?" Cynthia was caught off guard. She'd been listening to their bantering but never before had anyone purposely pulled her in to their conversation. The fact that someone had done so surprised her and for a moment she thought that maybe she'd heard the other girl wrong.

"MJ or Prince?" Cookie asked, still donning a sly smile as she awaited Cynthia's answer.

Ella sucked her teeth. "Ugh, just pick one already! Who would you choose?"

"Who do you think is best?" Theresa asked, as if Cynthia needed an explanation of the question they were posing to her.

Cynthia shrugged and cleared her throat. "Ahhh ... I think I'd have to say ... both." The last word she spoke was gobbled in her throat, strangled by her nerves.

Ella frowned. "What'd you say?"

"I s-s-said, I'd I have to say both. They're both equally talented and cute to me. I can't pick just one."

Ella shook her head. "You HAVE to pick just one! That's the whole point, to see whose best." She waved Cynthia off before the girl could defend her answer. "Your dad does music, you'd think that you'd know a lil' something about it."

"It's no surprise that she knows nothing about boys yet along picking whose cuter," Ana spoke up. "Choosing both." She laughed. "I bet you wish you had two guys to choose from. Never gonna happen."

All of the girls laughed and the music was turned back up. No one cared to hear Cynthia's argument. No one was concerned about her feelings of being shunned and hushed. She was nothing more than a confused, naïve, outcast in their eyes. Cynthia grabbed a sofa pillow and squeezed it tight as she just sat there watching the others have fun. She longed to be in the solace of her own room, blocking out the feelings of being unwanted and unseen in this crowd.

CURRENT DAY

Some things never changed. Cynthia stood holding the umbrella unsteadily over her head as she stared at the blank tombstone next to her mother's burial site. It had always been the plan for her father to be laid to rest with her mother and it broke her heart to know that this prearranged occurrence hadn't taken place. She wanted to throw herself down onto the wet earth, wrap her arms around her mother's marker, and scream out loud. Maybe then her mother's spirit would engulf her person and fill her with a sense to protection, some form of strength, because at this point Cynthia felt like she was losing.

Things were happening in rapid succession and she had little time to catch her breath and actually process it all. One minute she was in the middle of a petty argument with Ella and the next minute her father seemed to be losing control of his body. His coloring, his fatigue, and his inability to speak through his pain had been nothing short of alarming for everyone in attendance at his birthday bash. By the time the ambulance whisked him off to Emory Hospital everyone had questions but the only one who could answer them was Ebony and even she too was in shock—at least temporarily. Cynthia shuttered to think about all of the information Ebony and her father had been holding back. Apparently, her dad had been diagnosed with stage four liver cancer earlier in the year and neither he nor his wife felt that it was important to share that. The thought of him suffering in silence made Cynthia sick to her stomach. Didn't he know that she would have done anything for him? Didn't he ever think for a moment that she'd want to capitalize on her last months, days, and hours with him? She wondered whose idea it had been to sit on the news, but she knew that now she'd never get any answers. He was gone. The cancer had finally attacked all of his organs and he simply hadn't been able to hold on. Five days in the hospital and finally he was no longer with them. It was an experience that Cynthia would never forget and was much like a bout of dejavu from when she'd lost her mother.

She'd had no say over her father's care as he battled with end stages of cancer since she hadn't known. In the hospital, because she wasn't the next of kin—Ebony was—she'd also had no say over his treatment. Not that there was anything that any of them could have done differently by that time. It was a sad decision to make, but she did back Ebony's choice to take him off of life support and not prolong the inevitable. She'd never want to see her father laying around in pain and unable to do anything for himself; a plethora of machines attached to his body making horribly irritating sounds to remind them all that time was really ticking, that his life was hanging in the balance.

In the distance a clap of the thunder sounded and jolted Cynthia out of her thoughts. Her face was wet with tears and her chest heaved relentlessly. She'd always imagine that when it was time for her father to go, at least she'd always be able to visit her parents together; side by side. But, alas this was just another decision that she hadn't been allowed a hand in making. Her voice was practically silenced as Ebony made the choice to have her father cremated and then spread his ashes over the private beach where they'd had their second honeymoon. Sure, perhaps it was meaningful to Ebony but what about her? What about her feelings and need for closure? What about the way she wanted to send her father on to glory? None of it mattered. Her ideas weren't even considered for the overbearing memorial service that Ebony had planned in which left open to the public. It had been a mad house with camera crews, grieving fans, onlookers, and music industry professionals from all over coming through to pay their respects or simply to show their faces. Cynthia felt that it was no time for media coverage, but of course Ebony would take any given opportunity to place herself in the limelight. Playing the role of the grieving widower was right up her alley as cameras were shoved in her face and she smiled brightly, speaking about how difficult it was for her to come to terms with the fact that her husband was no longer with her.

"It's not right," Cynthia whispered to her mother as it grew dark from the storm. "It's just not right."

She tried to pull herself together for her appointment, but her emotions were flying high. She had no family now, aside from Preston, Amelia and Thea. She didn't phantom a relationship continuing between her, Ebony, Ella, and Ana. Without her father there to be the tie that bound them, they were nothing more than acquaintances now. Deep down, Cynthia felt an odd sense of relief. Perhaps now she wouldn't have to be subjected to the way her step-family treated her. But, she felt sad for Amelia. Not having a full family to call her own wasn't exactly something that she wanted her daughter to have to experience. She knew what it was like to feel alone and disconnected; she didn't want that for her child. Sure, Amelia would always have Preston's side of the family but his parents were all the way in New Hampshire and Preston was their only child so there'd never be any cousins for Amelia to grow up with. Still, Cynthia wasn't about to force a relationship with the women who had clearly never wanted her around to begin with.

"I'll be back," she promised her mother as she sniffed and dried up her tears. "I'll tell you all about it when I visit again." She blew her mother a kiss and turned away to head back to her car where her husband and daughter were waiting. Today would mark the last day of this entire nightmare and maybe then she could begin to find peace with it all. As she hurried through the rain, Cynthia trembled. Something told her that much like everything else pertaining to this family, she would be in for a surprise today. She could only pray that it would be a positive one instead of the opposite.

It felt strange sitting in formal living room of the home her father once inhabited. The absence of his presence, his unique scent and the authority of his voice when he spoke, made the room cold and uninviting. It was nothing more than an overly decorated room with furnishings and knick knacks in various shades of white. No one ever utilized the room much before, aside from when Ebony was trying to make a statement during an indoor function. Today she was making a statement for sure as she sat in a white oversized vintage round back chair dressed in a black lace dress that stopped just above her knees. Her hair was pulled back in a neat bun and her makeup was impeccable. She kept a straight face but to Cynthia it was far from the saddened expression of a woman who'd just lost her husband. Her mascara wasn't running and there were no streaks in her foundation. Cynthia wondered if Ebony had shed one tear over her father.

Situated on the Meridan pearl white marquee sofa that sat in the center of the room, Cynthia clutched a couple of Kleenex tissues in her fist. Her nose was raw from continuously wiping and her eyes were swollen. No makeup covered her face as she sat there trying to maintain her composure long enough to get through the family meeting. To her left sat Preston, holding a sleeping Amelia, and to her right sat Thea, her only surviving blood relative. Thea held her purse in her lap with her legs crossed at the ankles. She too held a straight face as she continued to look over at Ebony who of course was doing her best to avoid eye contact with the older woman.

Ella and Ana were both present, seated to the right of the sofa on the matching loveseat. Ella continued to look at her watch as if she had somewhere else to be and Ana fiddled nervously with the dark shades that she kept on her face though there was no sun in the room at all. Behind her stood Trey, his eyes fixated on his phone as he strolled through his Instagram timeline. He wasn't family yet, but no one questioned his presence. They were all too caught up in their own thoughts, worries, and concerns.

"Thank you all for taking the time to meet with me today," Kori Remington, Elton's estate attorney said in a somber tone as he sat in the second round back chair situated on the left side of a small antique armoire that separated him from being just beside Ebony. He cleared his throat before continuing. "As you know, Elton left a will behind and following the management of his final expenses, we're now able to disperse that which has been bequeathed to the family."

Ebony sat up straight and didn't bother to look in Kori's direction. Thea clutched her purse tightly and kept her eyes trained on her brother's wife. Cynthia kept her head down, struggling to get through the moment and wanting nothing more than to crawl into her bed and sleep off the grief. Preston was torn between paying attention to Kori and keeping an eye on Cynthia. Ana and Ella listened to Kori, but didn't seem particularly interested. But Trey abandoned his iPhone, stuck his hands into his pockets, and was completely tuned in as the lawyer shared the news.

"Elton was a generous man," Kori stated. "His final will made it adamant that $100,000.00 be rendered to the American Cancer Association in the family's name following the payoffs of any of his expenses. This has been done and the association has been wired the funds which will take a few days to be cleared." Kori took a breath and looked down at the papers in his hands. "As his primary beneficiary, he's left the bulk of his remaining assets to Ebony including $2.5 million dollars in currency and stocks, the primary residence, the summer villa in Florida, reigning control over GMG including the downtown recording studio, his percentage of the ownership of Right Touch—"

Cynthia's head shot up and looked over to Preston. "The center? He gave her his half of our center instead of turning the shares over to us? Why would he do that?" She looked to Kori for an explanation. "Why would he do that, Kori? If anything he'd want us to completely own what's ours."

Preston put his free arm around his wife. "Shhhh," he told her. "Let's not worry about that, babe. It's fine." He spoke the words but his bones were chilled with disappointment himself as his eyes cut over to Ebony who continued to sit stoically in her seat without any form of expression on her painted face.

"If I may finish," Kori replied, not bothering to answer Cynthia's question.

Cynthia looked over at Thea. "That can't be right. Is that right to you?"

Thea took her niece's hand and gave it a squeeze. It wasn't right but she needed to know just how foul this situation was going to be before she cut loose. "Go 'head, young man," she urged Kori.

Kori nodded and continued. "All vehicles in his name are turned over to Ebony minus the Lexus driven by Ella which has been paid off out of his remaining monetary assets and the MKZ driven by Ana which has also been paid off at this time. Next is the jewelry, clothing, and personal effects … he requested that they be given to charity at

Ebony's discretion along with the belongings stored away at his storage facility."

"Wait," Cynthia protested. "Some of the things in that storage unit belonged to my mother. Can't just give that away."

Kori cleared his throat. "I'm only telling you what's legally binded in his official will. You have the right to contest the will in court but I'm telling you now that suits like that take a long time to be tried and settled holding up the overall dispersement of the estate."

"We all want this matter to be done with so that we can grieve in our own ways, don't we Cynthia?" Ebony finally spoke, narrowing her eyes at her step-daughter. "Elton would never approve of bickering over something so trivial as mere things."

"Easy to say when you seem to have been given all of those mere things including the ones that don't rightfully belong to you," Cynthia replied.

"Really, dear? I'm a fair person. You know good and well that I don't wish to keep anything that belonged to your mother. You are more than welcomed to retrieve her items from the unit." She paused for effect and frowned. "I have to say I'm disappointed in your cattiness at this moment. Now, if you will," she said, holding her hand out to Kori signaling that he should continue on.

"Okayyy," Kori stated unsurely. "Uh, Cynthia, your father left you $50,000—"

"That's generous," Preston said interrupting Kori, trying to sound reassuring although they all knew that $50,000 from a man who had millions wasn't really all that generous.

"...left in a trust in Amelia's name to be disbursed when she's 21."

Ella snickered at the thought of what was just happening. "Well, you always said you didn't want his money."

Cynthia shot her a look and the fire could be seen in her eyes.

"What else?" Thea asked, finally speaking up.

"Excuse me?" Kori returned.

"What else? What else he left her?"

Kori shook his head. "That's it."

"Bull!" Thea shot back.

"Uh, Thea right?" Kori questioned.

"That's right," Thea replied. "And Thea wants to know what the hell's going on."

"You're the sister," Kori went on. "Elton left you his bible." He reached underneath his seat and grabbed the old weathered bible. He rose and handed it to the older woman.

"A bible?" Thea asked, looking at the book as if it was the strangest gift she'd ever received. "Hell I'ma do with this?" She opened the front cover and read the inscription on the front page aloud. "Bertha Mae Grayson ... this was our mama's bible."

Kori smiled. "I guess he wanted to pass on that sentimentality."

Thea laid the bible down between herself and Cynthia and clutched her purse once more. "That's all fine and well but what else did he leave this baby."

"That's it," Kori answered solemnly, taking his seat.

"That's it?" Cynthia asked in disbelief.

"That's it," Thea repeated, waiting for Kori to renege on his statement.

The attorney nodded his head. "I'm afraid so."

"What about us?" Ella asked motioning between herself and Ana. "I mean, surely he thought to give us something."

"Yeah," Trey chimed in. "Elton seemed more giving than what you're telling us. He wouldn't forget his children like that."

Ebony shot Trey a questioning glance but it was Thea that spoke up.

"Child hush," she insisted. "You ain't even family. You got no say here. Elton only had one child, one daughter. Ain't no way my brother done departed this world and didn't think to take better care of his daughter."

"Whatever happened to thinking of us as his own?" Ella chimed in. "I thought we were more than just step-children."

"He gave you your cars, greedy wench," Thea blurted out. "What more do you want? Work for something."

"I work for everything that I have."

"By work I don't mean work your body," Thea snapped.

"That is enough!" Ebony said, rising to her feet. "This has been a difficult time for all of us but this bickering isn't going to change anything." Her eyes honed in on Thea's. "And let this be the very last time that you disrespect my children or me."

Thea rose to her feet and took a step towards Ebony. "And let this be the last time that I ask this young man where's the rest of what's owed to this child!"

Ebony looked over at Kori. "Are we done here?"

He looked down at the papers, skimming over the verbiage quickly. "Yes. Yes, that's it. There's nothing left."

Ebony smiled wickedly as she crossed her arms. "That's it. I'm sorry if anyone here is displeased, but Elton made his choices and it is what it is. All we can do now is respect it."

"While you ride off into the sunset with nearly everything?" Cynthia questioned, the tears dripping from her eyes.

"I am his wife," Ebony stated. "I am the one that took care of him in sickness and in health, for better and for worse."

"That's only because you encouraged him to keep the cancer a secret," Cynthia replied through clenched teeth, feeling the heat of her tears as they rolled down her cheeks. "My father would have never decided to keep such a secret from me in a million years."

"Well since he isn't here to speak for himself I guess you'll just have to take my word for it when I say, and I repeat … Elton made his choices. All we can do is respect it."

"Respect my ass," Thea said. She pointed from Ebony to Kori. "The two of you did this. Elton ain't did this. Ain't no way that Elton did this. I know my brother and I know that above all he would have made sure that Cynthia was taken care of."

"For someone who was always so above the money, you seem real concerned about it now," Ella pointed out again, looking over at Cynthia. "I mean, God, get off it already. You can't make the will include an inheritance for you. Face it, you're just as broke today as you were tomorrow and you're always going to be struggling class."

Cynthia stood up and Preston quickly held tight to Amelia and rose himself. No matter what, he wasn't about to let anything happen to his wife.

"Shut up!" Cynthia said, pointing her finger at Ella who appeared unfazed. "Shut your face." She turned to look at Ebony. "How'd you do it?"

"Excuse you?" Ebony questioned.

"How'd you get my father to write something so unlike him? How'd you get him to decide to turn his back on his own flesh and blood?"

Ebony chuckled. "Dramatic much? I'd hardly say that he forgot about you, dear. Like Ella said, you were never a fame of the money or our lifestyle so it's only natural that he'd avoid imposing any parts of either upon you. He only gave you what you wanted: to make it on your own accord. On the bright side, he set up the trust for Amelia which even your husband stated was generous."

"But you must admit that it pales in comparison to all you've gained," Preston told her.

Ebony shrugged. "What did you expect?"

"I expected my father to be fair."

"I think he was more than fair. Did you think you could go your whole life looking down on us and then he'd reward you for your disdain? Really, you've been quite the pain in the ass for far too long, Cynthia. Grow up!"

"And my business?" Preston questioned. "You think it was fair of him to give that over to you?"

"I've managed Elton's affairs for quite some time," Ebony replied. "He trusted me to make the best, sound decisions on his behalf. Who else would he have left his shares to?"

"Us!" Cynthia cried out. "It's our business."

Ebony shook her head. "No, ma'am. It's our business. But no worries. I have no intentions of taking a more active role in the day to day operations. As long as the money comes in, I'm good."

"Nothing from nothing leaves nothing," Ella chimed it. "You should be very comfortable in that reality."

"I'm not going to tell you again to SHUT UP!" Cynthia yelled, raising her arms like a crazed woman. "This isn't right. None of it!"

She looked at Ebony. "You never wanted me around, never wanted my father to show me any kind of attention. You did this!"

"No, YOU did this. Always looking down your nose at us as if you were so much better than us."

"That's right," Ella said, standing and moving to stand beside her mother. "You and your holier than thou routine. Now look at you, crying because your own father didn't even think enough of your uppity ass to so much as leave you a cent. What's that saying? You reap what you sow."

"Honey, you need somebody to sew yo' mouth shut," Thea cut in. "Whatcha say we can do about this, young man?" she asked Kori. "To fix all this."

Kori looked at Ebony skeptically before answering the question. "You can uh … you can contest it … but like I said, it will hold everyone else up from getting what was bequeathed to them."

Thea caught the look shared between the attorney and Ebony and felt even more convicted in her decision. "Mmhhm. That's what we gon' do. Ain't no way Elton agreed to this. I wanna see where my brother signed off on this mess."

"You selfish ingrate," Ebony retorted. "Didn't he do enough for the both of you? Why would you want us all to live in agony by prolonging things? Just leave it alone and move on so that we can all handle or grief and heal!"

"How am I supposed to heal when you've left me nothing to remember him by? You're giving me nothing."

"It was Elton's will, honey. Not mine."

"You just told us how you controlled all his affairs," Cynthia cut in. "I'm pretty sure you had a hand in this too."

"You better believe it," Thea cosigned.

"Maybe he was just tired of your slaps in the face," Ebony countered. "Maybe he thought you would have declined anything he did leave for you. I'm with Ella, you made your bed honey." Her voice lowered as she gave Cynthia a slick smile. "Now lie it."

"I'ma tell you who lying," Thea cut in. "You. You and this fancy pants lawyer. You done did some shifty stuff and I'ma prove it."

"Good luck," Ebony spat out. "And while you're looking for Blue's Clues feel free to get the hell out of my house."

"You can't throw me out my brother's house!"

"Weren't you listening? This house belongs to me now. Elton's gone and I refused to put up with your shenanigans. Get your things and leave the premises at once with the understanding that I never wish to see you here again. We have no further business with one another."

"I ain't leaving here without what this child is owed."

"Don't make me have you escorted out by the police."

"Do you. But they ain't built no police squad strong enough to move or scare me, baby. I wants this baby's money."

"Forget it!" Cynthia said.

All eyes shot over to her in shock.

"I don't want any of it," Cynthia stated, wiping away her tears and stepping between Thea and Ebony. "From day one you treated me as if I was some parasite that you wanted to get rid of. You and your daughters are evil, conniving, and disrespectful. You talked about me, made me have low self-esteem, and made me wish that I was never born at times. If you thought that I thought I was better than you then maybe I am. If being who God willed me to be and not allowing some green paper to turn me into some greedy monster means that I'm better than the lot of you then so be it. I'm not apologizing for who I am or how I am. I never wanted my father's money. I only wanted my father and every chance you got you took him away from me! Now that he's gone forever, you can take everything he left you and shove it where the sun don't shine. We don't need it. I didn't need it then and I don't need it now nor do I need this false since of family that you all have created." She struggled for air and cradled her now cramping stomach. "You don't ever have to worry about me," she cried. "Ever!"

"Good," Ebony spat out. "Frankly, I never had the slightest bit of desire to play mother to your charmless ass. You can take your high-saddity behavior and your GI-Jane aunt and leave my house. As far as I'm concerned, you're dead to me."

Cynthia opened her mouth to speak but couldn't get the words out. She stormed out of the room and exited through the front door.

Preston looked at Ebony who squared off at him in return.

"Your wife's emotions tend to get the best of her far too often," Ebony stated. "But, just because there's a familial riff doesn't mean that anything has changed business wise. Elton's will stands ... I own his portion of your little practice and make no mistakes about it, I plan to be all over my investment."

"Your threats don't work here, Ebony," Preston told her. "It's just sad that Amelia won't grow up with a loving grandmother."

"That child is not my grandbaby." Ebony rolled her eyes. "You should go now."

"With pleasure." Preston grabbed Amelia's diaper bag, took a final glance at the remaining individuals and said with an intensity, "I've laid back before while you all viciously attacked her with your words like the true trashy people you are but I will not tolerate it anymore. Sooner or later your darkness will come to the light and you will be the one to reap what you've sowed."

"Evil," Thea spat out.

"Jealous," Ebony shot back.

"There's a special place in hell for you," Thea said.

Ebony smiled. "In that case, I'll just enjoy my riches on earth and I'll be impeccable standing at the devil's side later because one thing's for sure about me, I always come out on top."

"Hmmm. Is that how she got you to change my brother's will, young man?" Thea asked Kori.

"Huh?" Kori asked, sounding and looking guilty. "That's not how this happened ..."

"Shut it, Kori," Ebony ordered. "The door awaits you, Thea."

"I got something awaiting you too," Thea shouted out before lunging forward in an attempt to hit Ebony with her heavy purse.

Ebony stepped back and Kori rose to shield her. "Calm down. Calm ... down ..." he insisted, raising his hands to avoid the blows of Thea's purse. "Ms. Thea, please."

"Please nothing," Thea hollered, still swinging the bag and trying to connect with Ebony's head over Kori's shoulder.

"You crazy old woman!" Ebony screamed, taking cover behind her chair.

"Crazy?" Thea repeated. "I can show you crazy. You just hold on." She rummaged through her purse and pulled out her handgun, waving it in the air. "We gon' see just how crazy I can be."

"Oh my God!" Ana squealed, finally piping up from her place on the loveseat. She turned to look at her fiancé. "Don't just stand there, do something!"

"Shit, what you want me to do?" Trey asked. "I'm not strapped. That lady's nuts."

Ana sucked her teeth and pulled out her cellphone to call the police. "Yes, please there's a mad woman pointing a gun at my mother in her own house." She rattled off the address to the emergency operator.

"I don't care 'bout no police," Thea said. "You think you gon' scheme and steal from my niece and I'm not gon' do nothing."

"Nobody stole anything from her!" Ebony hollered. "You both try to make it as if she's so innocent but that girl's more judgmental and hateful than all of us combined."

"The police will be here any minute, Ms. Thea," Kori advised. "Put the gun down now before someone gets hurt. We don't want anyone to go to jail today. Most importantly, we don't want to lose another life."

"'Shoul not Ebony's million dollar life, huh?" Thea hissed. She scowled at the woman and her finger came dangerously close to pulling the trigger. "I'on know what my brother ever saw in you." She began to back out of the room with the gun still drawn and shaking her head with a frown on her face. "This ain't over," she said menacingly. "Don't let me catch you in the streets." The second she was in the foyer, Thea took off running to the partially closed front door, shimmied down the granite stairs, and hurried off to her car waiting at the top of the circular driveway.

"Oh my God," Ella let out, covering her chest. "That woman's nuts."

Ana rushed over to her mother and threw her arms around her

shoulders. "Are you okay, Mom? That was some real reality show type of drama."

Ebony withdrew from her daughter's embrace. "I'm fine," she said, shaking it off and adjusting her dress. "I wouldn't dare let some psycho shake me."

"She had a gun, Mom," Ana stated as if they all needed the reminder.

"It probably wasn't even loaded."

"Then again it could have been and you could have very well been shot." She took a deep breath and looked at her mother and sister. "I gotta wonder if it was all worth it."

"We're rich aren't we?"

"You maybe," Ella said. "You didn't see fit to have anything left to us."

Ebony huffed. "You're so dense. How would that have looked for you to have an inheritance and Cynthia to get nothing? You think they were pissed with the way things are imagine if I had done it the way you wanted. Relax. I got you the cars with no problem. I'll make sure that you both are fine financially, don't I always?"

Preston plopped down into his chair and cradled his head in his hands. His heart was racing and he wondered if the old woman would really petition to contest Elton's will. The thought of doing prison time for what he'd done for Ebony wasn't the least bit appealing.

Ebony's eyes darted over to Trey who was lingering on her every word as he toyed with his cell phone. "I'll set you up with allowances but for a limited time," she told her daughters. Meanwhile, focus on finding your own money source and don't expect Mama to carry you forever because I won't. Ana, do something with your man. You better hope his ass stays hot and turns out to be a true winner with all that you're putting up with. I sure hope you get something out of the deal."

Ana looked embarrassed as she pushed her sunglasses up from the bridge of her nose. "I don't know what you're talking about," she whispered.

Ebony didn't waste another breath addressing the couple. She looked to Kori whose entire demeanor reeked of fear and worry. "Meet me in the office," she told him before moving to leave the great room.

"The rest of you can see yourselves out. This family meeting has officially concluded."

The queen bee had spoken and the others could do nothing but comply with her demands. She was the boss now, the one holding all of the money and pulling the reigns not that she hadn't been doing so before Elton's death. Now it was all legit; she was the millionaire, the one they all needed. She now held complete power and intended to assure that they all never forgot it.

Chapter 5

Some things in life are constant ...
People get older,
Seasons come and go,
The rich prevail and the poor continue
to strive to come up,
Judgment is passed,
Lies are told,
Hearts are broken.
Some things in life are inevitable,
Beyond our control ...
No matter what we do,
These things will happen despite our
desire for them to cease,
Attempts to spark change,
Or the prayers we send up to help cope with the truth ...
The truth ... the reality that some things just are
And there is nothing we can do
But learn to cope

-Kenni York © 2016

SEVEN YEARS LATER

*O*ver time Cynthia fought to cope with the passing of her father and the fact that she'd basically been cut out of his will. Although it had hurt her to know that she'd spent the greater part of her childhood feeling like the Cinderella of her twisted family only to still be regarded as such upon her father's death. She'd tried numerous times to rationalize how he could have possibly been okay with treating her with little regard but each time she concluded the same thing: it was Ebony. There'd never been any love lost between her and her stepfamily but even the idea that perhaps Ebony had purposely poisoned her father's mind against her was unbearable. Still, she couldn't allow it to consume her. Life went on and day by day she was able to find peace and joy. She'd encouraged Thea to let it go and drop the notion of contesting the will. With Ebony, Ella, Ana, and the whole fiasco behind her, Cynthia was able to move on enjoy the real, immediate family that God had blessed her with; the family she and Preston created.

One year after Elton's death Cynthia gave birth to Elsa who was now six. Two years later the Durdens were blessed with their third child, Brooklyn, who was now four. Amelia was sprouting seemingly overnight and at seven years old she looked even more like Cynthia's mini-me. Family time was of the utmost importance to both Preston and Cynthia. By this time, Cynthia had quit her regular job to manage the office at Right Touch so that Preston could focus more on actually serving their clients. Her salary was modest but together they made a decent living that allowed them to attend to their children's needs and also supply them with extra surprises here and there.

With Elton gone, the summer family vacations that Cynthia dreaded were a thing of the past. However, it was Preston who had suggested that they start their own tradition of taking their family away at least once a year, typically during spring break when the weather was perfect and not unbearably hot. They enjoyed taking the girls to exotic places including beaches, historic cities, and even cruises. When Preston advised that he'd secured them all tickets for a ten day cruise sailing to Aruba, Jamaica, and Cozumel Cynthia had been overjoyed. She wondered if they could really afford such a lavish vacation, but it was already done and Preston assured her that all was well.

Seeing her daughters enjoy themselves while sailing along the clear blue sea was priceless. Being able to expose them to so much culture as they explored the various stops along their itinerary made Cynthia proud. They worked hard to give their children memories that would last a lifetime. Nothing was more important. As she stood along the side railing of their cruise ship one evening, Cynthia stared over at her husband as he posed for a picture with the ships mascot. Brooklyn was up high on his shoulders as he kneeled down between Amelia and Elsa. Cynthia's heart melted at the joy etched across their faces. I love this man more than life itself, she thought. Since the day they'd made their union legal and official, she'd always felt that Preston was her lifeline. With no other family now aside from Thea, that thought was even truer. Preston was her world. She envied his zest for life, loved his ambition, appreciated his commitment to her and their family, and adored the way he still made her feel as if she was the most important, worthy, and beautiful woman in the world. They'd been married for eight years now and he seemed to love her even more than when they'd first started out, if that was at all possible. The same was true for Cynthia; she couldn't imagine a life without the man who had given her a reason to smile so long ago when life seemed so bleak for her.

As she watched the girls playing with their father, a familiar chill ran through her body. Cynthia shook it off. Her mind was instantly programed to ignore anything that placed worry, doubt, or concern in her mind. In the past, those feelings of being ill at ease had given birth to nothing but misery and sadness. There was no way that she was going to succumb to any of that. Things were perfect now. Her daughters were a blessing, her husband was amazing, and there was no stress in their lives outside of the regular day to day responsibilities of being a working adult and a parent. She couldn't have asked for anything more and couldn't envision the wind ever shifting to change the way things were.

With one platinum album in his catalogue and a series of short-lived hit singles as well as a failed sophomore album, Trey was on a downward spiral. He'd been so involved in jumping right into the music scene that he didn't appear to be the man that Ana had originally met. Well, maybe he had always been a disrespectful opportunist at heart. Access to money—specifically her money—only seemed to bring it out of him more. They'd been married for nearly five years now following their long engagement which Ana had loathed. She'd pushed and pushed for him to commit to the marriage until finally he'd conceded. Deep down she knew that he'd only done so to solidify his claim to her bank account and her family's money since sales for his first album had begun to decline after reaching the platinum milestone.

Their relationship was strained at best whenever he decided to be at home. They'd given up her apartment which had been funded by the allowance from her parents originally, choosing to move into a condo that was almost outside of their means. But, it was important to Trey to be able to present a certain impression to his friends and colleagues whenever they visited. He popped expensive bottles of champagne and liquor on a regular bases, whether he was entertaining or not. On the road, he spared no expenses since GMG picked up the tab for incidentals while he was on tour. He never offered to take Ana on road trips with him, claiming that he didn't need the distraction. But Ana knew the truth. Hell, all of America knew the truth with the way that he carried himself in public. More times than she cared to admit, Ana had found pictures of Trey and various chicks on the internet. The blogs were eating her alive, calling her all kinds of stupid for staying married to a now B-list celebrity who would give it to any young thing that smiled twice at him. When he did radio interviews or the few television interviews he'd been granted, he always showed up to the studio with an entourage including some bimbo hanging on his arm. It was disgraceful.

Still, Ana tried her best to keep her wits about her and encourage him to stay focus. His dream had been to make it big as a rapper and her dream was to make it big as a celebrity's wife. Trey was making it difficult for both of them to get what they wanted. He had a new found habit that made his temperament even worse than it was before: cocaine. This realization had hit her hard when she found him in a hotel passed out while on tour. She'd been calling him for days and having gotten no response, she'd taken it upon herself to pop up on him. She'd expected to find a girl in bed with him, but instead she'd found him stoned out of his mind with the white powder out on the table open to anyone in the room. No argument and no threat she issued could get him to stop using, so she tried to ignore his dirty little pastime and focus on their mutual goal: elevating his career.

Over time, it became disgustingly apparent that Trey simply didn't respect her. It was no secret that he'd lash out and hit her from time to time. This habit had begun long before they'd finally said I do. Though others assumed it was happening, Ana never gave voice to the truth. It was embarrassing to admit that her husband was beating on her and that she was actually sticking around to put up with it. She'd made a choice to stick with this man so that they could succeed together; she dreamed of them being the next Jay-Z and Beyoncé, although no one took her musical aspirations seriously. She'd never mentioned to anyone that she often fancied herself a singer. Her talent was a secret only revealed in the shower for the most part. She'd been so focused for so long on attaching herself to a man who was going somewhere and being his backbone that it had never occurred to her that she should invest just as much, if not more, in cultivating her own dreams and focusing on a career of her own.

What hurt the most was that despite the fact that Trey treated her so horribly, she'd actually grown to love him. It was a sick thing that even she couldn't wrap her head around. Several times she'd thought about leaving him, but just couldn't bring herself to do it. Like many other battered women she'd come up with excuses for why she just couldn't walk away. Like the good team player that she tried to be, Ana threw herself into Trey's career even though it seemed as if he was giving up on himself. As he was somewhere immersed in booze, drugs, and women she was flying across the country meeting with people in California trying to figure out a way to boost his image. Within a week's time, she'd met with one of the hottest producers in the game, practically begging him to do a track with her husband. She'd also managed to secure Trey a spot on a popular night time talk show to give him an opportunity to appeal directly to the people. Ana prayed that he could sober up enough to make good on the two connections she'd put in place for him.

As she dragged her tired body down the ramp from the airplane's boarding dock and towards the gate of the airport, she felt the butterflies begin to rumble in her stomach. Trey had been left to his own devices in her absence and there was no telling what kind of self-destructive path he was on now. He hadn't answered a single call she'd placed to him while out trying to salvage his career and reputation. She'd tried emailing and inboxing him through Facebook a couple of times, but to no avail. Ana dreaded what she would return home to since his silence offered her no form of a heads up.

"Ana?"

Ana turned her head to the left to see who was calling her within the airport terminal. She squinted hard, peering through the crowd and then grimaced when her eyes fell upon her estranged stepsister and her sickeningly adorable family. The Durdens waltzed over to her looking like characters from some cheesy family sitcom and Ana resisted the urge to simply walk away and ignore them. She hadn't had any contact with Cynthia in years and that was just fine for her. She straightened her stance and tried to fix her face so that neither Cynthia nor Preston would get the impression that her life was anything other than fantastic. She was certain that they'd seen the blogs just like everyone else in America. It would be just like Cynthia to look at her knowingly and offer some kind of shoulder to lean on out of pity. Ana wasn't about to give the other woman the satisfaction of thinking that she was in need of any kind of help or compassion.

"It's been a while," Cynthia commented first, smiling as if all was forgiven.

"So it has," Ana replied. "Just as you wanted it if memory serves me correctly."

"Well …" Cynthia responded, not wanting to jump right into arguments of the past. She was over the shadiness of her stepfamily's behavior and the entire inheritance fiasco. She'd come to terms with it and in the end realized that she possessed something far greater, something she felt the others were devoid of: love.

"How are you?" Preston asked, setting the tone for the other adults to remain civil.

"Busy," Ana remarked. "I'm just coming back from closing some deals for Trey in Cali. I never knew just how taxing the music business is."

"How's Trey hanging in there?" Preston asked.

"Trey? Oh he's great. Trying to stay on top of his schedule and working on some new music."

Preston nodded. He'd seen the blogs and heard the stories spreading on the gossip entertainment shows. He knew that Ana was putting up a front, embarrassed by the antics of her husband. A part of him felt sorry for her. There was no way that he could ever treat his wife the way this man was treating his. It just wasn't in his pedigree. He cherished and respected Cynthia too much to ever have her walking around looking broken and tired the way Ana did in that moment.

"Who do we have here?" Ana asked, looking down at Brooklyn. She'd long since unfollowed Cynthia on social media. She was aware of the fact that she'd had Elsa, but seeing a third child was news to Ana. Maybe her sister had mentioned something about it years ago, but between battling depression and trying to keep up with Trey, she hadn't been able to pay much attention to anything or anyone else.

Brooklyn smiled brightly, her eyes lighting up with her grin. "I'm Brooklyn. What's your name?"

Ana couldn't help but to smile. "My name is Ana. It's nice to meet you Brooklyn. How old are you?"

Brooklyn held up four fingers proudly. "I'm this many."

"Wow. You're a big girl."

Brooklyn nodded. "Uh-huh."

"That's not humble of you," Amelia spoke up. "You shoulda just said thank you. Right, Daddy?"

Preston put his arm around his oldest daughter and chuckled. "It's okay Amelia."

Cynthia chuckled herself and looked at Ana. "Excuse them. We've been taking them to children's bible study and one of the most recent lessons was on humility."

Ana smiled back. That was just like Cynthia to raise her children to follow Treytian principles. A whole family of goody-goodies, Ana thought. Before she could issue an excuse to escape further conversation, her phone began to buzz. Quickly, she pulled it out of her purse and shuttered when she saw her mother's name on the display screen. "Excuse me for a moment," she said to the Durdens, holding her index finger up as she accepted the call. "Hello, Mother."

"Where are you?" Ebony demanded.

"At the airport. I just touched down. Why?"

"Get to the house now."

Ana sighed. "Mom, I'm exhausted and I really need to—"

"It wasn't an option. Get here now. This can't wait."

Ana didn't have a chance to protest before the line went dead. She had no idea what had her mother in such an uproar and frankly she was in no mood to deal with whatever grievance the old woman had. Still, it was her mother and the truth was that Ebony had been calling the shots for a very long time. She was basically indebted to her mother and it wouldn't do to rock the boat. Slipping the phone back into her purse, she smiled at the others politely. "That was Mom. There's apparently some kind of an emergency so I have to get over to her."

"She's okay isn't she?" Cynthia asked, concernedly.

"Oh, I'm sure she'll be fine. You know her. She's a resilient one."

Cynthia nodded. "Indeed she is."

Ana looked down at Brooklyn and gave her a huge grin. "Take care of yourself, Ms. Brooklyn."

"Byeeeee," Brooklyn sang, waving frantically.

Ana moved to walk away with her luggage.

"Ana?" Cynthia called out after her, feeling the strings of her heart being tugged.

Ana stopped and looked back.

"If you ever need anything, my number hasn't changed," Cynthia said, offering the other woman an olive branch.

Ana saw the pity in Cynthia's eyes and wanted to kick herself. This was exactly what she'd wanted to avoid. "I'm fine, really," she said, convincing no one. "See you around." She turned away and hurried off.

As she sashayed through the airport towards the exit, she resisted the urge to cry. She had to admit that Cynthia had a beautiful family and they all seemed to be genuinely happy. She'd wanted a family, but Trey had been against it. Instead of giving her a baby, he'd once given her an STD that she'd been mortified by. Since then, sex with her husband had been infrequent and not to mention unpleasant. She longed for the days when they were once so super attracted to one another and didn't have so much pressure and tension lingering between them.

A car was waiting for her outside. As the driver put her bags into the trunk, Ana slid into the back seat. She pulled out her cell phone and tried to call her husband. She wasn't surprised when the call was directed straight to voicemail. She took a deep breath, advised the driver to take her to the Grayson estate, and then leaned her head back against the soft leather of the car seat. Staring out of the window she wondered just how much she could take. She wasn't getting any younger and she was already giving Trey the best years of her life, which he was squandering away. She could just walk away from it all; divorce him and live off of the money her mother was fronting her as an allowance. But, the thought of living life as if she was some child dependent upon her mother's assets in order to maintain didn't sound as pleasing as it once had when she'd started out on this path. *I could have been great*, she thought. *If I had focused on me and actually embarked upon some kind of a career I could have been great.* She shook off the thought. It was too late now for all of that whimsical thinking. She was middle aged and no one would dare take her seriously if she decided to branch out on her own. Besides, what would she do? She had no real skills aside from her one hidden talent. She almost laughed out loud at the idea of beginning a music career at her age. *Never gonna happen*, she thought. Besides, she'd seen firsthand what the music business had done to her husband by turning him into some drug addicted, sex-crazed monster and the way that it had turned her mother into some unreasonable, tight-fisted tyrant. It wasn't the life for her. Sure, she enjoyed the things her mother and husband's money afforded her, but she was starting to wonder if the life of luxury was worth the cost of her soul.

When the car pulled up at the front door of her mother's home, Ana sat and stared at it for a moment. She only moved when the driver opened the door for her. Reluctantly, she slid out of the back of the town car. "Don't leave," she advised him. "I'll only be a few minutes."

"Yes, Ma'am," he replied, shutting her car door behind her and jumping back into the driver's seat to consult a book he had resting on the passenger's seat.

Ana waltzed up the stairs to the front door and rang the bell. She waited several moments before Maria finally let her in. "Ugh," she complained as the much older woman held the door open for her to enter. "What took you so long, Maria? It's hot out here."

"Lo siento, Senora," Maria apologized.

Ana waved her off as she walked through the foyer. "With the Spanish already! You're Americanized, honey. Speak English, Maria. English! Where's Mom?"

"En la officina" Maria answered.

Ana rolled her eyes at the woman's blatant disregard for her speech instructions. Ana began to walk in the direction of the downstairs office. "Bring me some lemonade on ice," she called out over her shoulder without tacking on the cordial phrase 'thank you'.

Ana entered the office to find her mother on the phone scowling. That seemed to be what Ebony did the most these days when she wasn't giving fake smiles to the media.

"I don't care how he feels," Ebony barked. "I'm done funding stupidity. I want it over and done with. Shut it down." She paused for a moment to listen to the other person on the phone. "Are you listening to me? I'm losing money left and right on this deal. Those hoodlums aren't doing anything but tearing up my property and costing me money. I'm not paying the staff to sit on their asses and let my money be flushed down the damn toilet. I could care less what it looks like to the community or the media. None of them are putting the coins back into my account."

Ana took a seat and snickered. It wasn't like her mother to claim not to care about the opinion of the public. If anything, she was the one always pushing their family into the public eye and impressing upon them how important it was to always stay on top of their game in the event that someone was paying attention to them. Truthfully, Ebony seemed to be happiest knowing that someone somewhere was paying attention to her and her family. She got off on being the center of attention and the talk of the town.

"Pull the plug already and let me know when it's done," she ordered. "Send out an official memorandum with my signature and I want it blind-copied to my email within the hour. Discussion over." Ebony disconnected the call and threw her cell phone onto the desk in anguish. "Ugh! Everyone's in my pocket for this reason or the other. I'm getting fed up with being everyone's benefactor."

Ana sat up straight and tried to look past the hit that she wasn't sure was aimed at her yet she was surely affected by. "What's going on?"

"That damn center that I let Kori and Monae talk me into opening is killing me."

About a year prior, Kori the attorney and advisor, and Monae, the business manager and publicist that Ebony hired, had encouraged her to open up a youth music academy in Elton's honor. The center was designed to help inner-city youth in Atlanta learn more about the industry, cultivate their talent while exposing them to actual equipment, artists, and music events, while keeping them off of the street. It was intended to make a positive impact on the community while taking the Grayson brand to greater heights. Investors, artists, and consumers like it when a company appears to be socially conscious and not just out for self.

"How so?" Ana inquired, though she could care less about her mother's struggles of pulling the puppet strings of the people who actually ran her inherited organization.

"The damn staff we put in place hardly shows up to work with the brats. They're letting them constantly tear up the state of the art equipment that we have. Hell, my artists refuse to go down there for workshops and whatnot because the little brats are so rowdy and disrespectful. Do you know that they've spray-painted the side of the building twice in the last three months?" She threw her hands up. "I'm over it. You walk through there and there's little baggies, blunt filling, ashes, and all kinds of mess on the premises."

"So hire a cleaning crew."

Ebony shot her daughter a perturbed look. "We have a cleaning crew, honey. But even they are complaining about the way these kids continue to trash the place. I'm losing money on repairs, equipment replacements, raised cleaning fees, paying the salaries of these bums that we're calling instructors."

"Maybe there's another way to get through to them," Ana suggested. "Something that can be implemented to keep the graffiti down to a minimum."

"The police were called last week because two boys from rival gangs got to fighting during a recording course. I'm done. No way I'm going to have my company's good name dragged through the mud in the media because of these hoodlums."

"But if you shut down the center then people lose their jobs and the kids that really were invested in the program lose their safe haven to learn the business."

"So" Ebony fired back. "If they wanted to keep their jobs they would have gotten a handle on the situation. Like I told Monae, I'm not funding stupidity. Anyway, when did you become such a Mother Theresa, down for the people and their rights?" She waved her hand at Ana. "Oh I know! When it comes to spending my money you're always down for the cause. Well, you and everyone else can kiss this venture goodbye. I'm sick of losing money."

Ana remained silent. She was certain that there was nothing she could say that would change her mother's mind, not that it bothered her much. She had her own problems and didn't see a need to try to hone in on those of her mother. Additionally, it was clear that Ebony was on the warpath. She didn't want to say anything that would cause her mother to begin spewing venom in her direction.

"Speaking of losing money, what the hell's going on with your deadbeat of a husband?" Ebony asked.

So much for staying out of the line of fire, Ana thought. "What do you mean?"

"Don't play coy with me, Ana, I'm not in the mood. Trey has been a thorn in my side for a minute now and because he's your mistake, I kept silent. But, now it's getting to be messy and extremely embarrassing for everyone involved."

"My mistake? That's a little harsh don't you think?"

"You don't really feel like your marriage is sanctified and purposed do you?" Ebony raised an eyebrow and shook her head at her daughter's silence. "Okay," she said, letting out a loud breath and sitting back in her chair. "Maybe you're okay with him whoring around and making an ass out of the both of you for all of the world to see, that's your business. But when his antics begin to affect my bottom line then it becomes my business. I have promising artists who won't sign with a company that allows its artists to go around slandering other artists, picking fights, behaving unprofessionally, and simply giving the label a bad name. No one wants to be attached to that."

Ana shook her head. "And what? You're going to allow the opinions of some unknowns to influence your decision about Trey? Surely he isn't the first rapper to act out and he definitely won't be the last."

"Be that as it may, GMG has a reputation to uphold and frankly Trey doesn't fit the bill anymore."

"Mom, come on! Let's be reasonable here. You're acting as if he's gone completely off the deep end here."

"And you think he hasn't? Ana, Trey has a drug problem."

"Granted, but how many artists do you personally know have the same issue? That's fixable. We can put him in rehab and get him cleaned up. Hell, let's give him a reality show that chronicles his road to recovery. The viewers would eat it up."

Ebony crossed her arms. "And what about your face?"

"Excuse me?"

"You gonna put him in a rehab facility that teaches him to stop beating on you?"

Ana's mouth hung open. She was completely speechless.

"Right," Ebony stated. "What? You thought no one knew? You sneaking in and out of the ER, 911 calls to your condo with no filed reports because you stupidly drop the charges, the dark shades you walk around with even when the sun's not shining." She paused and shook her head at her daughter. "Didn't I teach you to value yourself more? How dare you let a man have this much power over you?"

"Actually, mother, you taught me to latch on to a man but I don't really recall any pep talks about girl power," Ana snapped.

Ebony's palms hit the top of her desk. "I taught you to find a man that would die giving you everything you deserve. To find a man you could mold into being the king he should be so that you could live the life of a queen. Have you ever seen me knocked onto my back by some barbaric man?"

Ana shook her head. "No, but I've seen you roll over willingly to get what you wanted out of many of them."

"You watch your mouth!" Ebony said sternly, pointing her finger at Ana. "Everything I ever did was to give you and your sister the upbringing you deserved. Whether or not you picked up on the traits of survival that I tried to instill in you is your problem, not mine. I didn't raise you to be a stupid doormat. Look at you, it's hard to tell which one of us is the elder judging by your tired appearance. You're letting that man run you into the ground, honey, but he will not be allowed to do the same for GMG. Talking about put him in rehab and give him a reality show. You're crazy. I'm not putting another red cent into that crack head."

Ana opened her mouth to respond and was promptly shut down by her mother.

"Don't you dare come at me with an opposition because you and I both know that that's exactly what he is. Trey can continue to be your problem but he'll no longer be mine. The money wasted in studio time and having producers come out to work with him. The money he squanders on tour ... tours that I must point out ticket sales have rapidly declined for which is why I cut it short. And don't get me started on the repeated advances against his royalties."

"Advances?" Ana asked weakly.

"What? You didn't know that your hubby was milking your dear old mother for extra cash?" She shook her head. "Between your monthly allowance and the loans to your junkie, I'm over it. The two of you need to figure out what you're going to do because I'm cutting you both off. No more allowances for you and as of this afternoon, Trey is no longer employed by GMG."

"You can't do that!" Ana squealed. "Music is all he knows. It's all he loves. It'll kill him."

"He's killing himself already, but that's not my problem either."

Ana stood up and leaned over the front of her mother's desk, gripping the edges as if holding on for dear life. "Don't do this, Mom. How are we supposed to survive? What are we supposed to do now?"

"Get a job. If either of you had any sense you would have invested some of the money you both pissed away. You're too old to be sucking from your mother's money. Really, I'm ashamed to call you my daughter."

Ana hesitated for a moment and stared her mother in the eyes. "Well we'll just go to another label then. And we'll take his masters and release music on our own if we have to."

"Right. Because I'd be dumb enough to give that fool exclusive rights to anything. I own all of his music, dear, and I'm not giving him anything. You can bet your bottom dollar that no other label will bother with him, but feel free to try."

Ana stomped her foot. "Mom! Please," she whined. "Don't do this to me. Don't do this!"

Ebony stared back at her daughter with no remorse in her tone. "Do yourself a favor, Ana, and get rid of him. Until then, there's absolutely nothing I can do for you."

There was a light tap at the door and in walked Maria with a tray of lemonade. She stopped at Ana and offered her a glass. "For you, Senora."

Ana looked from Maria to her mother and back to Maria. "No thank you," she said. "I think I'll just be going now." She snatched her purse from the chair she'd been occupying and exited the office in a huff.

Everything was falling apart and she had no idea how to get her life back on track.

Cynthia closed her bible and sat it down the nightstand to her left. Heard the front door open and the alarm resound before hearing it reset followed by footsteps moving up the stairs. Preston had worked late at the clinic handling some late scheduled clients followed by some bookkeeping. Cynthia had cut out around four that afternoon to pick the children up from school and daycare, prepare dinner, and have a little quality time with the kids before bed. Having a flexible schedule was one of the perks of working for herself essentially; it was important that the children still had a very active mother in their life.

"Hey you," Cynthia said as Preston dragged himself into the room and over to his side of the bed where he perched on the edge and kicked off his shoes. "I left your dinner in the oven wrapped up."

Preston pulled his shirt over his head. "I don't have much of an appetite."

"Hard evening?"

"Nothing I can't handle."

Cynthia smiled. "Of course not. You're my warrior. Nothing defeats you."

Preston remained silent as he sat on the bed feeling a tightness in his chest. The feeling had been coming and going for months, but he attributed it to anxiety. He'd been working crazy hours around the clock trying to keep his clinic afloat. As the head of his household, he did his best to balance being a business owner with being a husband and a father. However, at times it wasn't always easy. Still, he was dedicated to doing whatever needed to be done so that his family was happy and secure. Outside of that nothing else mattered. To ease his anxiety, perhaps he'd just exercise more and practice some breathing routines. Anything to help him get through the day.

"I was thinking about signing the girls up for ballet," Cynthia stated. "They're offering classes at this cute little dance studio I drove past today."

"I'm sure they'd like that," Preston responded, wondering how much these classes would run them. No matter the cost, if the girls wanted to do it, he'd figure out how to front the bill.

"Yes, I'm going to call them tomorrow to see if we can sit in on a class or something. Just so that they can get a feel for it."

Preston turned around to respond but was halted by the sight of a luminous figure standing over Cynthia near her nightstand. His words got stuck in his throat as he narrowed his eyes and basically stared at the being.

Cynthia took notice of his expression and turned to follow the direction of his glance. He didn't have to say a word. The dim flare of light of the figure was evident to her as well. The hairs stood up on her bare arms and the back of her neck. Cynthia swallowed hard and tried to fight back the brief feeling of dejavu and sorrow that jolted through her spirit. Then, just like that, it was gone; both her feelings of trepidation and the ghostly figure. She turned to look at Preston who remained speechless.

"Say something," she whispered.

"You saw that?" he asked confusedly. "You saw the spirit standing over you?"

Cynthia remembered the last time she'd experienced the presence of a spirit. She also remembered what happened following what she felt were signs from the universe. Not wanting to address those memories or her worries, Cynthia decided that it was best to put her husband's mind at ease. There was no point in having them both on edge. She could tell that he'd already had a rough day and was in dire need of relaxation. She wasn't about to do or say anything that would have him up all night with his wheels steadily turning.

"No," she finally stated. "What's wrong?"

He looked at her as if he couldn't belief what she'd just said. "You

DIARY OF A BROKEN CINDERELLA   137

didn't see it?" he asked pointing over her shoulder. "The light ... the lady spirit ..."

Cynthia shook her head and crawled over to her husband. "No, but I'm sure it was nothing," she said softly, cradling his face in her hands and giving him a long, intense kiss. "I'll tell you what," she said, pulling away from the embrace. "Why don't you go take a nice long hot shower and when you get out I'll give you a massage for a change? How does that sound?"

Preston's mind was immediately deterred from the sight of the spirit. "That sounds like heaven. I love you beautiful."

"I love you too."

"It's hard to believe that it's been almost ten years already."

Cynthia smiled at the thought of their anniversary. "It seems like just yesterday when we got married. You've been so good to me, Pres, and the kids. I thank God for you every day."

Preston grabbed her right hand and gave it a squeeze. "And I love you more and more each day." He kissed the back of her hand.

An idea occurred to Cynthia. "I think we should plan a vow renewal," she stated.

Preston looked stunned. "You want to start planning now for the ten year anniversary?"

"No. Who said that we had to wait until our tenth year? We can do a vow renewal next spring on the beach with just me, you, and the kids. Just our family. It'll be beautiful."

The thought of an exotic trip within little over the next half a year didn't really put Preston at ease, but seeing the joy on Cynthia's face as she spoke about it made him smile. "Anything for you, beautiful."

Cynthia bobbed up and down with joy. "Yay! I'll start looking on Pintrest tomorrow at various themes and ideas and we can start planning. You're the best, Preston. Simply the best."

Preston rose from the bed and head to the bathroom. "Off to take that relaxing shower now."

"I'll be right here waiting for you when you get back."

Preston smiled again at the thought of his loving wife awaiting his return anxiously. There was no doubt about it; he loved that woman beyond belief.

He was between clients and trying to keep himself busy with office tasks. Cynthia was already gone for the day and the only other staff member around was Eva, their receptionist. Though the clinic was quiet as mouse, Preston's thoughts were loud within his head. He was in a panic, trying to think of a plan to fix the currently dilemma that the clinic was facing. There was no way that he could burden Cynthia with the truth. Truthfully, he was surprised that she hadn't already realized what was going on. As he went about trying to fix the office copier which seemed to malfunction at least once a month, Preston felt that familiar tension in his chest. You need to relax, he thought, fully believing that he was driving himself crazy with worry. He didn't know which he feared more; losing his business or disappointing his wife. Neither were realities that he wanted to ever encounter.

Preston reached around the copier to retrieve the unplugged cord, hoping that his tinkering had finally done something to correct the machine's glitch. His movement was a little too swift and caused a nearby vase situated near the edge of the work table beside the machine to tilt over. Water spilled as the flowers slipped from the glass container.

"Darn it!" Preston called out, as he continued to move towards the wall outlet. Quickly, he plugged in the cord and instantly felt a volt surge through his body. "Ahhhh!" he screamed out.

The electric shook caused the lights from the lamps and all of the devices within the clinic to blink on and off. It alarmed Eva and she dashed from her desk at the front of the clinic to the office space at the back of the open floor plan establishment.

"Mr. Durden, are you okay?" she asked as she made it to his side.

Preston sat on the floor in front of the copier, clutching his chest and leaning forward. His body shook and he was irresponsive.

"Mr. Durden?" Eva called out to him. Her hand lingered over his shoulder but she was afraid to touch him for fear that electricity was still radiating through his body. She covered her mouth with her other hand and gasped. "Oh my God, oh my God." Frantically, she dashed for the office phone on Cynthia's desk and hurriedly dialed 911.

"911, what's your emergency?" the response operator answered the call.

"Um, it think … well, my boss electrocuted himself and I think … I think he's having a heart attack now," Eva explained. Her eyes were trained on Preston who continued to grip his chest without making a peep. "Oh my God," she cried, as he kneeled over resting against the copier. Eva became panicked. "I think he's gonna die. Oh Lord, help me please! I think he's going to die!"

Cynthia burst through the emergency room doors like a mad woman possessed. Already, her eyes were red with tears as she led her daughters through the waiting room and up to the receptionists' desk. "I'm looking for my husband! Where's my husband?"

"Ma'am, calm down," the front desk clerk stated. "What's your husband's name?"

"Mommy, what's wrong with Daddy?" Brooklyn asked, hanging on to her mother's pants leg.

"Preston," Cynthia answered the woman at the desk. "Preston Durden. I got a call that he was transported here by an ambulance."

"Cynthia?" a shrill voice called out behind her.

Cynthia turned around and came face to face with Eva who looked distraught herself. Looking at the younger girl's face made Cynthia even more pensive. Something was wrong. Something was terribly wrong. "Eva, what happened?" she asked. "What happened?"

Tears leaked from Eva's eyes as she began to try to explain the situation. "He was working on the copier and I heard him scream … there was a spark through the clinic and he was in pain. Clutching his chest like he was in pain and …"

"Mommy!" Elsa now called out. "Daddy hurt himself, Mommy? Is he okay?"

Brooklyn began to cry at the thought of her hero being hurt. "I want my daddy!" she cried out.

Amelia, trying to be a big girl, put her arms around Brooklyn and held her close. "We can't see Daddy now. Mommy has to talk to the grownups."

"Ma'am, your husband is in trauma room one," the clerk advised. "Let me see if I can find nurse to give you an update and find out what's going on."

Cynthia stared at the woman with wide eyes. "I need to see him. I need to see him now!"

"If you'll just take a seat in the waiting room I will find someone who can update you."

To her left, Cynthia noticed a group of medical professionals talking and heading towards the heavy brown, power-operated doors that separated the exam rooms from the waiting room. She shot a quick look over at Eva. "Watch the girls." Before anyone could say a word, Cynthia bolted and followed the medical staff through the double doors before they could close.

"Ma'am, you have to get a badge to be back here," a nurse called out.

Cynthia ignored her as she walked at a mighty speed, searching for trauma room one.

"Miss!" another nurse called out. "You need to sign in and be admitted back by a staff member."

"Preston!" Cynthia called out, feeling desperate to find her husband. "Preston!"

"Call security," the first nurse advised a nearby tech.

"Ma'am, can I help you?" a doctor asked, approaching Cynthia in her irate search.

"I need to find my husband. Preston Durden. Please! Please, help me find my husband."

"I don't know if—"

Before the doctor could finish his statement, Cynthia's eyes fell upon the name plate on the wall outside of the nearest room; Trauma

1. She ran away from the doctor and rushed into the room where staff were all around Preston. "Oh my God!" she cried out at the sight of him.

"Ma'am you can't be in here," a nurse told her, trying to push her out of the room.

Cynthia wasn't having it. "I need to be with him," she declared, pushing past the others and making it to her husband's beside. She took quick inventory of the scene and concluded that Preston was in very bad condition. The tears were plentiful as she reached down and grabbed her husband's hand. "Preston! Preston!" Cynthia gripped his hand tightly while staring into his irresponsive face.

The color was completely drained from his pigment and his body lay limp as did his hand smothered by her loving hold. The machines attached to him began to beep loudly and erratically. This couldn't be happening. Tears blinded her eyes as she glanced over to the one device which flashed a consistent flat line as it squealed its truth relentlessly. She was no medical professional, but Cynthia had seen enough movies and hospital-based television shows to know that this was a fatal sign. She dropped his hand immediately and grabbed his face as if her touch would somehow return energy to his body.

"Preston!" she screamed, becoming irate and emotional. She was practically kneeling on her knees beside him on the hospital bed as she peered down into his face. Her hands moved down to his chest and she began to press sporadically against his flesh hoping that her actions would be fruitful. "Don't do this! You can't do this to me! I can't do this without you. Please … please … don't do this to me."

Pandemonium took place as the room began to fill up with nurses, doctors, and techs all trying to respond to the code they'd been alerted to. Cynthia's focus was centralized on Preston and her body strength became greater than she knew. Two of the male techs tried to remove her from the body but she refused to let go and step aside.

"Ma'am, please," a nurse begged of her. "We need you to get off of him."

"Get her out of her!" one of the doctors ordered.

"Come on, Ma'am," the tech to her left pleaded. "You have to let us do our job. You have to give us space to do our job."

Their words were falling upon deaf ears as she continued to pound on the chest that she'd spent years of her life falling asleep on, crying on, and inhaling the scent of. They wanted her to give it up; to move aside and just let him go, but she couldn't do it. She owed it to Preston to fight for him even when he couldn't fight for himself any longer. She owed it to him to hang on with love until the absolute very end when God stepped in to say that the fight was over. Right now her spirit wouldn't allow her to throw in the towel. Her heart was shattering into a thousand pieces as the hospital staff around her barked orders, tinkered with equipment, and tried to force her out of the way.

"You can't do this!" she yelled at Preston. "You can't leave me. You can't leave me."

The techs managed to remove her from her semi-straddled position over Preston's body, but she didn't venture far despite their instructions. Time was of the essence and no one in the room knew what to expect from their attempts to save the man on the table. His chest was exposed and the defibrillator was readied. The leading physician stepped forward and shut his eyes for a brief second before grabbing the paddles from the nurse to his right.

"Charge to 200," the doctor ordered.

His request was fulfilled and immediately he pressed the paddles against Preston's chest and issued a volt to the man's body. All eyes flew over to the monitor which failed to report a change in his status.

"Charge to 250," the doctor ordered, determined to get a satisfactory outcome. He mimicked his earlier actions, feeling the surge of the shock as he tried to rejuvenate activity within Preston's body.

Still, there was no change. The room fell silent minus the consistent beep that magnified the intense depression surrounding the team's failure. Cynthia stood clutching her chest with large, blood shot eyes. She could feel it; the end. The end of an era, their marriage, their friendship, and his life. It was over. The staff was conceding finding it pointless to advance their efforts and there was nothing that she or anyone else could do about it. In that instance, she felt her life shift to a cold emptiness that she knew she'd never be able to cope with, never be able to accept. A life without Preston wasn't a life at all, it was a tragedy.

"Time of death," the doctor stated morbidly as he handed the paddles back over to the nurse. "2:59 P.M."

"No!" Cynthia screamed out, her strength finally weakening as she lurched forward and threw herself over Preston's lifeless body. "Nooo! I can't do it, Preston! I can't do it. I can't live without you. What am I supposed to do?" she cried out. Her tears began to create a puddle along the ridges of his abs. A flashback of a dream she'd had jumped to the forefront of her mind. She'd been huddled over on her knees in a distraught manner. She remembered waking him to tell him about the dream but they'd both gone back to sleep, neither thinking much of it. Now, here she was feeling a sickening sense of dejavu as she felt the rip in her spirit due to reality tearing her apart. "What am I supposed to do without you?"

No one bothered to pull her away this time. She was grieving and they all understood that. As Cynthia cried and held on to the man she'd never again have the opportunity to hold a conversation with, the man who would never again embrace her, the hospital staff went about business as usual. The machines were turned off, the coroner was called, and the room was vacated. Cynthia was lost in despair and heartbreak. Preston was all she'd known for years. He'd been her sunrise and sunset, the lifeline that kept her going. Without him she knew she'd live a mediocre existence devoid of love aside from that of their three children. The thought of going it alone now without him by her side and no real support system frightened her.

"What am I going to do, God?" she asked in a whispered cry. "What am I going to do?"

Cyn tearfully closes her eyes to sing Tasha Cobbs songs, Gracefully Broken and For Your Glory as she reminisced on all the times she had with Preston.

Chapter 6

There are lessons even in the nightmares that we endure,
Teachings of how we must move
forward and deal with adversity.
At the end of that long tunnel of despair,
We must know some good exists just beyond the exit.
It is only our job to belief,
Not to understand;
To learn from it,
Not to dictate the lesson.
It's our job to know that he keeps us
even during the darkest hours,
For the nightmares are only lessons
disguised as pain and suffering,
Yet with his grace and mercy we will wake up
Renewed, enlightened, and even stronger than before

-Kenni York © 2016

ONE MONTH LATER

verything she'd ever known was now lost to her. The family that she'd once adored and thanked the Lord for often, was now broken. The faith she'd gained in love and her own self-worth was plummeting. She was in hell and couldn't phantom a way out of it. The house seemed quite and bleak without Preston's presence. For nearly forty days following his funeral, she couldn't even find the strength to get out of bed. The shades remained drawn in her bedroom and the she didn't know what day of the week it was. Thea and Eva took turns tending to the girls, giving her the time that she needed to grieve. They spoke to her but Cynthia never heard them. She was lost in her own thoughts and fears which were far louder in her head than any other noise around her. She was losing weight because she refused to eat anything. There were many days where she cried so much and so hard that she made herself sick, vomiting stomach acid because her body contained no nutrients due to her failure to eat. At times, it felt as if there was no point. Her lifeline was gone; the love of her life had done the worst thing in the world: he'd left her. For a few days she'd been in denial, telling herself that it was just a nightmare. But during the time that she'd been forced to pick out his burial suit, casket, and tombstone she began to realize that the nightmare was very much her reality. Watching him being lowered in the ground nearly made her weak to her knees. At some point, she passed out and couldn't recall who had gotten her back home and in her bed. There was a nagging, empty feeling in the pit of her stomach that kept her balled up, trying not to feel it. Her tears were all gone for she no longer possessed the energy to cry. Her heart felt as if someone had literally broken it in two and several nights she prayed that God that she felt like she would die of a broken heart, because there was no way that she'd be able to survive this massive blow.

The most she could manage to do on a good day was reach over onto her nightstand for her tablet and play K. Michelle's Bury My Heart repeatedly. The words spoke to the total despair she was experiencing and the ultimate pain that her heart was suffering from. Her eyes were sealed shut as she listened to the lyrics singing her troublesome truth and bringing her close to the brink of a break down. As K. Michelle, said she was so lost without Preston. She couldn't see how she'd ever bounce back from this type of pain and the notion of ever loving anyone again in life was unbelievable. Preston was that one great love of her life. They'd just been planning their vow renewal before the universe cruelly took him away from her. First her mother, then her father, and now her husband. How much heartbreak and grief could one person take in their lifetime? What was the point in trying to cope when everything she'd ever felt, believed in, and lived for was snatched away from her the moment Preston took his final breath. Remembering the sight of her husband slipping away threw her into a fit of loud sobs. She knew that he was with God, but she wanted to scream out and ask God why he felt the need to relieve her of that which had sustained her.

It was the suddenness of the tragic event which is probably what hurt the most. The cold abrupt truth that her husband was gone, perished from the Earth. Never ending thoughts of what she would've said to her one true love had she known she'd be without a husband by the end of that day. Cynthia thought to herself throughout her day which now consisted of a numerous amount of panic attacks and deafening silence. She thought to herself about the night before. It had been one of her worst yet. She had laid there in her bed sobbing uncontrollably as she clutched on to one of Preston's shirts as if it was the only thing keeping her alive. The sad truth of that is it actually was gone. She had passed out two times now from her emotional distress and wasn't sure how much more her body could take. That was when she saw his shirt, still hanging in the closet of his clothes she hadn't beard to look at since his death, it was too hard, but at that moment it didn't matter. Cynthia lunged up out of her bed to retrieve back what she could of Preston and held on to it for dear life and slowly descended into a deep slumber with tears still furiously streaming down her face.

There was no coming back from this dark hole she thought. She'd buried it herself with the oceans of tears shed, the worries of how she would go on, and the truth that she was broken into pieces that had no hope of coming together again.

The door swung open and suddenly the music stopped. Cynthia didn't budge. She was used to them coming into the room trying to engage her and just like any other day she had no desire to be engaged. Suddenly, the room was filled with light as the shades were opened. Cynthia pulled the cover over head to avoid the bright rays. She couldn't remember the last time she'd seen the light of day, but today wasn't about to be her reunion with the sunshine. She wanted to be left alone to wallow in the pits of her grief. There was nothing that anyone could say to alleviate the feeling of destruction and the overwhelming sadness that consumed her.

"Get up," she heard Thea say.

As much as she respected her aunt and was deep down glad that she was there to tend to the girls, Cynthia was unmoved. She was in no mood for the woman's tough motherly love or attempts to get her up and active. There was nothing active about her life anymore. She'd been robbed of the sunshine that she'd become accustomed to rising to, the love that she'd embraced and found solace in. Now there was nothing but darkness. Unless they could bring Preston back, there was nothing that anyone could do to help her.

"Get up!" Thea ordered, pulling back the cover.

Cynthia grimaced as the light hit her eyes. She squeezed her lids shut tightly and reached down blindly for the covers.

"Nuh-uh," Thea said, tossing the covers on the floor on the other side of the bed. "Now you done laid up in here like dis long enough. Get up! Get up and get on with your life, hunteee."

Cynthia's puffy eyes opened slowly and she struggled to focus her glance upon Thea's round body. She groaned, indicating that she wasn't up to it today.

Thea didn't care. "No more sad songs, no more sleeping, no more laying around all day in your pajamas, no more crying. It is time to get up and get going."

Cynthia shook her head. "No," she mumbled.

"No what?" Thea asked, leaning down to look at her niece as if she'd heard her wrong.

"No, I don't want to get up."

"Did you hear me ask you? Nobody asked you. I told you to get up!" Thea's voice boomed loudly as she spoke.

Rattled by her aunt's assertiveness, Cynthia relentlessly pulled herself up to a sitting position and stared at Thea.

"Now, you need to eat," Thea told her, motioning towards the tray she'd sat on her nightstand.

Cynthia eyed the food and felt her stomach turn. "I'm not hungry."

"Like hell. You ain't ate nothing in days. Today you gon' eat, you gon' get up, and you gon' handle yo' business."

Cynthia shook her head again and ran her fingers through her hair. "I can't ... I can't do this today, Thea. I'm not ready. I'm just not ready."

"And when you think you gon' be ready?"

Cynthia shrugged.

"Mmmhmmm. Today's the day," Thea said. "You gon' ahead and pick up that fork and eat that oatmeal. Put something in your stomach. You got things to do today."

Cynthia looked at her aunt curiously. "What is it that I have to do?"

"You need to get down to that office and stake yo' claim on yo' business before you not have a business."

Thoughts of the clinic began to fill Cynthia's head. She was in no position to go down there playing boss. "Eva can manage."

"Eva can ..." Thea's words trailed off as she placed her hands on her hips. "Who you think been here tending to these kids? Eva can't be in two places at once. Eva ain't been to work in three weeks. From what I hear ain't no work to go to."

"What?"

"Ebony is closing the doors, honey."

"S-s-she can't do that."

"Reason being why you need to get your strength up and stop laying up in this bed like some martyr. You need to go get what belongs to you."

The thought of Ebony coming out of the woodworks and taking

over Right Touch infuriated Cynthia. The clinic was all she had left aside from their home and daughters to keep her connected to Preston. It was a part of his legacy. If she thought that Cynthia was going to just step aside and let her call the shots then Ebony had another thing coming. It took everything within in Cynthia to pull it together. She forced herself to take a few bites of oatmeal and eat half a piece of toast before taking a long hot bath and getting dressed for the day. Eva stayed behind with the girls as Thea chauffeured Cynthia to the home that she vowed she'd never return to. They were pretty sure that Ebony would be there perched on top of her throne, wreaking havoc wherever she could. Pulling up into the driveway, it was clear that Ebony had other company. It mattered not to Cynthia. She was there to settle things and whatever else Ebony had going on would have to wait.

Maria graciously let them it. Secretly, she was intimidated by Thea's size and couldn't bring herself to inform the intruders that Ebony was in a private business meeting. Thea, being the direct individual that she was, burst into the office that had once belonged to her brother and startled Ebony and her two other guests.

"Hello-er!" Thea called out.

"Oh God!" Ella let out from her seat across from her mother's desk. "Must we be burdened with your presence today?"

Ebony rose to her feet, standing behind her desk. "What is the meaning of this?" she asked with a frowned brow.

"We came to get some answers," Thea advised.

"Answers to what?"

Cynthia stood beside Thea and eyeballed Ella, then Kori who was seated next to her, ultimately landing her glance upon her stepmother who had aged noticeably over the last few years. She'd seen pictures of Ebony in magazines, clips of her on television, and candid shots here and there in the blogs but seeing her up close and personal truly gave evidence to how the years of being mean and devious were catching up to her.

"What are you doing with my husband's clinic?" Cynthia asked her.

"In the future I'll advise you to call ahead before coming to my home and any business matters can surely be discussed by calling Monae at the GMG business office," Ebony replied.

"Well, we're here in the present and I want to know what you're doing with my husband's clinic."

"As luck would have it we were just finalizing some things now."

"We?"

"Yes. You see, being that I hold controlling shares of the business I—"

Cynthia held her hand up. "Wait! What? Since when do you hold controlling shares of our business?"

"Since your husband couldn't manage financially and came to me asking to invest more capital into the business so that you could maintain your payroll and the expenses for the company. That was what, two years ago."

"You're lying. He would never give you that much control over what we built."

Ebony smiled. "One thing I don't lie about honey is making my money."

Cynthia was dumbfounded. "But … why?"

"Why? You can't be that blind. That place was a money pit. Clientele was low, overhead was high. He had an idea that he just couldn't manage to see through."

"But … I mean, I know that things would get slow from time to time, but I thought that we were okay," Cynthia whispered. "Preston said that we were okay."

"And you were, so long as I made sure the money was still coming in. I'm sorry for your loss, dear, but truth be told, I was going to pull the plug on that place this year anyway."

Cynthia's eyes became cold and tiny. "You heartless tyrant! That place was his life."

"Was being the operative word," Ebony remarked.

"So disrespectful," Thea hissed.

Ebony waved them off. "Look, it's done. I'm issuing you a check to cover Preston's half of the company's worth. I've already taken the liberty of dissolving the corporation and sold the building to a new business."

"You can't do that!" Cynthia stated. "You can't just take my business from me."

"Technically, it was mine, and it's already done."

"And what new business did you sell to?"

Ella crossed her legs and smiled. "I've finally found my passion," she stated. "I'm opening a boutique. The contractors are coming in tomorrow to redesign the place to fit my specifications. I'm an entrepreneur now."

Cynthia shot Ebony a heated look. "You took my company and gave the building to your daughter!"

Ebony smiled. "I simply invested in a new venture."

"That was our livelihood," she cried out. "My livelihood. I don't have a job anymore."

Ebony shook her head in mock pity. "That's a shame. You might wanna start looking soon. Separation notices are being sent to all of the employees. You should be able to get a few unemployment checks."

"I have three children," Cynthia stated. "You stole my inheritance, you stole my husband's legacy, and you're basically forcing me and my girls to be destitute."

"As I recall, these were decisions you brought upon yourself. Had you been more grateful and appreciative of the life your father created for us then you would have had plenty to live off of. And no one told you to quit your job in order to work with Preston. That was all you, dear. Take some responsibility for your own actions."

Ella laughed.

Cynthia rushed over to her. "You think it's funny that I have nothing? You think it's funny the way you and your evil mother have swindled me out of everything that's rightfully mine?"

"I think it's comical that you spent so many years thinking you were of some moral superiority and yet now you come groveling and needing us."

"I don't need you!"

Ella laughed again. "Oh you don't? You just said it yourself. You're left with three kids. How do you plan on feeding them? Oh I know.

You'll go on downtown to the welfare office with your hand held out like all of the other slackers with no sense of direction."

Cynthia's tears trailed down to her mouth as she spoke. "You disgust me. You've tried every attempt you could to ruin my life."

"No one's giving you a second thought, honey."

"No? Then why'd you try to sleep with my husband? Why'd you have to come and take my building? And I'm sure you were more than willing to help spend the money your mother stole from my inheritance."

"Okay, it's time for you to leave with all of your wild accusations," Ebony chimed in.

Cynthia wiped at her eyes and looked at Kori who had been silent up until now. "How'd she do it?" she asked him. "How'd Ebony get my father to leave me out of his will? I know you knew him better than that. Please ..."

Kori held his hands up. "All I know is what's documented." He stole a glance at Ebony who now donned a satisfied expression in the wake of him corroborating his lie. His heart sunk to his stomach. He was completely sickened by the way this young woman's life was falling apart at the seams. He was even more disgusted to know that he'd played a role in it.

Cynthia turned to look at her stepmother. "Is this what you wanted? To see me miserable? To witness me as a complete failure?"

"So melodramatic," Ebony replied. "Listen, while you're here I might as well give you the heads up ... You might want to start finding yourself somewhere else to live."

"What?" the question was barely audible as it left Cynthia's lips.

"Your house. Preston was behind in the payments so to help him out, I paid the house off and he in turn was paying me back out of his salary."

Cynthia's head was spinning. How was it that she didn't know what was going on with her family's finances? Preston had always made it a point to give her anything she ever asked for, not that she asked for much. He never once advised her that they were in such serious debt that he had to turn to the one person who she despised and mistrusted more than anyone. She felt her body waver as she processed the news. Now she could truly say that she'd lost everything. "You're taking my house?" she asked softly, unable to believe that any one person could be so hateful.

"Technically, I own it. I figured that with your lack of income, you and the girls would be more comfortable in smaller accommodations. You'll be served with an eviction notice shortly giving you thirty days to vacate the premises. I've already contacted a realtor and I'm making plans to sell the property." She smiled. "I do wish you the very best though."

Cynthia was done. "You're the devil!" she screamed through her tears. "How could you be so heartless? I wish my father had never met you!"

"I bet you do." Ebony looked at Thea who was struggling to hold up her distraught niece. "Is this the part where you pull out your gun and threaten to shoot me?"

Thea gritted her teeth. "Naw. I'ma let the lordt deal with you 'cause ain't no sense in me going to jail over no whore. You done slept your way to the top now you snatching the foundation from under the feet of good decent peoples."

"Blah, blah, blah. If we're done here, I'd like you both to get out of my house. Kori, I think it's time that we file for a restraining order against the two of them."

"Is that really necessary?" Kori asked.

Ebony shot him a look of displeasure. "I don't pay you to question me, I pay you to do as I say." She refocused her attention on Cynthia who was shuddering with tears. "Really? Grow some tough skin and adapt, honey. Maybe now you'll realize how big of a mistake it was to ever get on my bad side."

Thea ushered Cynthia to the door. "Come on, baby 'foe I do something this wrench will regret."

"Will she be okay?" Kori asked Thea.

"The Lordt got her, honey," Thea answered. "I just pray that it ain't too late to save your soul from Satan since you seem so stuck under her power." Thea held tight to Cynthia and managed to get her to the car.

"What am I going to do?" Cynthia screamed. "What am I going to do? I have nothing!" Her body jolted as she cried hard, painful sobs. "I have absolutely nothing."

Thea pulled away from the property and abandoned her thoughts of burning it down to the ground. "You got more than them crooks. You got a good heart, a decent head on your shoulder, and faith."

"Why would God allow this to happen to me? I tried to do everything right. I tried to be a good person. And I lost everything! No one to love me ... no one to help me."

"Honey, you gotta roll up your sleeves and help yo' self. Naw you ain't ask for none of this and you didn't deserve it, but that which doesn't kill you makes you stronger."

Cynthia turned to face the door of the passenger side and curled up in her seat. "I want to keep trying anymore. There's nothing left ... I just want to give up!"

"You hush that nonsense! You ain't 'bout to give up. You stronger than that. This is not gonna break you. Ebony will not break you. You got three lil' girls watching you. You betta not roll over and admit defeat with them children watching you. You all they got now. You got the rest of this car ride to cry then you gotta pull it together and do what you need to do for them children. Remember, God has the final say. Don't you let them drive you to defeat."

Thea stopped lecturing and turned up the music in the car. As if on cue, Marvin Sapp's 'Never Could Have Made It' began to play. Cynthia stared out of the window, holding onto the door handle of the car, considering opening the door and throwing her body out into the flow of traffic. She felt weary and lost. There was nothing left in this world for her to call her own other than her girls, but now she had no means of taking care of them. She let the gospel singer's words flow into her soul as her tears stung her eyes. Why God, she questioned. Why is this happening? How was she supposed to bounce back from this? How were they supposed to survive? Thea seemed to believe that the Lord would see her though, but Cynthia couldn't see the light at the end of the tunnel. She needed some kind of sign, some sort of clue as to what it was that she was supposed to do now. With no other course of action, she closed her eyes and did the only thing that she had the strength to do: Pray.

Dear God, she began in her mind *I don't know where to go from here. I have no strength to go on. I can't think of anything that will change this situation. I feel so helpless and alone … so defeated and lost. I need you now, Lord, more than ever. I can't do this by myself. I can't make it by myself. I want to believe that some greater plan is at work here, God, and I know that you know best. I just wish … I wish that I could pull out the lesson of all this. I wish that I could see the greater good of it all. Please help me, Lord. Help my daughters. Shield them from the negative effects of all the changes occurring in our lives. Keep me in the hours when I just want to end it all. Shower me with your grace and mercy, Lord for I'm nothing … nothing without you. Lord, please show me the way … Amen.*

The car stopped but Cynthia's eyes remained shut. She wasn't ready to get out and deal with the reality of all of the crumbled pieces of her life. She felt something heavy pressed against her leg. Slowly, she opened her eyes and looked down to see a tattered bible resting in her lap. She looked over at Thea who simply sat in the driver's seat with her arms crossed. "This is grandma's bible," Cynthia said. "Dad left it to you."

"Mmmhmm. And I'm giving it to you. You need God."

Cynthia was confused. "I don't need your mom's bible, Thea. Dad wanted you to have it. I have a bible."

"You need this one," Thea said. "Trust me. Open the bible and get a word from the Lordt."

Cynthia shook her head, too tired to argue. She sighed and began to flip through the pages just to get a sense of closeness to her father who'd once held the very same book. Thea stared, waiting for the girl to find that which would give her encouragement, but without warning, Cynthia slammed the book shut and took a deep breath.

"I need some boxes," she said wearily. "If you can help me get some … so we can start packing the house up. I'll have to start looking for a place tomorrow. We should have enough in savings to cover a deposit and first month's rent somewhere."

Thea pursed her lips for a second, fighting back the temptation to yell at the girl and force her head back into the bible. But she knew that Cynthia had to process things and move at her own pace. She knew that she couldn't force the girl to receive her blessing. She'd done her part, now she had to sit back and allow the spirit to move the child towards her turning point. "I'll come by tomorrow," she finally told Cynthia. "You go on in there and spend some time with them babies. They ain't had yo' attention in God knows how long."

Cynthia wiped away her tears and looked at her aunt through tired and puffy eyes. "Thank you."

"You'on need to thank me. I ain't did nothing. You gon' be okay. The Lordt got you. Not gonna be easliy broken."

Cynthia nodded and slowly exited the car. She mustered up all the strength she could summon in order to go inside and put up a brave front for her daughters. They were all they had now. It was time to put her game face on, roll up her sleeves, and make the best of a terrible situation.

"Did you see her face?" Ebony asked, plopping back down into her chair after Cynthia and Thea's departure. She let out a hearty laugh which caused her chest to hurt. "My God! I swear I've never seen the girl look so pitiful in my life."

"Which says a lot because she's never really been the picture of poise and beauty," Ella chimed in.

Kori frowned in contempt. "The girl lost everything. I don't really see how that's amusing."

"You wouldn't," Ebony shot back. "You're too much of a stick in the mud these days. What happened to you? You had so much fire and ambition when we first linked up. Even your sexual vigor has dried up, darling."

"I guess that happens when you have a barracuda draining the life, morale, and decency out of you. I don't know how you sleep at night, Ebony."

"Very peacefully on expensive sheets following lots of sexual encounters, no thanks to you these days."

"Eww!" Ella said, raising her hands in the air as if pleading for a subject change. "I definitely don't need to hear any of this."

"Don't be such a prude," Ebony told her. "It isn't as if you didn't know."

"Ummm, it's not as if I ever cared." Ella rose from her seat and picked up the folder containing the signed documents that gave her a new start in life. "I'll just take this and get out of your way so that you can finish your little lover's spat."

Ebony reached across the desk and grabbed her daughter's hand. "Don't make me sorry that I did this for you, dear," she said sternly. "One disappointment of a daughter is about all that I can handle in this lifetime."

Ella looked down at her mother's wrinkled hand and then back up to her equally wrinkle surrounded eyes. Even the expensive foundation she wore couldn't hide the rapid aging that was taking over her face. "No worries."

"Uh-huh," Ebony simply replied, secretly wondering whose lap her daughter was sitting on these days to have concocted such a well-thought out plan for a clothing business out of nowhere.

Ella withdrew her hand. "You've been such an inspiration to me, Mother. I envy the way you play ball."

"Are you serious?" Kori asked. "Your mother has singlehandedly forced a family into destitution and monopolized a whole business which should have been split fairly."

"If I recall, I had a few helping hands, Kori," Ebony corrected him. "Don't go getting all high and mighty on me now."

Kori jumped to his feet. "That's it!"

Ebony chuckled. "Is this the part where you assert your beliefs and try to convince me to be a little more giving where Cynthia's concerned?"

"I've stood by and watched you practically steal from Elton."

"Bull! He was my husband. You can't steal from your spouse."

"You can if you're transferring funds from his business accounts to your own personal accounts without his authorization! Not to mention the changing of his will, the increase in his life insurance policy, making yourself the sole beneficiary of said policy. My God, how much money does one person need?"

"I deserve everything I want and I'll stop at nothing to get it."

"Clearly. But your greed has escalated to a point of pure evil, Ebony. I mean, shutting down the youth center and putting people out of work, snatching the Durdens' business from under them under the pretense of helping them, and now taking Cynthia's home away. Did you ever stop to think about what this would do to her children?"

"Did I not allow for her oldest brat to receive an inheritance?"

"At the age of 21! My God! How are they supposed to survive until then?"

"You seem to have a lot of sympathy for Cynthia but this is what she wanted," Ella stated. "She wanted to do it all on her own. She wanted to have nothing to do with our wealth, our money, our lifestyle. She's a smart girl, she'll figure something out, but don't try to guilt my mother for going for what she wanted."

Kori shook his head. "You're so blind. Don't you see that you're just a replica of your mother? And it isn't your wealth or your money. It was all Elton's and Cynthia was entitled to it. Maybe she was right to not want to have any parts of it because look at what it's done to you." He looked over at his former lover with regret. "Look at what it's done to all of us."

"Calm yourself down," Ebony suggested. "Have a drink or something and get off of your soapbox already."

"I quit, Ebony."

Ebony sat up straight in her chair and looked at Kori pointedly. "Excuse you?"

"I quit. I don't know how you can look at yourself in the mirror everyday but I can't do this anymore. I'm not your puppet! I'm not standing by working deals to help you screw people over anymore. We're both lucky to have never gotten caught, but this is the end of the road for me. Find yourself another flunky. I quit." He moved to leave the room.

"You can't quit," Ebony told him. "If you walk out of that door I'll make sure that no other firm hires you and no one takes you own as their private litigator. I'll have you blacklisted and begging to come back within a matter of months."

Kori ignored her. He focused his attention upon Ella. "You're right about Cynthia. She's a smart girl and I'm sure she'll rise to the occasion and come out of this thing on top. But what are you going to do once your mother turns on you and stops backing your whims and giving you handouts?"

Ella didn't respond.

"If you leave here, Kori, you're through!" Ebony exclaimed, now rising to her feet. "You can forget any chance of a reconciliation. If you utter a word against me I'll make you wish you were dead!"

"It's too late," Kori said over his shoulder. "I already do." Without another word he exited the room, leaving the two women to wonder what the fall out would be after losing their legal aid.

Ella barged in holding up a bottle of Cristal and speaking loudly. "Get ya' champagne glasses, sissy! It's time to make a toast to our future."

Ana shut the door and walked into the kitchen of her home, unsure of what was going on. Her body ached and she was in no mood for company. But, Ella hadn't given her an opportunity to decline the visit before just popping up on her. With her hair pulled back into a messy ponytail and dressed in a simple pair of jeans and an off-the-shoulder t-shirt, Ana looked every bit as weary as she felt. She retrieved two glasses and rinsed them off before placing them on her dinette table in front of Ella.

Ella popped the top on the bottle and champagne trickled from the opening. "Yasss!" She poured up the glasses and handed one to her sister. For the first time since entering the home, she took a good look at Ana. "You look like hell."

"Gee, thanks," Ana replied. "It's nice to see you too." She couldn't remember the last time that she and Ella had gotten together to just hang. "So, what's this all about?"

Ella took notice of the faded bruises around Ana's neck and wanted to ask questions, but decided against it. Word on the street was that her sister was allowing her body to be used as a punching bag, but Ella didn't want to believe that the girl was that stupid. Thinking it better to just leave it alone, she focused on the point of her visit. "So, Mom issued the final blow today."

"Final blow?"

"Mmmhmm. Cynthia came by the house today to ask about Preston's business. You know, Mom had taken over controlling shares of the company years ago and was just waiting for the perfect time to give them the boot. So now, Mom's dissolved the business, sold the building, and is even about to sell their house which she'd paid the mortgage off on."

"Wait, didn't Preston die just a month ago?" Ana asked.

"Right, so you can imagine how distraught little Miss Goodie Two Shoes. She lost her husband, her income source, and her house. Checkmate! We come out victorious and she comes out brokeeee!" Ella emphasized jovially just before taking a sip of her champagne. "I bet she wishes she'd been nicer to us all now."

Ana held her glass and stared into it. Imagines of Cynthia's doors danced around before her eyes in the bubbly liquid. "What about those kids?"

"What about them?" Ella threw back, shrugging her shoulders. "It's not like she let any of us have a relationship with them. Her brats, her problem."

Ana took a slow sip of her champagne. "Right," she said softly. "As for the business, I don't really foresee Mom running some physical therapy clinic."

"She's not," Ella said smiling. "I told you she dissolved the business and sold the building to another corporation."

"Who?" Ana asked, vaguely interested as she took a seat at the table.

"Me!" Ella squealed proudly.

Ana looked up in shook. "What?" She laughed. "What business do you own?"

"I'm opening a boutique. Le Chic."

Ana looked at her sister in amusement. "What do you know about running a business? When'd you come up with this scheme?"

"It's not a scheme," Ella answered, feeling offended. "I have a complete business plan, I'm working with a seasoned retail buyer, and I have an investor and it isn't Mom."

"Somebody's husband?" Ana said knowingly.

"Excuse you?"

"It's always somebody's husband or some random rich guy looking to get richer through Elton's empire. It's no secret, El. We've all known for years that you're the glorified mistress, but do you really think that it's smart to let this latest sugar daddy invest in your business? I mean, what happens when he dumps you? You think he's going to just walk away and let you have your company? Or what about his wife?"

Ella sat her glass down hard on the table. Her face was filled with rage as she glared at her sister. "I didn't come her to be insulted by you. I don't know what your problem is, but it surely isn't with me. You sound completely jealous and bitter. What? You mad because that degenerate fiend you married is kicking your butt day in and day out? Marrying that creep was a decision you made. Don't sit there lashing out at me because you've screwed up your life."

Ana massaged her temples, not wanting to get into an altercation with her sister. "I didn't mean it like that."

"Oh really?" Ella snatched her purse up and frowned. "And to think I came over here to offer you a part in all of this, thinking that you could use the opportunity to start making your own money and get rid of that jerk. But you can just forget it. I'd hate to have to fire you for my sugar daddy pulls the plug on my business since you think I'm stupid enough to let that happen."

Ana's cell phone rang. "Just gimme a second," she told Ella as she pulled the phone out of her pocket and answered the call. "Hello?"

"Ana? This is Rick down at the Sound Center."

"Oh ... okay ... hi ..." Ana was confused as to why the studio manager was calling her phone.

"I figured I'd call you to see what you can do. You see, Trey is down here in Studio B."

"Why? He's not recording anything is he? Did he book studio time?" Her wheels were rapidly turning, wondering if her washed up husband had taken money from their savings to book studio time at the one place where he wasn't supposed to be.

"No, he was sitting in on someone else's session, only now he refuses to leave and it's gotten a little … uh … rowdy. Mrs. Grayson has mandated that he be banned from the premises, you know. Technically, I'm supposed to be calling the cops but I feel kinda bad for the guy so I thought I'd call you to see if you can just come get him. But you gotta hurry and you gotta make sure he doesn't come back because next time—"

Ana rose from her seat. "I got it. I'm on my way," she assured the man.

"Ana, it's not pretty. He's in pretty bad shape. If he gets any more out of control—"

"I said I'm coming!" she hollered, disconnecting the call. She looked at Ella who was shaking her head. "I gotta go."

"So I heard." Ella took a good look at Ana. "You should let him deal with the consequences of his own actions."

"Don't come in my house telling me what to do. He's my husband and I love him."

"You love him?" At the mention of the word love, Ella turned away and headed towards the front door. "You're ridiculous. Was it love when he put his hands on you?" She opened the door and turned back to look at Ana who was standing right behind her with her purse. "You're such a disappointment. I don't even know who you are right now."

"You sound an awful lot like Mom. Thanks for stopping by and for the judgment," Ana said sarcastically.

Ella left without saying anything else. Twice that day she'd been compared to her mother. Somehow it didn't feel at all like a compliment and her spirit felt wounded by statements.

A few days into packing, Cynthia had to take a break. She'd been trying her best to keep the girls' spirits lifted but between her efforts and searching for a place for them to live, the little energy that she had was beginning to feel depleted. She wanted to give up. She wanted to scream out to God to take her home to be with her parents and her husband, but she knew that this wasn't an option. Still, she wondered how long it would be before the pain would begin to ease up and the strife would appear to be a little less difficult to work through.

For the past couple of days the weather had been unbearable with continued thunder storms. To Cynthia it was fitting; the darkness of the sky, the howling of the wind, and the clatter of the thunder all symbolized the turmoil within her. Today was the first day that the heavens had had mercy on the earth, sparing the grounds of the pounding rainfall. Needing a minute to herself after having booked up the last of Preston's things to donate to Goodwill, she ventured out onto her back patio. Standing there looking up at the sky, Cynthia wanted to cry. How could she enjoy any ray of sunshine when the light of her life no longer existed? Her chest tightened and she felt herself on the brink of a breakdown.

"I can't do this," she said aloud in whisper with her eyes close and face tilted upwards to the heavens. "I can't do this, Lord. I can't do this without him."

Suddenly she felt a breeze whip past her followed by a pleasantly warm beaming kissing the skin of her face. Slowly, she opened her eyes and was greeted by the beautiful hues of a crispy, sparkling rainbow. She sucked in her breath, completely in awe of the wonderment of the Lord's work. Tears began to trickle from the corners of her eyes but for the first time since Preston's passing, they weren't tears of sorrow. Cynthia felt a spiritual connection in that moment. The sight of the rainbow gave her renewed faith that soon her troubles would be over. In the midst of wanting to give in, just as she was laying her burdens at the feet of the lord in prayer he'd purposely showed her this rainbow as an sign for her to keep the faith and know that a new, prosperous beginning was in store for her.

"Please keep me, Lord," she whispered. "Keep me wrapped in your grace and mercy."

Taking a deep breath, she turned away from the majestic symbol of his promise to her and returned inside to do more packing. She didn't know when and she didn't know how, but she felt assured that change was going to come.

Chapter 7

The greatest surprise of all
Is when love finds you unexpectedly
At a time when you had no desire to ever love again.

-Kenni York ©

*I*n a funny way, life was starting to get better. Things were looking up although the world as she knew it still seemed very different to Cynthia. She'd developed a strength that she never realized she had, standing firm in the face of adversity and making things happen for herself and the girls. The day that she'd taken her donation to Goodwill she'd also come across a Help Wanted sign. The organization was looking for a resource liaison, a person who could help clients who had fallen on hard times to build themselves back up be it through linking them to hiring agencies, signing them up for life skills courses, or getting them hooked up with community programs to get food or utility assistance. Thinking that getting hired on would be a long shot since she herself was in transition, Cynthia had filled the application out anyway. Apparently, the center's director had found her personality to be pleasing during the interview and before she knew it Cynthia was employed. Let her tell it, it was nothing but God. She'd gone in to make a donation and be a blessing to someone else, only to turn around and receive her own blessing in return.

Just before the start of her new position Cynthia and the girls had to move in with Thea. Ebony had wasted no time in sticking a for sale sign in her yard and Cynthia didn't want to risk the chance of coming home one day only to find that the witch had thrown her and her children's stuff out. So, for half a month the family were squatters until another act of faith proved to be beneficial and she was granted a three bedroom apartment within a gated community. It wasn't as big as the space they were used to but it was theirs and they didn't have to go on taking up any more of Thea's space.

Over time, they fell into a routine and Cynthia actually caught herself smiling and enjoying life again. There wasn't day that went by that she didn't miss Preston, but she was managing to do the one thing she never thought she'd be able to do without him: survive. She'd even managed to make friends with a couple of the ladies from her job. Tina and Joyce made the work day go by quickly and before she knew it, their cordial office relationships had become out of office companionships.

"I'm telling you, there's this brother at my gym who would be perfect for you," Joyce told her one day after they'd returned from an hour lunch break at a nearby eatery. "He's a little on the short side, but he's muscular and fit with rock hard abs. Girl, if I wasn't married!"

Cynthia laughed. "If you weren't married nothing! You know you and Gabe were destined. There's no way you'd ever be without that man."

"Mmmhmmm," Tina chimed in, taking her seat at the receptionist desk of the Goodwill Business Center where they all worked. "That's a true statement there. That's that 24/7 kinda love. Gabe got you chained down, honey."

Joyce smiled earnestly. "Truth! But I just want the same thing for you," she told Cynthia.

Cynthia shook her head. They'd been over it time and time again. She wasn't ready to get back out there. She'd just gotten to a point where she wasn't crying over Preston. Trying to get to know another man at this point seemed like a milestone that she'd never reach. Frankly, she had no desire to ever be with anyone else. Love was all consuming when it was real and true. Her heart had broken into a million pieces when Preston died. There was no way that she'd ever find another man that could hold a candle to the one who had been the love of her life.

"I'll pass," Cynthia said politely.

"God didn't intend for you to spend the rest of your life alone," Joyce stated.

"And I'm not alone. I have Brooklyn, Elsa, and Amelia." Cynthia smiled goofily. "And you two nuts."

"That's different," Joyce persisted. "Woman was designed to be a man's partner. Yeah, you've got us, but we can't love and care for you like a good man can honey. And you have to admit that you could use a little adult stimulation outside of cackling with us."

"I'm fine," Cynthia insisted. "I don't need a man. Really, I think I'm over that era in my life."

"Era? You say that as if you only can have love for one period of your life."

Cynthia shrugged. "I don't know. I kinda believe that you only get one great love of your life and when that relationship's over no other one can compare."

"May I help you?" Tina asked.

Her question reminded the other two that they were in the middle of their work day. Each one fixed her attention upon the man that had just waltzed into the office looking like a million bucks. His fair skin was flawless and the low-cut wavy texture of his hair was a dark luxurious black that seemed to sparkle under the florescent office lights. He had strong features that one couldn't help but to notice; from his six foot, one inch stance, his broad shoulders, his large round light brown eyes, and his full lips.

"I have a one o'clock appointment with Samantha Chambers," he said in English but with a distinct accent that put them all in mind of the Caribbean.

"I'll let her know that you're here," Tina told him, as she picked up her extension to advise the director of her appointment's arrival.

"Now that's a great sight to behold," Joyce mumbled, before walking way to return to her own desk.

Cynthia's eyes met the man's and she immediately felt embarrassed for staring. Realizing that she too needed to get back to work, she turned to walk away.

"Ah, excuse me, Miss?" the man called out.

Cynthia looked back but hadn't really believed that he was speaking to her, yet he was. She stopped awkwardly in her tracks as he walked over to her. She couldn't formulate words as the scent of his cologne followed the wind and settled within her nostrils. She hadn't been that close to a man since Preston's death and suddenly she felt like a fumbling school girl.

"I don't mean to hold you up," he said. "But I wanted to say that you have the most enchanting eyes."

She was stunned. "I do?"

"Yes. My grandmother used to say that the eyes were the windows to a person's soul. Looking into yours tells me a lot."

She didn't know whether he was running game on her or she should feel her privacy was being invaded in the event that he really was able to tap into the depths of her soul. She felt compelled to humor herself and ask him what it was that he saw, but the way that he held her glance began to make her uncomfortable and the best she could do was put some distance between them. "I … uh … have a good day," she stuttered before hurrying off to the solace of her desk.

Joyce came and stood at the threshold of her cubicle. "You're all flushed," she noticed. "It's good to know that the woman within you is still alive. So, I'm going to set you up with Michael from work."

Cynthia frown. "No, please don't."

"Come on, what's the worst that could happen? You'll either like him or you won't. Either way, you deserve to get out and be kid-free. I'm gonna set it up."

And so it began; her friends' mission to hook her up with someone in hopes of her finding love again. Cynthia wasn't thrilled about the idea but for a second she warmed up to the thought of getting herself out there and meeting new people. There would never be another Preston, of that she was certain. But she also thought that perhaps she could use some other adult stimulation as the girls had suggested. Reluctantly, she agreed to try it, but deep down she knew that Joyce and Tina would only be disappointed in the end. Love was over for her. It was a simple truth that she'd accepted.

"So, how long have you known Joyce?" Michael asked.

"Um, about six months," Cynthia answered, looking at her companion from across the table of the steak house restaurant he'd taken her to. "You?"

"About a year. She was in one of my hip hop dance classes at the gym where I work. Do you work out?"

Immediately, she became self-conscious. Although she'd lost a considerable amount of weight following Preston's death, she was still a thick girl. She had no desire to sit and listen to some health and fitness guru attempting to analyze her and put her on some fitness plan. "Not as much as I should," she admitted, hoping that he'd let it go and change the subject.

"A good work out thirty minutes every other day or so can do wonders for a person."

Cynthia nodded. "So they say."

"A good cleansing never hurt either."

"A cleansing?" Surely he wasn't talking about what she thought he was talking about.

"Yes, Ma'am. A good ole' colon cleansing. Man, those things work miracles."

Cynthia was speechless. He definitely was going there. She understood that health was his expertise, but she felt it was a little off-putting for him to be discussing colon cleansing while at the dinner table.

"You've got to be careful what you put into your body," he went on. "Some stuff will stick with you forever. You know, animal products. That's why I try to stick to a vegetable and protein based diet."

Cynthia didn't want to comment about the nine ounce steak he'd just ordered.

"You should let me work you out some day," Michael said, biting his lower lip and giving her the once over.

His erotic stares made her feel as if she was sitting there naked on display. "Excuse me?"

"You know ... like, train you."

"I'm really not in a position to employ a personal trainer," she told him. *And I don't think I want you anywhere near my body*, she thought.

"For you, there's no fee, baby. I've got you. Stick with me and I'll have you being a lean mean, toned machine. Not that you're not gorgeous with all those curves."

Cynthia's brain began to scan through possible excuses to bring the date to an abrupt end. She could already tell that Michael wasn't her type in anyway. She wanted to kill Joyce for even thinking that this hypocritical pervert could be ideal for her.

"Well, well, well. Look what we have here." A relatively short woman with her hair pulled back in an old-school French braid approached their table dressed in tights and a tank top. "When you said you were meeting with a client this evening and wouldn't be attending class tonight, I figured you were up to your old tricks." Her eyes darted from Michael to Cynthia. "From the looks of it, you should have opted for training her instead of dating her."

"What's going on?" Cynthia asked, completely confused

Michael shifted in his seated uncomfortably. "Um … I can explain. Baby, this is Cynthia," he stated.

"Baby?" Cynthia nearly choked on the word.

"Cynthia," the woman repeated. "Cynthia do you know that this is my man you're sitting up here chatting it up with?"

"Your man?" Cynthia was stunned. Not only had this loser turned out to be a pervert but he was also a cheater.

"Come on Ronnie, baby," Michael pleaded. "It's not like that. We were just talking about training and stuff. Right, Cynthia?" He looked at her pleadingly, as if begging her to cosign his lie.

Cynthia rose from the table. "I'm not doing this. Lesson, Ma'am, I don't want your man. Trust me, you can have him. In fact, I pray that you find someone better who will honor you."

Ronnie was taken back by her statement. Quickly, she grabbed the steak knife from Michael's place setting and aimed it in front of Cynthia's face.

Cynthia screamed in response, starting a ripple of shrieks and gasps throughout the restaurant.

"Are you taking shots at my husband?" Ronnie asked.

Cynthia shook her head but remained silent, afraid that the crazy woman would cut her.

"You fat cow, you wish that you could get a man like him instead of sitting around trying to seduce other people's men," the wife insulted Cynthia.

Michael put his hand on top of Ronnie's. "Calm down, baby. Put the knife down."

"Sir, I'm afraid that we're going to have to ask you and your company to leave," the restaurant manager told Michael as his staff busied about trying to calm down the other patrons.

Michael nodded. "We're going, we're going." He managed to pull the knife from Ronnie's hand and place his arm around her waist. "Come on, baby. It was nothing. Really."

Cynthia grabbed her purse and made a bee line for the front door. She wasn't about to stick around and talk things out with this irrationally scorned woman nor could she any longer stand the sight of Michael's lying face. As she hurried to her car she cursed herself for having listened to Joyce. Her friends meant well, but sending her on the date from hell was totally unacceptable. This couldn't happen again.

"No!" Cynthia protested. "No more dates." She shook her head as she exited the break room. "That was a complete disaster."

"Okay, okay, so I didn't realize that Mike was scum," Joyce stated. "But that doesn't mean that this guy Tina knows will turn out to be the same."

"Right," Tina chimed in. "That's what dating's like ... you gotta weed through the bad ones in order to find a good one."

Cynthia moaned. "Uhhhh. This isn't for me. I mean really, I don't have the patience to sift through a barrel of creeps hoping to find a Prince Charming."

Cynthia tells Tina and Joyce that she appreciates their efforts with trying to get her back out into the dating scene. They tried to get Cynthia to do online dating (swipe right if you like, swipe left if you don't like) and speed dating which were full of jerks too. It seemed that all the guys she met lack respect for women. They took Cynthia out to restaurant lounges and music concerts to keep her good spirit since she liked listening to music all the time. She felt so out of touch and didn't know how she would even really get her groove back.

Later on while they were at work, "Speaking of," Tina whispered, looking up the hall as the center's director led the handsome island brother from the other day towards them.

"Cynthia," Ms. Chambers called out.

Cynthia's body temperature immediately rose as the two newcomers stood before her. Remembering the way that the man had stared at her so intently had her shaken. Again today she could smell that fresh clean scent mixed with some oil fragrance that lingered upon his skin. She had no idea why he was back or what it was that he wanted with her, but she was ready to put some distance between the two of them.

"Cynthia, this is Jay Torres," Ms. Chambers made the introduction. "His charity One Love Incorporated is partnering with us to sponsor an outreach event next month. I need you to get with him to provide some leads on business willing to do onsite interviews, vendors who can provide grooming services, stuff like that."

Jay smiled at Cynthia again with those dazzling white teeth glimmering and those beautiful eyes sparkling. He held out his hand to her. "We meet again."

"So we do," she responded softly, shaking his hand quickly before withdrawing her own. "Um, you can follow me to my desk. I can compile a list of contacts for you."

"Lead the way."

Cynthia turned and headed to her cubicle with Jay trailing her as the others looked on with suspecting smiles.

"You've gotta admit, that's one fine brother," Tina stated, then caught herself as she looked over at her boss in embarrassment. "I'm so sorry. That was so unprofessional of me."

Ms. Chambers waved it off. "Relax. You were just telling the truth. And it doesn't help that he's loaded."

"Come again?" Joyce's interest was piqued.

"Mmmhmm. One Love is solely funded by Jay's family ... The Torres' own a chain of resorts throughout the Dominican Republic and have branched out to build a couple in the states two. One in Florida and one in California. But, Jay has always been big on giving back and helping displaced individuals. There was an entire 20/20 interview on him when that whole racial purging thing was happening in the Dominican Republic. With his own resources, the man helped many families who were being banned to Haiti find adequate shelter and obtain citizenship in the D.R. somehow or get green cards to reside in the states. That man is a humanitarian with deep pockets. His family's like royalty in the DR. He is actually a really cool billionaire. He's generally referred to as the Dominican Prince. I can't believe you aren't familiar with him."

Joyce and Tina were speechless. Who would have thought that Caribbean royalty would be just a few feet away from them? The two women looked at one another, each forming the same idea as their eyes locked. Jay sounded like quite a catch and they both knew someone who was in need of being caught up in the right guy.

As the others lingered in the aisles of the office space, Cynthia did her best to stay focused on the task at hand. She kept her eyes glued to her computer and as she created a spreadsheet of feasible contacts for Jay's event. She was well aware of him sitting to her left at the side of her desk watching her as she worked. She tried not to let on that she knew his eyes were piercing through her skin, but wondered if her face looked as flushed as it felt.

"So, what made you decide to partner with our region for your event?" Cynthia asked, trying to make conversation so that the silence in the cubicle would be filled and he wouldn't be aware of the rapid beating of her heart.

"Fate," he told her.

"Fate?"

"Do you believe in it?"

Cynthia shrugged. There was a time when she did believe in faith wholeheartedly. That was during the era of her marriage to Preston when it seemed as if the two of them were destined to live a long, full, happy life together. But, the moment he was snatched away from her life her faith in kismet connections and the phenomenon of fate dissipated quickly. Now, she just believed in getting from day to day and doing everything she could to make whatever she wanted to happen, happen because who was to say that there was any purposed occurrence waiting to fall in her lap?

"I believe in it completely," Jay went on. "I could have gone to any major charity in America, public or private organization. I could have settled upon any regional branch of Goodwill in any state. But, I believe that fate led me to you."

Cynthia pressed a command on the computer and the printer to her right came to life. "Or you could have researched an area with one of the highest unemployment and homeless rates respectively and decided to pinpoint an organization that served that particular demographic." She pulled the list of contacts off of the printer and turned to face him. "That isn't fate," she said. "That's due diligence. Here's your list. I'm sure you'll find these places more than eager to participate."

Jay took the sheet from her, glanced at it and then looked up at her with that million dollar smile. "You're very astute, not to mention good at what you do."

"Thank you, but you don't know me," she shot back. "You have no idea how proficient I am or am not at my job."

"I know that it only took you a matter of minutes to assess who you thought would be a good fit for this event." He looked at the paper again. "Listen, my time is split tightly between working on this and handling some other business. Do you think that you could—"

"You want me to call the contacts for you and secure their participation," she cut in. *How nice,* she thought. *You want me to do your work for you.*

Jay caught the contempt in her tone and chuckled. "Actually, I was going to ask if you could take half of the list and I'd manage the other half. Then perhaps we can meet to discuss our progress and other plans for the event. Maybe over dinner on Friday night when I return from my visit to California, if you aren't busy. I'd really like to have your input on how best to serve the needs of the community during the event."

Cynthia was caught off guard. It was already nerve racking that this man had her feeling uncomfortable in her own skin, but now he wanted to see her again and no less outside of the office. "Um, sure," she agreed without really thinking it through.

"Great. I'll have my assistant email or call you with the details of our reservation and I can meet you there." He stood before she could respond. "Thank you for your time, Cynthia. I hate to be so abrupt, but I have another appointment within the hour."

She nodded in understanding.

"'Til Friday," he said in his unique drawl before turning around and exiting her cubicle.

Cynthia stared at the empty spot he'd stood in for just a moment, trying to figure out how they'd gotten to the point of her agreeing to have dinner with him. *This isn't a date*, she told herself. *This is work and as soon as my business with him is over I never have to see this man again.* Something about Jay gnawed at her spirit and Cynthia wasn't sure that she wanted to tap into the feelings to see what they were all about. All she wanted was peace and to live a distraction free life as she tried to take care of herself and her daughters alone.

Joyce and Tina hurried into the small, confined space drawing Cynthia out of her daze.

"So how was your impromptu meeting with the Dominican hottie?" Joyce asked, grinning from ear to ear.

"Quick and uneventful," Cynthia answered, not about to give in to any girl chatter about how sexy Jay was.

"He left out of here looking like he was on cloud nine," Tina informed. "What did you say to him?"

"Nothing. I gave him a list of potential participants for his event and we agreed to meet later to discuss it further."

"So he's coming back here?" Joyce asked.

Cynthia hesitated before answering the question. "We're meeting out."

"He asked you out?" Joyce's voice was filled with zeal as if she'd just scratched off a winning lottery ticket.

"No!" Cynthia hurriedly corrected her. "It's not a date. We're having a business meeting over a meal to discuss this company sponsored event. That is all."

"That's all my foot!" Tina snapped. "Honey, let me tell you about this brother. He is—"

Cynthia held up her hand. "No! No, no, no! I don't wanna hear anything about his background, his interests, or your critique of the kind of man he is. No! It's bad enough that the two of you keep trying to set me up with losers, but I simply draw the line at trying to make a work thing be more than what it is. Come on. Have some scruples. You ever heard the term you don't eat where you—"

"Okay, you don't have to be so crass," Tina cut her off. "I'm just trying to tell you that he is—"

"Ugh!" Cynthia let out. "No, I said. I don't want to talk about this man anymore you guys. He's off limits. Anyone pertaining to work is off limits. For that matter, anyone with a boo, without a job, living with his mama, or is arrogant, judgmental, obsessed with anything, or way too talkative is off limits."

"But, really, Cyn," Joyce chimed in. "You should hear us out on this one. Everything that you just mentioned is fine, but—"

"No buts. Look, Tina just set up the date with the guy you were telling me about. Just get it over with. Now, can you ladies please leave me be so that I can get back to work?"

Cynthia wasn't really keen on the idea of yet another blind date, but at least that would get her friends' mind off of Jay Torres. Truthfully, she wanted nothing more than to take her own mind off of the man that had her riddled with goose bumps. No, there was no way that she would dare give the notion a second that.

Le Chic's grand opening came and went and Ella was doing wonderfully, businesswise. She'd been fortunate enough to have a team that helped her secure the best clothing designs wholesale, unique store furnishings, a reliable sales team, and of course marketing that caused shoppers to come out to her location in droves. She found herself spending whole days at the store even though she had store manager who was more than capable of holding things down. Le Chic was all she had, especially since her flavor of the month was beginning to go sour despite his initial interest in her venture.

Braxton Thurmond was a wealthy politician. The thing about him was that he was able to spoil her with all of her material desires while also investing in her business, but she could never tell if he was sincere in any of the things he said to her when he promised to be there, promised to take care of her, and even promised that he'd eventually leave his wife. The last guarantee she'd always known was a bunch of bull, but yet deep down she wanted to believe that maybe, just maybe, she was worth it to him. That notion was immediately dispelled when he failed to put in an appearance at her grand opening celebration, opting instead to send a wine basket with a thoughtless note attached to her condo. Ella hated him for letting her down, especially since he'd made it a point to stress to her before how he wouldn't miss the occasion for the world. Not only had she wanted to share the moment with him, but she also wanted to bask in the limelight on his arm for the world to see that he was indeed her man.

"Foolish girl," she chided herself as she drunk straight from the last bottle of wine left from the gift basket.

It was just a couple of weeks after her opening and she was beginning to spiral into a bout of depression. She'd spent the time alone without him dropping by or flying her out to wherever he was conducting business. Maybe it was time for her to move on and find a new bank account to withdraw from. It wasn't unusual for her boyfriends to finally decide that they wanted to play the good husband or father and put their sidepiece down for a while. She wasn't oblivious to the game; in fact she played her position well. But nights like these, filled with Golden Girl reruns and bottles of wine made her momentarily wish that she was more than just a rich, married man's good time; it made her long for something permanent.

"That's what you have the store for," she told herself aloud. On average, Ella was solid in her belief that she didn't need a man or the faux emotion of love. Love left you high and dry without anything to cling to in order to piece yourself back together again. To her, Cynthia was a classic example of that. Secretly, there'd been times when she'd envied Cynthia's resilience no matter how much she, her sister, her mother, and anyone else tried to knock her down. But, her entire goody-two-shoes demeanor and lovesick behavior had led her into the pitfalls of heartbreak the moment the love of her life died. Love had left Cynthia completely distraught with nothing; no job, no home, no support system, no man ... nothing. "That's what you get," Ella slurred as she took another swig. "That could never be me. That *will never* be me."

Her cell phone began to chime from its resting place on the foot of her bed. She struggled to reach down and grab it only to be surprised at who was calling. Sitting up straight, she tried to pull herself together. "Hello," she answered.

"Miss me?" the male voice asked.

"I'm sorry, who is this?"

"Braxton are we? I'll be in town this weekend. I'm taking you to dinner Friday at Park 75. Wear something sexy and I'll pick you up around eight."

It wasn't a question, it was a mandate. That was one of the things she liked the most about Braxton; his domineering personality. She knew that he felt bad for standing her up at her opening and leaving her alone for so many weeks. Dinner at a five-star restaurant wasn't even the tip of the ice burg with regards to how he would go about making up for the frown he'd placed on her face. Such were the perks of being the mistress: she could have him how she wanted him without having the tire of having him all the time and whenever he was around she'd get whatever she wanted no matter the cost.

Braxton said that he was taking Ella to a show. Cynthia was also there that night with her own date. Braxton hadn't said that it was a comedy show at a hole-in-the-wall establishment in the heart of the hood. Cynthia felt uncomfortable with the way the comedian of the night was going through the crowd heckling everyone. She'd lost some weight within the last year, but she still felt slightly self-conscious about her appearance.

"You enjoying yourself, baby?" Cynthia's date Mark said.

They'd gotten halfway through their chicken tender basket dinners and the man had already donned her as his. Mark called her his baby and his boo a total of sixteen times. Cynthia wanted to remind him of her name so that he'd stop calling her by these presumptuous pet names.

"I'm fine," she assured him, more than ready to go home.

Following the show, Mark walked her back to her car. She didn't know whether to be grateful for his chivalrous gesture or annoyed that he was lingering on. During the course of their date, she'd done her best to keep some distance between them because from the time he greeted her hello with a hug she'd noticed that his breath was highly offensive.

Standing at her car, she immediately pressed the unlock button on her remote and turned to smile at him politely. "Thank you for inviting me out. I had a good time."

Mark stepped forward and reached out to place his hand at the top of her door causing her to be partially blocked in by the frame of his body. "I wanna see you again," he told her. "I'd like to get to know you better."

The sting of his bad breath assaulted Cyn's nose. She couldn't mask the look of disgust on her face. "I, uh … I'm not sure it that's something I'm ready for," she told him.

"Not ready? Baby, we can be good together. I can see us now, making babies and being in love. With yo' sexy self. Gimme some time to show you I can be the man. Let me make you feel like a woman again." He leaned down in an attempt to kiss her.

Cynthia shoved him away, completely turned off by his bad hygiene as well as his gall. "Don't put your crusty lips on me!" she screamed, pointing her purse at him. "This date is over. Do us both a favor and lose my number. The last thing in the world I want to do is to see you again ever!" Without another word, she hopped into her car and sped off. She wanted to get as far away from the man as possible.

Driving down the highway, Cynthia had to laugh at the horrible caliber of men that were being presented to her. There was just no use. She'd already had the best of the best. Seemingly, she was wasting her time by going out on these pointless dates with men she was completely out of tune with. "I miss you, Preston," she said aloud. "Why'd you leave?"

She tried turning the ignition again but nothing happened. "Great!" she screamed, punching the steering wheel and managing to sound the horn at the same time, startling herself and her neighbor who'd just hopped out of her car in the parking spot beside her.

"You okay?" the woman called out

Cynthia got out of the car. Dressed in an all-black cocktail dress, she was doing her best to remain composed. "My car won't start. I don't know what's wrong with the thing."

"Maybe you just need a jump," the woman suggested. Following her hunch, she asked her husband to come out and attach the cables to jump start Cynthia's car. Unfortunately, this action yielded no results. "I'm so sorry," the woman stated, looking Cynthia up and down. "And you look so pretty. I really thought that would help. Can I offer to take you to wherever you're headed?"

Cynthia shook her head. "That's okay. I'll manage." She sulked back up the two flights of stairs to her apartment where Thea was babysitting the girls.

"What you doing back here?" Thea asked with her eyebrow raised.

"My car won't start." Cynthia took a seat at her modest kitchen table and sighed. "I'm not going."

"Nope. You got ya' nice dress on. Gon' take my car. Go on ya' date."

"It's not a date Thea and no, I'd rather not take your car. How would that look pulling up to valet in your old getup? This is a five-star establishment."

"Somebody somewhere ain't got no car," Thea told her. "And you one of them somebodies today."

"I'm just going to call him and cancel. I need to figure out how I'm going to afford to get my car fixed and still make rent this month. I haven't really been able to save the way I'd like to."

Thea took a seat across from her niece. "Have you taken it to the Lordt?"

"I pray every day, Thea."

"No, hunteee, have you read your bible."

Cynthia shrugged guiltily. "Not as much as I should, but that doesn't explain why my car just died on me or how I can get it fixed."

"If you were looking in the right part of ya' grandma's bible it would," Thea said, trying to give the girl a clue.

Cynthia pulled her cell phone out of her purse and dialed the number that Jay's assistant had forwarded to her in the event that she needed to reach him. She had no time to listen to her aunt's rambling at that moment.

"Hello?" Jay's voice boomed in her ear.

Cynthia was stunned that he had actually answered the line instead of the assistant. "Um, Jay … hi. It's Cynthia Durden from Goodwill."

"Yes, hello. I'm in route to the restaurant. Is something the matter?"

"It is actually. You see, I'm not in route. I'm not going to make it."

"Should I push back the time of our reservation?"

"No, I'm not running late. I'm just not going to make it. My car died," she finally explained, feeling a tad bit embarrassed.

"Ah. Well, these things happen. Still, we can't let it stop us from going on with our lives. Text me your address and I'll just come get you."

Cynthia's brow raised. "No!" she said instinctively, unsure that she wanted him in her private space or even knowing where she resided period. Her neighborhood wasn't horrible, but for some reason she had no desire to invite him to it. "You don't have to do that. You can just come by the office on Monday and we can discuss things then."

Thea shook her head. Watching her niece try to talk her way out of going out made her want to hit the girl with her purse. "You let that young man come for you," she whispered.

Cynthia shook her head. "I uh, I'll just see you on Monday."

"Nonsense," Jay insisted. "I'll push the reservation back and hour and head towards you. Text me your address. The night is young. Let's not waste it."

"But I—"

"Go ahead and send the text," he went on, cutting her off, "and I'll see you soon."

"Really, you don't have to … hello? Hello?" Cynthia looked down at her phone and noticed that the call had been disconnected. "He wants to come get me. He wants me to send him the address so he can come get me."

"Then send the address," Thea stated matter-of-factly.

"I can't do that."

"Why you can't?"

"I just can't. He doesn't need to know where I live. All of this to plan an event. Surely it can wait."

Thea snatched the phone out of Cynthia's hand and headed over to the kitchen counter.

"What are you doing?" Cynthia asked.

"You said you couldn't do it," Thea said smiling. She pressed a series of buttons and then laid the phone down. "So I did it for you," she said, looking at Cynthia.

Cynthia's eyes grew wide. "Oh my God, Thea you didn't!"

"Yeah I did. Now you go on and touch ya' makeup up and wait for the nice young man."

"How do you know he's a nice young man? You haven't even met him."

"Honey, he offered you a solution when you had a problem. He's adamant about taking you to a nice place for dinter," she said, purposely mispronouncing the word. "That tells me he has a thing for you and that this ain't about no work."

Cynthia was flustered. "Why would you say that? It's all about work. That's it. Just … work."

"Mmmhmmm. Keep telling ya' self that. Honey, you're a beautiful girl. If this young man is interested in you, let him be interested in you. There's nothing wrong with that. Just relax."

Nearly twenty minutes passed and still no Jay. Cynthia paced the living room feeling as if she'd been played. Just as she started to peel off her cocktail dress, there was a knock at her front door. Thea was sitting on the couch reading to Ana. Her eyes darted from Cynthia to the door.

"You gon' open it?" Thea asked.

Cynthia nodded, grabbing her clutch from the coffee table. Taking a breath, she headed to the door and opened it partially. The sight of Jay made her want to just melt to the floor. Dressed in a finely tailored black suite, the man looked like he'd just walked away from a menswear photo shoot. He handed her a bouquet of white roses and flashed her that heartbreaking smile of his.

"Good evening," he said. "I hope I didn't have you waiting too long."

Cynthia took the flowers and shook her head. She sniffed the fragrance of the roses and closed her eyes briefly. She couldn't remember the last time she'd received flowers.

"Are you ready?" Jay asked.

"Um …" Cynthia was at a loss. She held the flowers tightly and couldn't take her eyes away from the man standing before her. Something about the moment felt funny. She couldn't quite put her finger on what it was.

Thea was by her side, reaching for the flowers. "Go on. I'll put these in water." She looked over at Jay and smiled at him approvingly. "How you doing young man?"

"I'm well, Miss," Jay responded. "I'm Jay."

"I'm Aunt Thea. Y'all two go on and enjoy ya' selves." Thea looked at Cynthia and gave her a slight head nod. "Go on."

Catching on, Cynthia moved her feet and exited the apartment. Jay reached for her hand and led her down the stairs to the parking lot.

"You look beautiful this evening," he told her. "Very radiant and eloquent."

"I bet you say that to all the women you take to business dinners," Cynthia remarked.

"Only the ones who make my heart flutter at the sight of them and leave me wanting to hear and see more of them."

As they entered the parking lot, Cynthia's eyes fell upon the black stretch limo in front of them. The driver stood patiently with the back door open.

Cynthia looked over at Jay. "That's your car?"

He nodded and gestured towards the limo. "After you."

As she slid into the back seat of the luxury car, Cynthia realized what it was about the moment that had her so jittery. The tingles of magic were taking over her.

She'd never been to such an upscale eatery, even with her father. She wondered if her bemusement was evident to Jay. If it was, he didn't let on. From the moment he'd picked her up from home, he continued to impress her. Upon arriving at the restaurant, their table had been waiting for them. Jay managed to get them seated at the chef's table and resting in front of Cynthia's seat was yet another extravagant bouquet of white roses. Their waiter wasted no time in pouring up the bottle of champagne that he'd informed them that the chef had sent over to them as his gift for being his guests that evening. Cynthia began to wonder how it was that Jay had so much pull. All she knew about the man was that he was some sort of humanitarian given the project they were working on together. The way the staff at Park 75 seemed to jump for him and the lavish way in which he'd begun their evening, Cynthia knew that there had to be something more to the man's existence. He was truly a complete gentlemen on so many levels.

Jay had taken the liberty of ordering their cuisine ahead of time. So, without hesitation they were presented with spinach salads, she-crab soup, short rib rolls, and roasted duck entrees. The champagne flowed endlessly and before she knew it, Cynthia was having a wonderfully relaxed time as she sampled the dishes and sipped from her glass all the while losing herself in Jay's accent and his soulful eyes.

"So, tell me why such a beautiful woman is not out with her husband on Friday night instead of here with me."

Cynthia's smile faded as she sat her glass down. "My husband passed away. Apparently, he had a weak heart."

"My condolences," Jay offered, genuinely saddened by the look of pain that lingered in her eyes. "I'm sure that he loved you very much. I know losing someone that close to you cannot be easy."

"At all."

He cocked his head to the side. "I pray you don't let the loss harden your heart."

"What do you mean?"

"I mean, I can sense the fear and pain in your spirit. I can tell you have an unwillingness to accept the fact that someone else would want to love you other than your late husband. Your soul is guarded … your heart is fragile. It's all understandable. But once one passes the stage of grief they must find the strength to open their heart once more to the possibility of love."

Cynthia shook her head. "I don't know about that. The last time I loved someone … he left me."

"An occurrence you cannot fault him for. God calls us all home in his time, not ours."

"I don't think I have it in me to love like that again. Before Preston, no one had ever loved me … the way he did."

Jay reached across the table to stroke her face and surprisingly to Cynthia, she didn't flinch or swat his hand away.

"Perhaps you shouldn't expect anyone to love you the way he did. Allow the one intended for you to love you in their way. It is not to say whether it is a greater or lesser, better or worse love. But if you close yourself off to the blessing of the enchantment, you'll never know how good it could be."

His words were like poetry to her ears and his touch was like silk. Her eyes narrowed to slits as she allowed the allure of the expensive alcohol, the romantic ambience, and the enticing company she was in the presence of to wash over her spirit. *Lord this man is stirring something up within me*, she thought. She could recall him telling her previously about the looking into her soul. Before, the thought had spooked her, but right then in that moment she desperately wanted him to delve into the depths of her being and uncover everything she couldn't say, everything she'd ever felt, every fear she was clutching to, and every need she possessed including the ones that she no longer had the desire to pay attention to. *You don't even know him,* she reminded herself as she opened her eyes and sat upright in her sit, regaining her good senses. *This is a work relationship. Crossing the boundaries might be dangerous so just stay focused and stop allowing herself to get carried away. This is real life, not some fairy tale.*

"Cynthia?" Jay called out to her. Apparently, he'd been speaking to her as she daydreamed and mentally chided herself.

"Huh?"

"I asked you to tell me about you."

"What do you want to know?" she asked, taking a tiny bite of duck.

"Anything you desire to tell me."

"Well, I haven't been working at Goodwill very long, but I'm dedicated to the job. I'm passionate about helping other people especially since I know exactly what it's like to need help myself. Starting over definitely isn't an easy thing."

Jay smiled.

"What?" she asked defensively.

"Nothing. I just hoped that you'd share something a little more private about yourself. You're so ... all business."

"Well, this is a business meeting isn't it?" Cynthia asked, realizing that they hadn't once discussed the list she'd compiled for him or his other ideas for the event. There wasn't even a sheet of paper on the table to so much as pretend that there was any work being done.

"If I may be honest."

"By all means"

"My assistant covered the entire list while I was closing a deal this week. Many of them had great things to say about you and how you go beyond to help those in need, if I may add. I invited you here because I feel we're kindred spirits. The moment I met you I felt an electrifying connection to you."

Cynthia remained silent. She'd felt that exact same surge of energy upon their first meeting but hadn't thought it to mean that they were meant to be. They were simply strangers who seemed to be unable to take their eyes off of one another.

"I just wanted an opportunity to get to know you outside of that office," he went on. "To learn about the woman who has given me such a jolt to the point where I can't close my eyes without seeing your face or hearing your voice."

"All of that and you don't know me from Adam," she said softly.

Jay pointed to his heart. "I don't know the finite things about you, true enough. But here is already connected to there," he told her, pointing towards her heart. "I feel something in your presence, Cynthia, that can't be ignored. And I've been taught that when the spirit speaks, you must listen. My spirit's drawing me to you and my heart knows that it's attracted to yours. Everything else comes secondary to what's naturally occurring."

He was talking a good game, but Cynthia couldn't bank on that. She was fragile and now carried a lot of baggage that she wasn't sure any man would be equipped to deal with. Looking him dead into his eyes and trying her best not to turn to mush, she hit him with her harsh reality. "You want to know me?" she asked. "I'm a single mother with three beautiful, young daughters. When my husband died I was pretty much left with nothing because my family, my extended family, basically made certain that I got what they felt I desired. They took my house, my husband's business, and all of my inheritance minus the small lump sum that was willed to my oldest daughter via a trust fund. I'm struggling to get through each day and take care of my girls on my own with my modest salary." Tears welled up in her eyes as she spoke. "Right now, I'm worried about how I'll get to work on Monday and how I'll manage to get my car fixed since I'm on a tight budget. My life was once completely a mess and within the last half a year or so I've been working diligently to pick myself up … but I'm scared that now that I'm somewhat on a path to making things happen that I'll find myself in a relationship with some man and once it ends, because let's face it … all good things come to an end, I'll be right back in the pit of hell, struggling to get myself together.

"For forty days I didn't want to eat. I couldn't talk to anyone. I was frail and empty. My kids didn't have a 100% of their mother ... I was a zombie. If it wasn't for my aunt and my husband's former receptionist, Eva, I don't know what would have happened to my children. Depression is real. I've been there. Some days, I find myself sliding right back into that darkness and then I have to realize that my children can't afford for me to be sad or disheartened. So I carry around that quiet, private fear. Every day gets a little easier, but my greatest fear ... is falling in love and leaving myself open to the possibility of having to go through any of that again."

"Good evening, folks," a baritone voice interrupted her speech.

Jay was none too pleased to tear his attention away from Cynthia, but was polite enough to acknowledge the strangers standing before him. "Hello. Have we met before?"

The muscular man with the shifty eyes reached his hand out to shake Jay's. "I don't believe we have. I'm Senator Braxton Thurmond and this is my uh ... business associate. When they told me the chef's table was reserved I just had to come over to see who had bumped my reservation." The Senator chuckled heartily. "Didn't mean to disrupt your dinner. I just wanted to put in an appearance." He looked at Cynthia and winked mannishly. "I'm sure Chef Hoke is treating you well this evening."

"Indeed he is," Jay stated. "My apologies regarding your reservation."

"Money talks, right?" the Senator replied.

Jay ignored his statement. "I'm Jay Torres and—"

"Oh yes, I'm familiar with you and your family's brand."

"This is my date, Cynthia Durden," Jay went on, beaming with pride to be accompanied by her.

Cynthia was mortified. Her eyes never left the glare of one of the people she hadn't expected to ever see again.

Ella eyes were filled with envy and hatred. She hadn't seen Cynthia since the day her mother had broken the girl's spirits. Now here she was dining in one of Atlanta's most elegant restaurants with one of the world's wealthiest men as if she deserved to be his arm candy. She wondered how long it would be before Jay grew tired of her wholesome, boringness and moved on to someone much sexier, trendier, and liberated than she. She felt he was very handsome and far too much man for Cynthia. Ella made a mental note to pool her resources to see how she could make the Prince of the Dominican Republic her next conquest. There was no way he could have any real interest in this homely being she'd once had to call her stepsister.

"Well, you two enjoy," the Senator said, placing his hand at the small of Ella's back.

"Likewise," Jay responded. Once the other couple was out of earshot, he looked to Cynthia with concern. "Are you okay? You look like you've just seen a ghost."

Cynthia took a gulp of her champagne. "Remember what I said about my stepfamily ruining my life?"

Jay nodded.

"Well that was wicked stepsister number one. She took the building where my ex-husband's physical therapy practice once was and turned it into a clothing boutique. Not to mention, she tried to sleep with my husband."

"Your stepsister ... she's very popular among affluent men."

"If you want to call it that."

"I'm using the term loosely. I have an associate, Ramaro, who once showed me pictures of her from a succession of weekends they'd spent together. Ramaro's known for bedding American socialites and taking, uh ... compromising photos of them."

"What does he do with them?" Cynthia asked, intrigued.

"Sells them to the rags, flaunts them to his friends. Whatever he feels like doing with them."

Cynthia took another sip of her champagne and snuck a peek over in Ella and the Senator's direction. She'd seen Senator Thurmond on the news and knew enough to know that the man was very much so married. Cynthia shook her head. As much as Ella hated her it seemed that the girl hated herself even more to have so little respect for herself.

Jay raised his glass and smiled at Cynthia. "A toast," he said. "To new beginnings."

Cynthia hesitantly raised her glass. "Oh?"

"Absolutely. I know with all certainty that you will one day be my bride."

"Did you hear anything that I said?"

"I heard everything you did and didn't say, my love. And now, I need you to trust that the universe will not fail you. You once believed in fate. Take a chance on it again."

Cynthia searched his eyes for so much as an ounce of insincerity and found nothing but softness, kindness, and genuineness with a tiny spark of affection that was unmistakable. She clinked her glass against his. "To new beginnings," she finally said.

They each took a sip and their eyes smiled at one another.

"I'll have a car get you to work on Monday," Jay stated.

"Huh?"

"You said you were worried about how you'd get to work. I don't want you to worry about anything else this evening. Consider that taken care of and just trust that the rest will fall into place. All I need you to do from here on out, Cynthia, is believe. That's all."

The fact that he was so willing to help her without her asking spoke volumes. She didn't feel that his actions were led by an ulterior motive other than to care for her. She didn't feel that he was moving too quickly when he reached over and grabbed her hand. For the first time in a long time she felt something she had to admit that she'd been missing; secured and cared for. It was a feeling that she could once again get used to.

Chapter 8

When the truth reveals itself
You can either open your eyes and see it for what it is
Or
Close your eyes, ears, and heart to the reality out of fear.
The latter may hinder you from the beauty of a love
So pure, profound, and surreal.
But, the former may afford you the experience
That seems only to be present in fairy tales.
Happily ever after is what you make it,
Unless you decide to ignore it.

-Kenni York © 2016

*J*ay and Cynthia became inseparable. He'd kept his word about making sure she got to work the Monday following their first date, but went above and beyond by providing her with $25,000.00 via a cashier's check to replace her automobile. His generosity was far too great for her, but though she'd tried her best to decline the offer, Jay insisted that she allow him to do something for her. So, thanks to him, she was able to purchase a modest Toyota Camry and add some funds to her savings account. She tried to keep quiet about their budding relationship, but Joyce and Tina were well aware of how fond the two had become of each other. Several times they tried to get her to dish out what it was like to be spoiled by such a wealthy man, but two things had been made very evident to her friends; firstly, Cynthia was not wowed by Jay's ability to spend lavishly on her, but by the way he made her feel and secondly, she was apparently oblivious to the truth of whom she was dating.

Cynthia didn't feel the need to Google the man, ask others questions, or even listen to the gossip that her friends seemed to be dying to share with her. She wanted to get to know Jay on her own terms, learning about him through their interactions and simply being in his presence. Sure, she realized that he was a rich businessman but money wasn't new to Cynthia. Her father had made plenty of money and died without ever really having enjoyed his life. Working so hard to cash the paper that his wife worked equally as hard to spend had only helped push her father into an early grave. Money didn't buy you happiness nor did it offer you true love. Cynthia wanted more than just expensive dinners, great gifts, and luxury trips all over the world. She longed for that feeling of understanding and acceptance, affection and attention, as well as suitable companionship all of which she found herself discovering within Jay the more they were around one another.

As the weeks turned into months, she realized that she was falling head over heels and didn't want to jump too deep into something she wouldn't be able to pull herself out of. Her life was elevating and she felt that a lot of it had to do with this new energy, this new force, in her life. Through their discussions, Jay had her thinking about her greater purpose. Sure, she was good at her liaison position at Goodwill, but she longed to be and do so much more. In keeping with her desire to help others, Cynthia was now on a path to discovering a way that she could impact more people on a greater scale. Everything was so exciting; the progression of her relationship with Jay and resting at the brink of a new endeavor. But, from time to time doubt still frolicked within her and she was uncertain as to what to do to shake the feeling.

"What's the matter with you?" Thea asked, walking into the living room to find Cynthia staring down at her lap.

"Huh?"

"You in here acting lost. What's the matter with you?"

The children were outside playing at the playground and she'd been taking a moment to regroup. Somehow, that moment had turned into nearly half an hour as she reviewed her life and began to feel the pressures of uncertainty.

"Is it real?" she asked, turning to look at Thea with questioning eyes.

"Child, what are you talkin' 'bout?"

"Everything. This thing with Jay. How he's got me wanting to do more ... start something meaningful, like an organization or something."

"Your minds all cluttered with thoughts. You over here stressing yourself out over nothing." Thea took a seat beside her on the sofa. "That young man loves you."

"You think so?"

"What you gotta ask me for confirmation for? You see the way he looks at you?"

Cynthia nodded.

"You see the way he takes care of you?"

Another nod.

"You see the way he cares for those kids?"

It was true. A month into dating, she'd finally allowed Jay to meet her kids and they all seemed to be smitten with one another from that point forward. When it was time to purchase school clothes for them, Jay paid so that she wouldn't have to tap into her savings. Elsa had taken a terrible fall just a month prior and the insurance they had wouldn't cover the full cost of the surgery and medicines that she needed. It was Jay who had come to the rescue making sure that Elsa had the best care she needed. He'd even gone so far to be there at the hospital each night of her stay, being sure to read her favorite bedtime story. It was the simple things like that which made him appear to be such a loving man; in turn, it melted Cynthia's heart and made her feel safe and secure with him. That alone scared her. What if she allowed herself to take hold to him like a safety net only to be cut loose later? Not only would it crush her, but now that the girls were invested it would affect them too.

"You worry too much," Thea told her. "You gon' miss out on your blessings by worrying too much and not looking to the Lordt. Everything you want, everything you need is right in front of you. Right within your grasp. You just gotta have faith, honey. Have faith, turn to the Lordt."

Thea's advice was never ending. Ever since Preston passed, all she'd ever recommend when times were hard was for Cynthia to turn to the lord. She prayed daily, went to church most Sundays, and believed in the heavenly father, but for the life of her she couldn't understand why Thea was constantly pressing her to turn to her maker.

"The Lordt got you," Thea said, patting Cynthia's leg and rising from the sofa. She was becoming frustrated, but if it was one thing she knew how to do, she knew how to follow directions. She knew that in time, all would be understood and all would be as it should be.

He was spending more and more time in Atlanta since the love of his life resided there, but Jay's home was in the Dominican Republic. Still, he kept a cozy penthouse suite at the Crowne Plaza to accommodate him when he was stateside. From time to time, Cynthia would stay over and he loved the way she looked walking around in his white hotel bathroom, her hips filling it out nicely. He'd even had her and the girls over for a day at hotel's spa, spoiling all of his girls with a family day in. He was beginning to feel that sense of responsibility for Cynthia and her daughters and knew without doubt that he'd finally found what he'd been looking for; a woman of virtue, grace, and poise with intelligence and a strong sense of loyalty and morale. Jay wasn't the type to fall in love easily, but he'd known from the moment he'd saw her that Cynthia was meant to be his bride. He'd told her such, but was certain that in that moment she'd brushed his comment off as his simply telling her sweet nothings. But, he also wasn't the type to say or do anything that he didn't mean wholeheartedly. It was the basis of his business and community dealings; operating from the instinct that propelled his spirit. His grandmother, the head of his family's dynasty, had always told him to listen to his spirit for it would never failed him. In this case, his spirit was encouraging him to love Cynthia with all of his being for as long as he existed and he had every intention upon doing so.

Knock, knock. As Jay browsed over papers sent over to him by his realtor, he was disrupted by the abrupt knocking at the door of his suite. Clad in silk lounging pants and his princely robe over top, he head towards the door. Looking through the peephole, he frowned with confusion. He recognized his visitor but was unaware of why she was there.

"I must say that I am surprised to see you here," he said, opening the door slightly.

Ella smiled at him as she held on to the large collar flaps of her black knee-length coat. "Pleasantly so I hope."

"That depends upon the reason for your visit."

"Direct are we?" She smiled. "May I come in?"

"The gentleman in me would like to invite you in, but the realist in me doesn't know if that's a good idea," he answered, closing the gap of his half open door with his body to discourage her against pushing past him.

"I take it you remember me."

He nodded. "How is Senator Thurmond?"

Ella winced slightly. She had no desire to talk about the man whom she hadn't heard from in the last two months. The night they'd ran into

Cynthia and Jay, he'd presented her with a rock that left her speechless. She'd then given him the best sex of his life which had left her with one bad thing in the end: a broken heart the moment after he informed her he was going back to his wife and would no longer see her again. She was miserable and alone. She was always attaching herself to yet another wealthy man and causing someone else the same misery she suffered from. It seemed that Cynthia was always the punching bag in these situations and Ella knew that taking Jay from her would be the ultimate gut punch.

"We're no longer affiliated," Ella answered, loosening the belt of her coat. "I was hoping that you and I could talk and figure out a way to uh ... combine forces." She completely untied the belt and allowed her coat to fall open, exposing her body. She smiled seductively and licked her lips. "I promise you that you won't regret it."

Jay moved forward, ignoring the excitement in Ella's eyes. "You're a beautiful woman," he said softly, pulling at the ends of her coat and drawing them together. "It's just a shame that you don't realize it." He began to tie the belt of her coat. "I pray that you one day encounter a man that sees you for the person God intended you to truly be ... someone who sees past this temptress façade and shows you what it's like to be honored."

Ella was speechless. She'd never had a man shut her down without putting her down. Was he really that into Cynthia or did he just not find her desirable?

"Is something wrong with me?" she asked meekly, sounding as if she'd breakdown at any moment.

"That is something that only you can answer."

She studied him for a moment, surprised that he was still standing there instead of rushing back into his suite. Maybe she still had a shot. "If I could just talk to you for a minute," she said, working the sad girl angle. "Maybe there are some things that I need to work out ... I just need someone to talk to."

"I can assure you that I am not that person. I have to be honest with you. I'm a very compassionate person, but I'm also very loyal.

Cynthia's been through a lot, I'm not about to give her any reason to doubt my love or fidelity."

At the mention of Cynthia and his feelings for the other woman, Ella was infuriated. "So you know we're related?"

Jay nodded.

"And you're telling me that you're actually into whatever it is that you're doing with her? I mean, your family has plenty of money. You're a prince for heaven's sake. You know she has nothing right? She has no claim to her father's estate at all whatsoever. You'd have a better chance of tapping into a new money source by getting with me."

"Money doesn't buy you happiness," he told her. "Perhaps if you'd have less, you'd value what you have more."

She was done listening to him analyze her. "You've got to be out of your mind to turn down all of this."

Jay shook his head and took a step back into his suite. "We'll keep this meeting between the two of us, but I think we're done here." Without another word, he softly shut the door.

Ella remained standing in the hallway for a moment staring at the closed door. She felt foolish, standing there half naked throwing herself at a man who preferred the likes of Cynthia over her. Suddenly, she felt the need to have a drink. Turning away, she headed for the elevator. Lonely nights and wine; this is what her life had been reduced to.

"I'm hungry," Trey complained.

Ana was busy going over the lyrics of a song she'd written for an up and coming artist. She'd decided to try her hand at music since her husband had long since given up on his artistry as well as life itself it sometimes seemed. Her mom had cut her off financially and Trey had no royalty checks coming in. They were screwed. She'd had to kiss her dream of being an artist goodbye, but with music lingering in her from being around Elton and then Trey, she still found a way to turn to it in order to keep them afloat. Who knew that writing music could prove to be lucrative? Because she had practically been disowned by her mother, she hadn't tried to hit up GMG artists with her songs. Instead, she tapped into companies who were focusing on their budding talents and made sure to supply them with hits that would spark their careers. So far, she was off to a good start. Royalties were coming in for a few of the songs she'd written and they'd been able to save the home they'd almost lost. Sure, they'd had to scale back drastically since they only had her income to rely upon, but even that money had to be budgeted because of the way her pay periods ran. Still, it was something. The only problem was that Trey still battled with his expensive habits and maintained his abusive disposition.

"I'll throw something together as soon as I'm done," she told him, not bothering to look up from her computer.

"You'll take care of your man now!" he yelled back, tossing his half full beer can at her.

The can hit the computer and screen and the liquid rained out onto her keyboard.

"What the hell!" she hollered," quickly tossing the can aside and searching for a cloth to soak up the beer that was drenching her keys. "You can really be a pain in the butt, you know that?"

Trey was livid that she would have the audacity to speak to him that way. "Do you know who I am?" he asked, staring at the back of her head as she struggled to clean up her computer. "I'm the man of this house. I am still the man of this house and you will respect me."

Ana remained silent.

"Do you hear me talking to you?"

She didn't respond. Experience had taught her that if she simply ignored him as he ranted that he'd just go on about his business and her face would be saved from any pounding that he was itching to give it.

"You're just like the rest of them aren't you?" he went on. "Think you don't have to respect me! Think just because that bitch you call you mother took everything from me."

"You took everything from yourself!" she shot back. Immediately, she regretted uttering a word.

"What did you say?"

"Nothing." She sat back down and started typing again.

"No, you said something. What was it? What did you say?" he asked again, grabbing her by the arm.

"Trey please! I'm trying to work."

"Work? You think I care about your work? You think I care about what you're doing? Writing for other people, helping them come up. You can't even help your own man." With all of his might, he shoved her computer off of the desk and onto the floor. Picking up the cordless phone, he tossed it at the monitor's screen as it lay on the carpet.

"What are you doing?" Ana screamed.

The phone crashed against the front of the monitor and instantly the screen began to fade to green starting in the middle and spreading across the entire span of the screen.

"My computer!" Ana tried to get down beside it, but Trey snatched her up by her arm, forcing her to face him.

"You and that witch stole my life," Trey told her. "I hate the sight of you because every time I look at you I see her and I just want to bash your face in."

Ana braced herself, unsure of what he'd do next but quite certain that her body would be inflicted somehow. "Please," she whimpered, hoping to appeal to the part of him that was still the good man she'd once known. "Please, let me go."

He grinned at her sinisterly before shoving her to the floor. As she scampered to crawl away from him, he towered over her and raised his foot just above her abdomen.

"I wish I could squish you like a bug," he threatened. "Squish you, you disrespectful twig. Look at you. Used to be such hot stuff. Now I wouldn't touch you with another man's penis!"

His insults hurt, but not as bad as she knew his blow to her midsection would. Sure, she'd lost a lot of weight during the course of their marriage; partially because there were times when she couldn't afford to put food in the house due to his addiction and partially because of the stress that being with him caused.

He lowered his foot to ground and leaned down to look at her as she cowered underneath him. "I never wanted you," he taunted her. "I just wanted the money but you messed that up for me. I should have been banging Ebony. Maybe then she'd have a little incentive to do right by me."

When Ana didn't respond, it seemed to only infuriate Trey more. "You're worthless!" he shouted at her.

Without warning, he punched her in the face, his fist landing against her nose. Blood oozed out and she tried her best to move away from him. Trey grabbed her neck and squeezed it as tightly as he could, watching as her eyes popped open wide and her blood dripped down to her lip. She tried to pry his hands away, but to no avail. She was becoming lightheaded, but it didn't stop her legs and arms from flailing in a wide attempt to stop him from extracting life from her body. She bent her right leg at the knee and with all of the force that she could muster up, she brought her knee up impacting his groin area as hard as she could.

"Owww!" he hollered, letting go of her, stepping away, and grabbing his manhood. "Ana!" he squealed in a soprano tone she'd never heard him use before.

This was it. She'd come so close to losing her life by his hands and finally reality hit her. As long as she stayed with him, things would never get better. He'd forced her to alienate herself from everyone and everything. She didn't even have a good relationship with her sister anymore. She had nowhere to go but one thing was for certain; she couldn't stay there. Quickly, she pulled herself to her feet, wiped her nose with the back of her hand as she grabbed her purse, and made a dash for the front door. Her clothes, her files, and all of her personal effects didn't matter to her. All she cared about was being free from the man who had been punishing her relentlessly for his own shortcomings.

Ana found herself driving around crying and racking her brain trying to figure out where to turn. She considered getting a hotel room but didn't want anyone to recognize her and call the tabloids. She didn't need any more blog stories about her stupidity popping up. She thought about going to her mom, but she knew that the woman would only gloat about how she'd told her so, if she even allowed her into the house. Ana managed to dial Ella's number but received no answer. Feeling as if her sister was purposely ignoring her phone calls, Ana felt frustrated. She'd been such a horrible person to others, looking down on people and relying on her mother's money and connections to get her through life. Now, here she was in a bind and had no one that she could trust to take her in temporarily as she sorted out the mess that had become her life. As she scrolled through her contact list she came across Cynthia's number. She lingered for a moment wondering if it was a good idea. She'd been especially horrible to Cynthia, they all had, wishing bad for the woman's life only to be kicked in the butt by karma given all she was enduring. Still, she had no one else.

The phone rang three times before she finally answered. "Hello?"

"Cynthia?" Ana asked, sniffing.

"Ana? Ana what's the matter?"

"I'm really sorry to bother you, but I just … I don't have anyone else to call and … I need help. I'm in trouble, Cyn. I need you."

"Lord, please show us the way," Cynthia prayed aloud. "Please help us as we deal with our own insecurities, troubles, and fears, Father. Show us the path you wish for us and guide us as we faithfully succumb to your will. Help us to know that all past transgressions have been forgotten and that you will never leave, hurt, nor forsake us. We may not understand the journey you've set us upon, but we turn it all over to you, God. We ask that you keep us in your grace and mercy father, as we come to realize that this too shall pass; that there is nothing we can't conquer with you at the forefront. We speak healing over our souls in your name, Lord. Amen."

"Amen," Thea seconded from her position in the oversized chair in the living room.

"Amen," Ana whispered, opening her swollen eyes and looking over to Cynthia apologetically. She'd said 'I'm sorry' over a thousand times in the last two hours that she'd been there, but that just didn't seem like enough. After filling Cynthia and Thea in on the way her husband had been beating her for years and practically driving them into poverty with his addiction, she'd vowed to make up for the years of pain and heartache that she'd helped Cynthia suffer from.

Cynthia sighed as she held tight to the bible resting in her lap. She needed some extra spiritual guidance after listening to Ana's confessions. As usual, Thea had encouraged her to look to the word of God.

"Why you'd let me come?" Ana asked. "I mean, after everything we've done to you, I'd think that the last thing you'd want to do is help either one of us."

"God said to love everyone," Cynthia told her. "Even your enemies too. I'd never let you suffer if there's something I can do. It's just not who I am."

Ana looked down at her hands and balled up her fists. "I don't know who I am anymore. When did I become some battered wife afraid to stand up for herself? And then, even when I knew they were doing you extra dirty aside from purposely honing in on Elton's money I ignored my instinct to speak out against it and look what it's gotten me. Look where it's all gotten me. Karma's no joke."

"What a minute," Thea interjected. "Not to discredit what you're going through, but what you mean 'purposely honing in on Elton's money'?"

Ana looked from Thea to Cynthia, afraid to tell the truth for fear that they would surely put her out. But, if she was going to turn over a new leaf, now was the time. "Mom had Elton's will changed before he died and tricked him into signing off on it. It was her plan to make sure that you didn't get any of his money. She had herself renamed as the sole beneficiary on his insurance policy too at the same time that she increased the amount."

"That's illegal!" Cynthia hollered. "I knew something wasn't right. He would have never intentionally done that."

"I'm sorry. We all just felt that you despised us and the money so much that she just … took it from you."

"Evil troll," Thea stated.

Cynthia shook her head. "Why would anyone stoop so low to try to hurt someone. Was the money that important to you all?

Ana lowered her head in shame. "I'm so sorry."

Cynthia gripped the book tightly and closed her eyes, fighting back the tears. She'd always known that Ebony had done some underhanded mess to cut her out of Elton's will, but hearing Ana confirm it made her blood boil.

"Give it to Lord," Thea warned her. "Don't you let that evilness corrupt your heart. Give it to the Lordt."

Cynthia opened her eyes and slightly turned her head to look at Thea. "You're always telling me to give it to him but how am I supposed to deal with all of the crap that the world keeps throwing me?" She absentmindedly shook the bible and watched as an envelope slipped from the middle of the pages. "What in the world?" She opened the bible and pulled out the envelope that she'd never noticed was there before. "What is this?" she asked Thea.

Thea sat still with her arms crossed.

Curiously, she opened the envelope and pulled out a letter. Her eyes poured over the words quickly. *Dearest daughter, I don't know what to expect when I'm gone but I want to assure that in your darkest hour I can manage to provide you with some light. Enclosed is the banking information for the account that I've set up for you. I've poured into this account since the time your mother passed, even when I barely had two cents to rub together. I know Ebony isn't perfect and can be a little excessive at times, like all of us, my wife is flawed. But, I'm leaving this to you so that you won't ever feel that I didn't have your best interest at heart. I always have and even in death I always will. I know you never wanted any parts of the GMG empire, that you sought more than money, fortune, or even fame. Still, a few extra dollars wouldn't hurt anyone. I love you. Your Dad.*

She switched the page bringing into view a statement form Liberty Mutual indicating that a savings account had been created in her name. Saying nothing to the others, she pulled out her cell phone and called the customer service number listed on the letter. After entering in the appropriate information via the automated prompts, she finally heard what she was seeking; the account balance. Mystified by what she'd heard, she pressed the button to hear it again. Disconnecting the call, she looked at Thea in disbelief. "I'm a millionnaire?" she asked slowly.

"Look at God," Thea answered.

"What?" Ana asked.

"My dad ... he opened an account for me and was constantly saving money all while he was alive. Since he's been gone, it's only been accruing interest. I'm a millionnaire." She looked at Thea again. "All this time ... did you know?"

"He wrote me a letter too," Thea explained. "Left it in that bible that he bequeathed to me. Told me to hold it for you until you were open to the gift he was giving you. You know your stubborn. Even when you was struggling the most, I kept telling you to give it to God, to turn to the Lordt. Your answer was always there. But I think over time you got something so much more than this here money. You learned your own strength and worth and that there is priceless."

Cynthia looked down at the old bible and cried tears of joy. Soundly, the words of Whitney Houston's "I Turn to You" began to play in her mind. It was so true; the Lord knew exactly what you needed when you needed it and had a funny way of being right on time. This was a lesson that she knew she'd never forget; there was no way that she could ever not trust God's timing and plan even when she felt confused and wasn't sure she was strong enough to endure. Through him all things were certainly possible and he would never forsake her. The lord sure did work in mysterious ways.

No longer troubled by whether or not she should give in to her feelings for Jay, Cynthia gave it over to the Lord. She realized that he'd brought Jay into her life to show her that it was possible to love again even when you'd gone through something heartbreaking and traumatic. He was a great man and he'd helped her to uncover strengths she hadn't even realized that she had. Upon learning about his true worth, only after sharing the news of her new-found wealth, Cynthia felt even closer to Jay. To her, it was a plus that he hadn't told her about his royal upbringing and family fortune, so that she was able to get to know him and love him without fearing that money would destroy them. Their union was much more blessed and destined than they thought. Together, they pooled their resources and gave life to the vision that Cynthia had been struggling to give birth to: a resource center for women. The center specialized in counseling women who struggled with domestic violence, depression, low self-esteem, or any other occurrence which hampered them from loving their self or realizing their full potential.

It had now been a year since Jay and Cynthia got together. Cynthia began to experience the happiness that had been absent from her life before and was falling more in love with Jay by the second. He was an eternal light for Cynthia and she could not of felt more blessed to be where she was right then. Jay had spontaneously decided to take Cynthia on a trip to the Dominican Republic and as soon as they arrived, he scoped her to the breathtakingly romantic beach for horseback riding. As they both strolled down the beach along the shore, waves from all directions came sliding in, becoming one and softly colliding with the land that glistened from the golden sand. The sun had just begun to set leaving a blend of colors to dance within its reflection upon the sea. It was in this moment, when everything around them seemed to unify into a captivating and ravishing scene, that Jay revealed a stunning diamond ring that shined almost as bright as his smile. With a sense of pride and the utmost admiration Jay said, "Cynthia, I want to spend the rest of my life waking up next to you. I want to spend the rest of my life knowing that I will be coming home to an amazing lady that gets even more astonishingly beautiful every time I lay eyes on her. I want to spend the rest of my life having my best friend by my side who I know will stay by myside through the good and bad with unwavering love, I want to spend the rest of my life with you. Cynthia, will you marry me?" She was in shock, at a loss of words, how she was blessed with a man as stunning and genuinely good guy as Jay was beyond her. Cynthia soon recovered and happily replied, "Yes, of course!" she exclaimed. Jay placed the ring on her finger as they immediately embraced passionately with a kiss.

Following the engagement was the jaw dropping wedding festival that would without a doubt be the hot topic for the remainder of the year. It had only been a few months but it seemed like an eternity as they counted down the weeks, the days, the hours, the seconds. Finally, the time arrived when both Cynthia and Jay could at last display their affections for one another to all of the people that loved and cared for them the most. Jay had done everything in his power to make sure that Cynthia had her dream wedding, and that's exactly what she received. As she elegantly strides down the aisle, the sand on the private beach they'd chosen glimmered as the sun shined down on them enlightening the joy within them all. There was a peace that seemed to surround and transfixed them all in perfect harmony. This scene of tranquility reminded Cynthia of what had occurred shortly before. As she was getting ready a tingling sensation sent chills through her body as though a presence was around her. She took notice to an enrapturing, bright beam of light coming through her window. As though trapped in a spell Cynthia moved towards it and began to see the image of her loved ones reaching out to embrace her. What she saw were the angelic spirits of Preston, her dad and mother; and just like that they were gone. Despite being partially confused by the event that just happened, she still thanked them for always looking out for her and being her guardian angels. Installed with a new-found happiness, Cynthia counted to get ready and add her final touches. Shortly after, she finished applying her make-up and stepped back to examine herself in the mirror which displayed a new woman. Cynthia's white, enchanting dress flowed freely down to the floor as the small finishings throughout the dress glistened. On her feet were a pair of clear shoes and on her neck was the reminder of her mother, as the diamond necklace that was once hers tied together her outfit. There was a specific beauty in the way her dress outlined her figure and it was in this moment, that she felt more like a princess than ever before.

As the night continued, the couple did a bride and groom dance one of their favorite songs by Charlie Wilson called "You Are." There was other live music from Kem who sung Share my Life, I Can't Stop Loving You, and Promise to Love. Of course, there were the traditional wedding shuffle songs played during the reception like Cupid Shuffle and the Wobble. After they were united as husband and wife, and having their exceptional honeymoon, Cynthia was announced as the official Princess of the Dominican Republic. They split their time between living in the Dominican Republic and living in the states to afford their children the best of both environments. Shortly afterwards being married, they welcomed a beautiful baby boy into their family; Jacob. Amelia, Elsa, and Ana were thrilled to have a baby brother.

As for the others, Ana went on to divorce Trey but was gracious enough to allow him to keep the house so that he wouldn't be homeless. It was her last kind gesture towards the man that had hurt her so badly. She began to focus on her music, pouring into herself as she worked to become a better person overall. When Cynthia told her that she'd be holding annual conferences at her women's center, Ana eagerly volunteered to speak to the women about overcoming domestic abuse. Over time, Ana and Cynthia got to really know one another, building a new relationship built upon trust and mutual respect. Ana felt that she owed Cynthia so much for showing her genuine compassion at a time when she was truly at her lowest point.

Eventually, Ana found it in herself to reach out to Ella. It took a lot for Ella to humble herself, but she realized that she needed help and simply couldn't do it on her own. With Ana by her side, she finally turned to the women's center, seeking the help of one of the many professionals employed by Cynthia. It was funny how things had turned out. She had been so overly consumed by the problems troubling her, taking it all out on Cynthia stemming from blind resentment, that she didn't realize that all along Cynthia would of been there for her in a heartbeat. That's just what a family does.

In the end, it had been Cynthia and her center that helped her regain respect for herself and the ability to love herself enough to want more than just being a man's trophy or running up someone's charge card.

Ebony never apologized to Cynthia. She never was able to put her feelings aside in order to reconnect with her daughters. She became very ill from back to back strokes but she still managed to be the same way that she always lived; lonely, rich and selfish in a world of her own.

Cynthia stayed empowered over her life and refused to allow the evil and toxic components of life impact her anymore. She stood strong every time she was faced with curveballs of life and as a result, blessings overflowed when least expected. Yes, there were going to be some tough times, that is just what comes with life, but Cynthia finally had her happy ending with her devoted husband and compassionate kids, allowing her to love peacefully and happy forever.

I AM PRINCESS, I AM PRINCE, WE ARE ONE

I am Princess
I once was easily broken
I once was distressed
I am free from blockages
I am restored and renewed
Ready for anew mindset
Still standing by grace, mercy and favor
Dreams and aspirations still awaits
Yes, I'm ah superwoman

I am Prince
Declaring seeds of greatness
Exploring new possibilities
With a mission to provide
With a mission to protect
With a mission to lead
Yes, I'm ah superman

We are one
Destined to cross paths
Equally yoked, our souls tie
The challenges we face
Are the challenges we'll overcome
Selfless unconditional agape love
Your love makes me whole again
Yes, ah real kind of love that's everlasting

Engage Lyfe © 2017

SUMMARY AND
CLOSING REMARKS

Love isn't always picture-perfect fairytale or storybook.

Love doesn't come easy and perhaps impossible to live without.

Love is about working together, confronting challenges and overcoming obstacles.

Love comes in different forms, colors, shapes and sizes.

We love our pets and jobs!
We love our friends and family!

We learn to love from every perspective.
We learn to love through the good and the tough times.

Are you able to withstand the tests? Have you been broken when already broken? Have people tried to knock you down at the lowest point in your life?
When your strength is tested and you don't know how you're going to get through it but you somehow miraculously found away, it's because of God and his guardian angels that watch over you.

All it takes is a little faith of a mustard seed to flourish.
Then when you combine faith with strength, it's even more powerful.

As the old saying goes, "Nothing last forever." These challenges are temporary.

Turn your focus on, fulfilling your purpose and your dreams.

Learn happiness.

Learn empowerment.

Learn God's will and control of your destiny.

Learn people don't dictate our life.

Learn this order to life that will help you live amazing life, be stronger, be wiser and have empowering relationships.

THE ORDER TO LIFE

1st - Trust in God.

God is the starting point of all wisdom.

God should be first in everything and anything we do.

God possesses all power not people.

God gives grace, mercy and favor to us.

God provides our every need and blesses abundantly.

2nd – Make everyday count.

Love and make the best of every moment.

Life is too short to not let everyday count.

3rd – Seek self-love.

Love yourself.

Find the value in yourself and be true to who you are.

Cherish the skin you're in. Cherish the spirit from within.

Self-love not self-hate. Self-love not self-destruction.

Happiness originates from within.

4th – Understand your true given purpose in life.

Discover, pursue and fulfill your destiny.
Listen to your passions, talents and gifts.

5th – Love one another (sisterly and brotherly love).

Women to women empowerment (sisterly love).
Men to men empowerment (brotherly love).

6th - Don't rush love during the dating phase of life.

Don't just settle for less.
Don't gravitate to "fake sort of kind of" love.
Don't rush into false companionship.
Seek true happiness and true love.

7th - Honor marriage and families.

Respect, love, honor and cherish marriage you're in.
Exemplify and pass down good strong family values to your children.

Live To Love Life

Printed in the United States
By Bookmasters